HAWKSHEAD

THE ABDUCTION CYCLES

JOHN ELIJAH CRESSMAN

MAVERICK-GAGE PUBLISHING

ISBN: 978-1-7351302-7-9 (Paperback)
ISBN: 978-1-7351302-6-2 (Hardcover)
ISBN: 978-1-7351302-8-6 (Amazon Kindle)
ISBN: 978-1-954524-00-2 (Audiobook)

Any references to historical events, real people, or real places are used fictitiously. Names, characters, and places are products of the author's twisted imagination.

Front cover image by Christina Myrvold

Editing By Celestial Rince.

Printed by Maverick-Gage Publishing in conjunction with IngramSpark, in the United States of America.

First printing edition 2021.

Maverick-Gage Publishing
Allentown, PA
info@maverick-gage.com
www.maverick-gage.com

John Elijah Cressman
www.johnecressman.com

❀ Created with Vellum

This book is dedicated to my friends and family, who continue to support my crazy dream of being a writer.

1

———

"Take that!" Ethan screamed into his microphone as the second of the lava ogres fell, his own voice mixing with those of the rest of his party over his headphones.

"That's --- way --- do it!" came Wyatt's voice, crackling and breaking up over the audio. Wyatt was always crackling nowadays. His dog had knocked over a 2-liter of soda on his headset two weeks ago and he didn't have the money to replace it. It made him hard to understand half the time and it had nearly caused deaths in their dungeon excursion several times.

Wyatt was the group's healer. His avatar was a Pandarian shaman, a large bipedal panda-bear-like race. The Pandarian stats didn't really lend themselves to being the best healing race, but shaman was their favored class so they received certain bonuses. Shamans themselves were a healing hybrid class, so not even a full healer. But Wyatt made it work.

No one in his group were power-gamers; they played whatever class/race combination they liked. The group wasn't the most powerful bunch, but they worked well together. So far, they'd been able to conquer all of the content in CastleBlaze, their current MMORPG of choice.

They'd been playing MMORPGs, online role-playing games, since their high school days, moving from game to game as they conquered it or became bored - or the next big thing appeared.

"Get a new microphone, you loser!" Hunter joked. Hunter was their Froggog witch doctor, an amphibious race that looked like a frog on two legs. Like Wyatt, he had chosen the race because he liked frogs, not because it made a good spellcaster. Luckily, Hunter was great at his class and the Froggog's affinity for water gave them bonuses to water magic, which he had specialized in.

"I - new - one - but - mama - it," said Wyatt's crackling voice.

Hunter laughed. "Did you just make a my mama joke? Because it totally loses the impact when we only hear every other word. But you're right. That was a great fight!"

Ethan heard Hunter's tone turn more somber then. "Sometimes the game is better than real life. I wished I lived in the game sometimes."

"Come on, guys," said Gage, their Cornicus thief. The Cornicus race were humanoids with the bodies of muscular humans and the heads of unicorns. It was an unusual choice, and they teased him mercilessly but he made it work, plus he was able to do sneak attack damage with his horn. He was also great at disarming traps and when the occasional trap exploded, the Cornicus' luck ability usually saved him. "The big boss fight is next, the Ogre Volcano Lord."

Ethan looked over at the digital clock on his bookshelf. It was after 1am. He sighed. So much for getting a full night's rest before work tomorrow. According to the forums, the boss and his adds could take up to an hour to defeat. There was no way he was getting to sleep before 3am. And he had to be at work tomorrow at 8am.

Ethan groaned as he thought of work. He was a computer tech for the TechTeam, a mobile technical team that made house calls to fix people's computers. The work was neither glamorous nor did it pay well. But he still enjoyed it from time to time when he came across a particularly challenging problem.

Of course, now he'd be exhausted tomorrow since he lived in the middle of nowhere and it took him over an hour to drive into the city where he worked. He groaned again as he thought of how early he would need to get up.

He frowned and briefly considered telling his friends that he needed to go to bed. Yet, he knew that some of them had been looking forward to their Wednesday night dungeon run. He was their tank. If he left, the dungeon run would be over.

Ethan's avatar was a Ratatol, a small rat-like race who made excellent thieves. But of course, he didn't play a thief. Instead, he played a paladin and was clad head to foot in shiny platemail armor. On his left arm, he held a large kite shield and in his right hand he had a longsword of holy avenging.

"Come on, you wussies," Ethan said through his headphone and popped the lid on another soda. "Let's go kill us a Volcano Lord."

The others muttered agreements, with Wyatt crackling incomprehensibly. They quickly searched the dead ogre corpses scattered around the room, earning a ton of coins and minor magic items. All of them had better gear and they gave all of the items to Gage so he could deconstruct them for crafting materials.

For some reason, Gage loved the crafting part of the game almost as much as the rest of them liked the combat portion. He enjoyed finding the various recipes, blueprints and rare materials and crafting powerful gear.

The Shield of Reflection Ethan carried in his left hand was testament to Gage's skill. It was made from mythryll and was not only light, but reflected 15% of damage back on the attacker. It was as good as any dungeon drop for their level.

The looting complete, they moved to the far end of the grand entryway. The chamber was meant for the twelve-feet-tall ogres so the room was enormous to creatures his party's size. Ethan hadn't done any measurements, but the chamber had to be at least 100 feet long and 30 feet wide. Large pillars lined both sides of the walls and the craftsmanship looked too good to be made by ogres.

"Anyone read the lore on this quest?" Ethan asked as they walked through the chamber to the double brass doors at the far end.

Unsurprisingly, it was Hunter who answered. "This was some dwarven fortress a long time ago, before the dwarves were wiped out. Some orcs lived here for like a hundred years before the ogres invaded and defeated them. Their descendants were the slaves we freed in the lower levels."

Hunter was the lore man. He enjoyed reading all of the backstory to the quests and learning the storylines that the developers came up with. Usually, he took the time to explain everything to the rest of the group as they were fighting. Tonight Hunter had been mostly silent and Ethan knew why.

Normally more jovial, Hunter had been down all day. They'd been texting earlier in the day because Hunter's girlfriend of two years had decided to break it off last night. His friend was taking it very hard and had needed to vent to him. He had almost decided not to play tonight but Ethan had managed to talk him into it.

Ethan was glad he had. Despite not being his normal talkative self and spouting off on the lore, he'd caught his friend getting into the game and laughing at some of their corny jokes and one-liners. He made a mental note to text him tomorrow and make sure he was okay.

He frowned, glad his friends couldn't see him. Ethan was

sad for his friend for losing his girlfriend but he was also a bit jealous. Ethan had never had a proper girlfriend. None of his other gaming buddies had. Only Hunter.

Sure, he'd "gone steady" with a girl in high school and gone out with a few girls in college but they'd never gotten to the girl-friend-boyfriend stage, let alone moved in with him. Being a skinny, glass-wearing computer geek who fixed computers by day and played MMOs by night meant he didn't exactly have women lining up to date him.

He sighed as the group reached the large brass doors and stopped in front of them. Focusing back on the game, Ethan turned and faced them all in the game, glancing down at the notes on his tablet to refresh his memory. While Gage was the crafter and Hunter was the loremaster, Ethan was the tactician. He scoured the Wikis and forums to find the best tactics and then adapted them to his eclectic group.

Most tactics were geared for the perfect mix of classes and races, playing to the different characters' strengths. Since his entire group was composed of non-standard, and some might say sub-standard, race/class combinations, adapting the tactics was sometimes difficult. Now was one of those times.

"Alright," he said, looking up from his notes. "The boss is a level 100 ogre berserker with a flaming sword and a set of platemail that radiates heat and also grants him fire immunity...."

"Good thing I'm not a fire mage," Hunter said, using an emote to make his frog-like tongue shoot out about ten feet. The others groaned or gave him half-hearted chuckles before Ethan cleared his throat and continued.

"He's got a half-dozen elite ogre guards who he will send to deal with us first," Ethan told them. "We'll defeat them and then fight the boss until he gets down to 90%. Then he summons more guards as he backs up to the throne."

"Yeah, yeah," Gage said. "We kill them and then fight the boss again."

"Right," Ethan agreed, a little annoyed at being interrupted. They were all tired, he knew, and just wanted to get the boss fight over with. Glancing back at the clock, he sympathized. "We kill the adds, fight the boss and this happens until we get him to 50%. When that happens, you all back up all the way to the doors and switch to ranged attacks."

There was a collective groan from the group. Other than Hunter, who could hurl magic, none of the others specialized in ranged weapons. It was a weakness of his group, but they all liked being melee fighters.

"Yes, he goes berserk," Ethan said again. "That means he will randomly switch to any target within 30 feet. So, switch to ranged attacks until we get him to 40%, then you can close back in. After that, he'll retreat and call for the shaman for healing, getting him back to 50% while we fight more guards. If we kill the guards and shaman quickly enough, he won't get healed all the way."

Taking a deep breath and a sip of his soda, Ethan continued. "We'll get him down to 25% and he'll go berserk again, so same game plan. And then again at 10%."

"Special attacks?" asked Hunter.

"That sword he has can do a fireball, centered on him," Ethan replied. "When he holds the sword up in the air with both hands, run out of range as fast as you can."

"How often - - use -?" Wyatt asked, the crackling of his voice difficult to understand.

It took a moment for Ethan to realize what he had asked. "The fireball has a five-minute cooldown. Just watch for the sword lift."

"What else?" Hunter asked.

"The armor generates a damage-over-time flame effect to anyone within 10 feet," he told them and listened to their expected groans and complaints. Some boss monsters had some sort of effect around them that caused damage or gave a debuff. Since everyone but Hunter were melee fighters, it had been a constant challenge.

He heard Wyatt sigh over his headset. "That's a lot of healing, guys. I'm going to use up a ton of magic potions for this fight."

"Don't worry. We'll all donate to the 'Keep Us Alive' fund," Ethan said and heard the muttered approvals of the others. Most of the gold they found tonight would probably end up going to Wyatt, but that was fine. It was the price they all paid for wanting to be different. "Just do your best to keep us all up."

"I always do," Wyatt replied.

"You guys ready?" he asked, facing the door. When they all checked in that they were ready, Ethan pushed open the doors.

2

The boss was down to 15% health. The battle had been brutal so far with Hunter going down to one of the ogre elite guards. Wyatt had been able to cast a Raise Dead spell on him, but it had really drained his magic.

Ethan's health bar was down to 20% as the boss continued to rain blow after blow on him with its massive greatsword.

**Potbelly Cuddlebear heals you with
Growth of the Earth for 4718 health.**

His health bar shot up to over 50% as Potbelly Cuddlebear, Wyatt's shaman, healed him. Letting out a sigh of relief, Ethan swung his own sword at the boss's armored leg.

**You slash Omogg the Volcano lord for 192
damage.**

From behind the boss, Gage struck out with his two curved daggers and his horn.

> *Rainbow Sparklehorn stabs Omogg the*
> *Volcano lord for 592 damage.*
> *Rainbow Sparklehorn stabs Omogg the*
> *Volcano lord for 531 damage.*
> *Rainbow Sparklehorn gores Omogg the*
> *Volcano lord for 307 damage.*

Gage's bizarre name for his Cornicus avatar never ceased to amuse Ethan and he could see the thief was getting in some good backstab damage.

> *Tadpole Bugsnatcher casts Greater Ice*
> *Shards at Omogg the Volcano lord for*
> *1319 cold damage.*

Hunter's witch doctor, Tadpole, was doing really good damage to the boss with his water attacks, but like Wyatt's shaman, he was getting low on magic as well.

Omogg the Volcano lord suddenly stopped attacking and started raising its greatsword to the sky. Ethan recognized the boss was about to use his special attack. "FIREBALL!"

The group rushed out of range as flames burst from the ogre lord, erupting into a huge ball of fire. Ethan glanced at his health bar, thankful that it hadn't moved and then rushed back in, using his Taunt ability to once again force the boss to focus on him.

He spun the boss back towards the throne, keeping its back to his companions. While this boss didn't have special forward attacks, its greatsword did splash damage, damaging everyone in an arc. By keeping Omogg facing away from the rest of the group, he was sparing them that damage.

The group continued their assault on the boss until he hit 10% and then they all ran back to the door as the huge ogre's eyes went bloodshot and its muscles bulged. The volcano lord let out a mighty roar as it began raining blows down on Ethan.

> *Omogg the Volcano lord slashes at you*
> *for 1122 damage.*
> *Sword of the Volcano burns you for 311*
> *fire damage.*
> *Omogg the Volcano lord slashes at you*
> *for 1097 damage.*
> *Sword of the Volcano burns you for 319*
> *fire damage.*
> *Potbelly Cuddlebear heals you with*
> *Growth of the Earth for 4718 health.*

The ogre lord's barrage continued while his friends threw knives, hit it with slings and cast spells to get it down to 5%, when his rage would end.

"OMG! - out - potions!" came Wyatt's frantic voice over his headset and Ethan knew exactly what he was saying. They'd run out of magic potions. Wyatt was out of healing.

"I'm out!" Hunter said.

"I gave you mine already," Gage said apologetically.

"I have 2 potions!" Ethan yelled into his headset. "But you can't get them until he's done with his berserk!"

Looking at his health bar plummeting, he checked the boss. The ogre was only at 8%. They still had to get it down 3 more percent before the rage would stop. He wasn't going to last that long without healing.

He checked his timers. Ten more seconds and his divine shield ability would be up and he could use it for 60 seconds of invulnerability.

> *Omogg the Volcano lord slashes at you*
> *for 1299 damage.*

*Sword of the Volcano burns you for 298
    fire damage.*
*Omogg the Volcano lord slashes at you
    for 1328 damage.*
*Sword of the Volcano burns you for 313
    fire damage.*

His health bar dropped into the red. Less than 10%. He wasn't going to make it another ten seconds. Gritting his teeth, he used his daily paladin ability, pure soul.

Immediately, pure white light surrounded him and his health bar climbed all the way to maximum. It was the paladin ultimate ability, giving him a complete heal once a day. But now it was gone and the boss was still at 8%.

The boss continued to hammer its greatsword against his shield, whittling down his health bar. Divine shield had reset and he'd quickly used it, but now it was down for another 5 minutes. If they didn't get the boss down to 5% soon so Ethan could trade the potions to Wyatt, they were going to fail.

Ethan continued his attacks while his eyes flicked from his own health bar to the boss's health bar. He was at 74%, the boss at 7%. More damage. He was at 58%, the boss at 6%. His own bar kept falling. 43%.... 37%... 30%... 25%... 19%... 13%.

Suddenly the boss stopped its attacks and shook its head. The rage was over. He looked to Wyatt. "QUICK!"

The fat panda waddled over to his side and opened a trade. Ethan moved his last two magic potions into the trade window and clicked the "Accept Trade" button.

And everything went black.

Ethan blinked, unsure what had happened for a second and then screamed. "NOOOOO!!!!"

His power had gone out! Right at the end of the boss fight. His avatar would stay in the game for a few minutes but then he'd be automatically logged off. Not that it mattered. Without him controlling his avatar, he'd be dead in a matter of moments.

Ethan scrambled around for his phone in the pitch blackness. He felt his arm hit his can of soda and then heard it drop to the floor. He cursed as he realized he'd have to clean the carpet before he went to bed.

He felt around the floor until his hand closed on his phone. He pressed his finger on the back of the phone to unlock it, then brought up the flashlight app. Nothing happened. Ethan swore. Had the phone gone dead?

Ethan's eyes were beginning to adjust to the dark and he made out the outline of the window. Hands out in front of him, he slowly made his way to the window and opened the blinds. It was dark outside too, but at least there was a small amount of illumination from the stars.

Tilting his head, he looked outside to see if he could see any light from the neighbor's house. He lived an hour from the city, in a small rural area. It was mostly farms around him, separated by acres or even a mile or two of fields. The nearest neighbor was Jack and his wife, Francis, up on the hill.

He strained to see their house but it was too dark and too far away. He thought he remembered them leaving their porch light on at night, so maybe they lost power too. That was one thing about living in the country. One never knew when some drunk redneck was going to drive his truck into a pole and take out the power for the entire area.

He swore. No power meant no alarm clock and with his phone dead too, he had no way to wake up in time for work tomorrow. And with no phone, he had no way to even call work and tell them he was going to be late.

Intense bright-white light suddenly flooded into the room through the window, blinding him. He held up his hand to ward off the light and tried to blink away the after image.

Squinting, he moved back to the window, trying to determine where the light was coming from.

Next to the window, the light was so bright, he could barely keep his eyes open. He looked out through slitted eyes and could see that the light seemed to be around his house. That was strange. It must be coming from above. Was there a helicopter out there? If so, why? Was it the power company?

With the light streaming in, Ethan walked over to the bedroom door and opened it. He saw light streaming in through all the windows, illuminating the inside of the house. Still using his hand to shield his eyes, he staggered down the hallway to the front door.

Not for the first time, he wished he had a gun. All the other residents seemed to have guns, or at least, they had rifle racks in their pickups. He had a few katanas that he had collected from back in his martial arts days, but they were cheap replicas and not even sharp. Walking into the living room, he took one from its stand and, brushing the dust off of the scabbard, drew the katana.

Because the sword was a cheap replica, it didn't have the right weight or balance, but he could still pummel someone with it. Feeling better, he went back to the front door and turned the deadbolt.

Opening the thick wooden door, he stepped onto his porch. He walked to the edge of the porch and looked up, trying to see the helicopter. That's when he suddenly realized that it was quiet. Too quiet. There was no sound of a helicopter. There weren't even the normal sounds of the country - crickets, bugs, frogs, etc. It was deathly quiet.

The light around the house narrowed until the circle which had been around the entire house shrank to about a six-foot circle, centered around him. Ethan broke out in a cold sweat. This didn't feel right. He needed to get back into the house.

Turning, he went to move he realized that he couldn't move.

His body had stopped responding, frozen in midturn. He really began to panic, trying to force his arms and legs to move but it was as if he'd become a statue, locked in his weird pose.

Then, he felt his body lurch as he began to rise off the ground. He wanted to swear but his mouth was frozen too. Only his lungs seemed to still be working as his breath was coming in quick rasps.

He realized, too late, what was happening to him. He was being abducted. This was some sort of alien spaceship and he was being abducted. The crackpots were right after all. There were aliens. And alien abductions. Where were Mulder and Scully when you needed them!

As he rose into the air, a terrifying thought occurred to him. He remembered other alien stories. Were the anal probings real? What about those stories of alien surgeries and mutilations. His breath came faster as he mentally struggled against whatever paralysis held him.

Then a high-pitched noise started and grew rapidly louder. He tried desperately to move his arms so he could cover his ears, but it was no use. The sound grew in frequency even as the light became brighter and more intense.

Then he could see nothing but white and hear nothing but the high-pitched whine until finally, darkness swallowed him and he knew no more.

3

E than awoke with a groan. His head hurt. His body hurt. Everything hurt. Eyes snapping open, he sat up quickly as he remembered the events from the previous night. He instantly regretted it as pain shot from every part of his body and fireworks erupted behind his eyes. Unable to take the pain, he closed his eyes again and collapsed back down.

He tried to think. Tried to remember. He felt like he had the biggest hangover in the world and he'd gone 10 rounds with a UFC champ. The last thing he remembered was that painful noise and the bright light. And floating in the air!

Feeling himself beginning to panic again, Ethan nearly tried to sit up before he thought better of it. The pain of his previous attempt was still rebounding in his brain. He didn't need a repeat of that. Keeping his eyes closed and thinking through the fog and pain, he tried to figure out his surroundings.

During the brief moment he'd had his eyes open, Ethan had realized he was outside. And it was daytime. He'd seen the sunshine before the light drove daggers into his brain. Feeling around with his hands, he could feel grass and dirt. That made sense, he'd seen the sunlight and he could feel the ground. That meant he was outside on the ground.

Ethan was trying to think things through but it was difficult. He felt like he was thinking through molasses. He thought back to the last thing he remembered. The light. And being carried up into the air. Total X-Files stuff. But that was impossible. That was the stuff of movies and bad novels.

Had he gotten drunk? He didn't remember drinking. Before the whole close encounters episode, he'd been playing Castle-Blaze Online with his friends. He nodded, mostly to himself, and instantly regretted it as bombs went off in his head. Right. No moving the head.

This pain was not normal. Even in the worst hangovers of his college years, he'd never woken up feeling this bad. Was there something serious wrong with him? Like a brain tumor? Had he hallucinated the whole alien abduction scene outside his house? While terrifying, it certainly made more sense than actual aliens.

He tried sitting up again, but this time, he did it very slowly. It hurt and the pain in his head got worse as he moved. Finally he pulled himself up and sat cross legged on the ground. He noticed he was still wearing his sweatpants, T-shirt and sneakers. That was good at least. He wasn't naked.

Ethan was woozy and felt like the world was spinning but he was able to stay seated. The next step was to open his eyes. That was more difficult than sitting up. The light seemed to burrow directly into his brain, causing excruciating pain. He had to take it very slow. He wasn't sure how long it took, but gradually, he forced himself to get used to the light. After what seemed like an eternity of pain, he was able to keep his eyes open, if only slitted.

Once he could keep his eyes open, he was able to get a better look at his surroundings. He was in an open, grassy meadow that was filled with tall grass and dozens of varieties of flowers. None of them looked familiar, but he wasn't really a flower guy.

Now that the pain was starting to subside, he paid attention to the sounds around him too. He could hear birds singing and chirping. He also heard the sound of water flowing, maybe a small river or a brook. Thinking of water made him suddenly realize how parched he was. It was like he hadn't drunk anything in a week.

Moving his head slowly to minimize the pain, he zeroed in on the sound of the running water. He pushed himself forward onto his hands and then gingerly crawled towards the sound of water on his hands and knees. He didn't have to go far.

Ethan had crawled about ten feet before he pushed through some grass, revealing a three-feet-wide stream. Seeing the cool water, he rushed forward and began to scoop large handfuls into his mouth. The water was more refreshing than an ice coffee mocha.

As he did, something flashed in front of his eyes. At first he thought it must be light reflecting off the water of the stream. But it wasn't a reflection. There were words in the water. Glowing green words. He moved his head to get a better look and the words moved with him. He froze. As he turned his head slightly, the words stayed in the same relative spot. He moved his head the other direction and again they stayed in the same relative place.

The words seemed to be displayed in the air in front of him, almost like a HUD, a heads-up display in first-person-shooter and RPG games. He squinted and read the words.

Cool brook water restores 1 Stamina.
Stamina: 10
Cool brook water restores 1 Stamina.
Stamina: 11

Cool brook water restores 1 Stamina.
Stamina: 12

Ethan read the words and then re-read them. They were like the system messages from a MMORPG. Only he wasn't in front of his computer and he wasn't logged into any game. Feeling his heart pounding, he reached up to his head, feeling around for any sort of virtual reality helmet.

Was he in some sort of bizarre government experiment? Was he strapped into a chair in some underground top secret base with a virtual reality headset on? Ethan shook his head, causing shooting pain again. No, even virtual reality headsets weren't this real. He had actually felt the blades of grass under his hands as he had crawled through the grass. Heck, he'd felt the cold water going down his throat.

His mind went back to the white light he'd seen in his house. The floating sensation. Had he been abducted and put into some sort of advanced virtual reality game? Why? Why would aliens do that? It made no sense.

He looked up into the sky, half expecting aliens to be looking down on him from outside some sort of virtual reality snowglobe. Instead, he gawked at the enormous ringed planet that took up most of the sky in the direction he was looking. Turning, he saw two suns in the opposite horizon, one yellow and one blue.

But that wasn't even the strangest part. Between the two suns was a huge black sphere. The sphere seemed to be siphoning light from the two suns in an intricate spiral pattern. Ethan had watched enough scifi movies to know what it was: a black hole.

Ethan swallowed. He wasn't in Kansas anymore, that was for certain. Although it seemed impossible, it appeared more and more like he was in some sort of advanced VR game or world. Did that mean there really were aliens? If so, what did they want from him? Why put him in a game?

Still thirsty, he leaned back down and took several more handfuls of water, each one throwing up another message that he was restoring *Stamina*. He was familiar with the concept of stats from playing RPGs like Pathfinder and Dungeons and Dragons as well as all of the MMORPGs he and his friends had played.

If he had some sort of HUD, did that mean he could see more information? Did he have some sort of character sheet?

As he thought of a character sheet, information flowed into his vision. The earlier messages were replaced by what appeared to be some sort of representation of his body along with additional information. Just like the earlier messages, the text seemed to hover in midair like a hologram.

```
Name: None
Class: None - Default: Commoner
Race: Human
Level: 1
Experience: 0
Fame: 0
Strength: 10
Agility: 13
Hardiness: 13
Intellect: 17
Intuition: 14
Charisma: 10
Health: 20
Stamina: 20
Mana: 34
Karma: 28
```

Ethan soaked in all of the statistics. Most of them seemed

similar to statistics in other RPGs he'd played and he wondered how they applied to him. Without knowing the upper limit of the scores, he had no way to measure whether he was the biggest weakling on the planet or a god among men.

One thing that immediately struck him was the race designation. It said human. How did the aliens know that's what his species called themselves? And why was he even seeing writing in English? It seemed a strange detail to add to some sort of virtual simulated world.

Was there some sort of translation going on? Or was information being fed directly into his brain and this was how he was interpreting it. Did that mean he could just think about commands?

He thought about the character sheet going away and it disappeared. Ethan grinned. He had to admit, it was cool. Thinking of it again, it reappeared instantly. He thought of it again and it reappeared.

This time he focused on Name and an overlay appeared.

No name chosen. Choose a new name? (Yes or No)

Shrugging, Ethan chose Yes and a blank appeared. He started to think of the letters of his own name and they began to appear. E...T... H... A... N. A new prompt appeared.

Change name to Ethan? (Yes or No)

He frowned. Did he really want to be known as Ethan in whatever this virtual world or virtual game was? He always made up unique names for his characters in MMOs and RPGs but his head still hurt and he just didn't have the energy to come up with a new name. Hopefully he could change it later. Selecting Yes, he received a new message.

**You have successfully changed your name
to Ethan.**

At least he had a name on the character sheet now. He moved down to Class. It said None, Default: Commoner. Did that mean he was a commoner? He mentally selected the field.

**No class chosen.
Default class: Commoner.
Choose a class? (Yes or No)**

Ethan chose Yes and another overlay popped up with a list of classes.

**Knight
Swordsman
Tempest
Warrior
Acrobat
Brigand
Duelist
Ranger
Channeler
Summoner
Warlock
Wizard
Cleric
Druid
Priest
Templar**

The list of classes was impressive, more than most MMORPGs he'd played. He wasn't sure what the advantages and disadvantages were to each but he noticed that Magician, Tempest and Wizard were highlighted in a different color.

He thought of each one, trying to see if the HUD would give him more information but it only prompted him if he wanted to change to that class. That was frustrating. How was he supposed to choose a class without knowing what it did, what its abilities and perks were.

Ethan had never been a power gamer, though he was definitely a little more of a min-max meta-gamer than his friends. He liked to find interesting combinations of classes and races that seemed weak but which gave unexpected bonuses.

But now, he had no information at all to base his decision on. Should he just stay a commoner for now? He felt like he should, rather than making a rash decision. If whatever simulation he was in was like regular MMORPGs, once you chose a class, you were locked in.

Letting out a frustrated breath, Ethan mentally dismissed his HUD and the text disappeared, leaving with normal vision. He drank a few more handfuls of water before trying to stand up.

He rose shakily to his legs, standing tall in the knee-high grass, only to come face to face with a woman whose eyes narrowed as she caught sight of him. Ethan started to smile and say hello until he realized the woman wasn't human.

4

The woman on the other side of the stream looked to be about five feet tall with a slim, athletic build. She was dressed in some sort of outfit that looked to Ethan like a worn leather climbing harness. There were various straps and buckles that hid very little but at least covered her crotch and the nipples on her small breasts.

A normal woman in that outfit with a body like hers would attract a lot of male attention. But that wasn't what caught Ethan's attention. Well, not all of his attention.

The woman, if he could call her that, wasn't human. At least, not completely. She had the same shape as a human: arms, legs, neck, head and even fingers and toes. But that's where the similarities ended.

She was a fox girl. Like in some of the Japanese anime shows he'd seen. The woman's body seemed to be covered in fine, short rust-colored fur, which was an off-white on her face, and the front of her torso, but he could see black tiger stripes on her back. And that was just the beginning.

The fox girl had long, red-orange hair, streaked with cream highlights, from which rust-colored fox ears poked out. Even as he stared at her, the ears twitched and rotated slightly. She also had a fluffy rust-colored tail with a cream-colored tip.

Growling, the fox girl revealed slightly pointed canines. Fingernails like claws suddenly extended and the girl crouched down, ready to spring. Ethan opened his mouth to try and talk to the fox girl but she suddenly pounced at him.

Ethan barely had time to react. He tried to stumble backwards and the sudden motion caused pain to explode in his head. The little fox girl slammed into him, knocking him to the ground. Blinding pain exploded through his head as he hit the ground and he nearly passed out. As he blinked away tears of pain, he felt the foxgirl's claws digging into his throat as she grabbed him by the neck.

"What are?! Why have you brought me here?!" she snarled down at him with large grey eyes. "Take me back! Now!"

"I..." Ethan coughed. "I didn't... do... anything."

"Where is my pack?!" she snarled again, tightening her grip on his throat.

"Kidnapped," Ethan gasped. "I... was... kidnapped... bright light... in sky... floating."

The foxgirl sat up and loosened her grip on his throat but didn't release him completely. He gasped for air as she frowned down at him.

"What are you?" she asked, looking at him with undisguised disgust.

"Human," Ethan breathed, still sucking in air. "What are you?"

She puffed out her chest and stared down at him. "I am Fire-Storm pack, rulers of the Northern Forest. Craftiest warriors in all the lands. And you will return me to my pack!"

"Did you... encounter a bright white... light and then float..." he asked her but her eyes grew wide.

The foxgirl growled at him. "Yes, sorcerer! Take me back!"

She started to squeeze his throat again and he put his hands up in a gesture of peace. "Not... me... didn't... do it. Same thing... happened... to me. Bright light... floating... and I woke up here."

What Ethan guessed was a look of uncertainty crossed the foxgirl's face and her grip on his throat and she sat back, still straddling him. She bent down slightly and sniffed, then wrinkled her pink nose. "You stink, human."

She rolled off him, somersaulting into a crouch a few feet away, facing him. Ethan saw her eyes dart to the stream as he sat up but she quickly flicked her eyes back to him.

Sitting up again, he rubbed his throat and coughed. It was sore and he guessed it was bruised. Massaging his throat, he saw a small blinking icon in the lower right of his vision, and as he thought about it his HUD opened up again. He scanned the new lines of code.

Unknown
Foxling
Commoner
Level 1
You have gained: Analyze Skill.
Skill increase: Analyze +1%.
Unknown pounces on you for 1 crushing damage.
Unknown squeezes you for 1 crushing damage.
Unknown claws you for 1 piercing damage.
Unknown squeezes you for 1 crushing damage.

Dumbfounded, he stared at the words on the screen. This was just like some sort of MMORPG and he had apparently gained a new skill, *Analyze*, which he guessed allowed him to see the names and some information about other creatures in the game.

He frowned as he read the damage messages and quickly pulled up his character sheet again.

Health: 16

The foxgirl had done four points of damage to him and he had the bruises to prove it. He was down to nearly three-quarters of his *Health*. That begged the question: What would happen if he reached 0 *Health*? Would he respawn like in a video game? Or would he die for real?

Considering the consequences could be permanent, Ethan didn't want to find out. Which meant he needed to keep his *Health* up.

"You know you did 4 points of damage to me," he said, more to himself than to her. If this was some sort of bizarre simulation or alien VR, that might mean she was a game character. In MMORPG terms, was she a player or a non-player character, or NPC?

And if she was a player, what was she? Another victim, like him, or one of the aliens who abducted him, testing him and gauging his reactions? Did that make him some sort of lab rat?

He saw the foxgirl tense and growl, once again baring her canines. They weren't exactly Dracula fangs, but they looked like they would hurt if she bit him. Considering how much damage he'd already taken, he really didn't need any more. She snarled. "You are lucky I do not kill you!"

He held his hands up, not even sure if that gesture would mean anything to her in whatever culture she came from or was programmed with. "Thank you for not killing me. I mean you no harm."

She snorted but seemed distracted at something. He wondered if she was seeing a HUD as well. "Do you see a HUD?"

"Where is HUD?" The word was obviously awkward on her lips. Her brow wrinkled but then she frowned again.

"It's in your head," he explained but then realized that if she were a NPC, a computer-generated character, she wouldn't have a HUD. "But it looks like writing in the air in front of you."

She bit her lip and looked at him curiously. "In my head. You mean, the glowing signs in front of my face that never move?"

As if to illustrate her point, she moved her hand in front of her like she was trying to catch something in the air. He almost grinned but thought better of it and nodded instead. "Yes. It's writing that appears in front of you but doesn't go away."

Narrowed eyes and a snarl were her only answers. He wanted to ask her questions and compare their experiences to try and make sense of what had happened to him. As he looked at her, still crouched and watching him like a ... well, like a cat watches a mouse... he didn't think she would cooperate. Maybe if he offered her an olive branch.

"You can make the writing go away, if you tell it to go away in your mind. Just think about the HUD and then think: go away," he told her, smiling.

She narrowed her eyes more at him but then her eyes went wide and she looked around with what he thought might be a smile. Her hand pawed at the air like she was trying to make sure the HUD was really gone.

Then, the foxgirl seemed to remember him and dropped back into a crouch, her brief smile replaced once more by a snarl. "What is that magic?"

He was going to try to explain it but wasn't sure he understood it himself. And without a reference point like the MMORPGs on Earth, how could he really explain it. And he assumed it was some sort of technology that he was experiencing but he didn't know for certain.

"I'm not sure what it is or exactly how it works," he told her truthfully. "But I think whoever or whatever brought us here is doing it to us."

"Who?!" she demanded. "Where are they?!"

He shrugged slowly, making sure it didn't seem threatening. "I don't know. I only woke up a few minutes ago."

She made an unreadable face, an expression that didn't seem to have a human equivalent. "I have only been here a few minutes too."

A sudden thought struck him and he was surprised he hadn't thought of it before. "How are you speaking English?"

She wrinkled her furry brow. "I am not speaking the Engleash. You are speaking T'cha'raa. You speak it very well for a who-man."

He kept a smile on his face but wasn't sure what to make of her reply. There was no possible way they could have the exact same language. The odds were too astronomical. Not even everyone on Earth spoke the same language.

That meant something must be translating for them. That did seem to lend credence to the idea that he was in some sort of alien version of a virtual reality game. Either that or he had some sort of translator implanted in his head.

If the aliens that abducted him had the capability of crossing the stars, they probably had much more powerful computers than anything on Earth. It would stand to reason they could do some sort of translation between various species.

It was hard to wrap his mind around. To him, it seemed he had only been on Earth a few minutes ago. Now, he was in some sort of alien equivalent of CastleBlaze. Thinking of CastleBlaze, the question he'd asked himself before came to mind. What would happen if he died in this simulation? If in fact, it was a simulation.

He caught the fox girl's eyes darting to the stream again and then jumping back to him. He gestured to the water. "Go ahead and drink. I'm not going to attack you."

She bared her teeth, clearly not believing him.

Ethan smiled at her. "It's not like you didn't already prove you could take me down without breaking a sweat."

The foxgirl made a noise in her throat that might have been a chuckle and her face broke into a smirk for an instant before resuming her snarl. But she flicked her eyes to the water longingly before fixing her gaze back on him. Slowly, she began to move sideways towards the stream still facing him.

She was almost to the water when the grass on the opposite side of the stream was pushed aside. The figure of a stout, female form in a leather tunic, blue canvas leggings and large, metal-bound boots stepped into view. The squat figure looked down at the stream and grinned broadly. "Odin's Beard! Something to drink! About knockin' time!"

5

The foxgirl seemed to jump ten feet straight, hissing at the newcomer, before coming back down to earth and scrambling behind him. Ethan cast a confused look at the woman behind him. Hadn't she just been wary of him? And now she was hiding behind him?

Ethan looked back to the newcomer, who had been startled by the fox girl. His first impression was that she was a dwarf. She literally fit the description of the quintessential stereotypical fantasy dwarf from the RPGs and MMOs he'd played. Minus a beard.

The stocky woman was about four and a half feet tall, with dark ebony skin, as if she had been hewn from black volcanic rock. She was broad shouldered with thick, stout limbs. Her chest was large, in every sense of the word. She had breasts that would make a pornstar jealous, but the dwarf looked to have a good deal of muscle underneath.

The ebony-skinned dwarf's hair was long and jet black, pulled into a topknot, with the remaining hair flowing down her back to the small of her back. In her thick right hand, she had a large wooden cudgel that seemed little more than a thick branch she had found.

The woman scrunched her face as she looked at Ethan and at the foxgirl with bright-red eyes, squinting at both of them and then at nothing in particular. He realized she must be reading her HUD.

"Ethan and unknown," the dwarf muttered. "Those are stupid names." She looked down at the stream and then back to them, slapping her club into her opposite hand. "I'm parched and I'm going to get me a drink of this water. Don't either of you try anything or you'll get twacked! You hear."

No waiting for a response, the dwarf bent down, keeping her club in her hand and plunged her face into the water. Ethan glanced back at the fox girl who was staring at the strange dwarf too. He chuckled. "I guess she was thirsty."

The foxgirl nodded and then seemed to realize she was hiding behind Ethan and crawled a few feet to his side, angling herself so she could see him and the dwarf.

"Ah!" cried the dwarf as she pulled her head from the stream. "It's not mead, but it'll do in a pinch."

Ethan took the opportunity to examine her, willing himself to *Analyze* her.

Ainslee Arnbuckle
Dwarf
Knight
Level 1
Skill increase: Analyze +1%.

Ethan cocked his head at the dwarf as he read the information on the HUD. According to the HUD, she actually was a dwarf! And unlike him, the dwarf had a class. She also had a name. Had she figured out how to work the HUD?

"It looks like you're a knight," Ethan said cautiously. "Did you choose that class from your HUD?"

"HUD?" The dwarf squinted at him. Her face brightened. "You mean see-thru scroll? Is that what's it called?"

"Where I'm from we have similar things and we call them HUDs or heads-up display," he told her.

"Heads-up display." She tilted her head, playing with the phrase. "Heads-up display. HUD. I like it! Easy to say! To answer your question, yes, I saw the class and I assume that's something like profession, so I chose knight - even if I don't have a goat to ride. I put my own name in too. Didn't want to be unknown."

"How did you figure out how to do that?" he asked her.

"We dwarves are good at figuring things out," she grinned. "And I'm the best smith in all of Inverasdale! It didn't take long." Her face became serious and she pointed to the ringed planet and then to the double suns. "This isn't Inverasdale though. Not even Ninzeon."

Ainslee eyed them both again before shrugging. "Neither of you look capable of bringing me here unless you're a better craftsman than me and even then I don't know about the science."

"Ninzeon? Is that the planet you're from?" Ethan asked. Unlike the foxgirl, she seemed to understand concepts like planets and had even figured out the HUD and had chosen a class. That was more than he had done.

"Space flight? You mean, between planets?" she chuckled. "There are dwarfs who dream about going into the stars, but no one's ever succeeded. Our best balloons will only go so high. They just prove that what goes up, must come down. And usually with a big crash."

The dwarf threw her head back and roared in laughter for almost a full minute before wiping her eyes. Ethan and the fox girl exchanged looks but said nothing, neither apparently finding Ainslee's words as funny as the dwarf did.

"So what's your story?" the dwarf said. "Do you live in this place? And why did you bring me here?"

Ethan started to speak but the fox girl hissed. "No, I do not live here! I was stolen from my lands and brought here against my will."

The dwarf looked to Ethan with a raised eyebrow. "What about you?"

"Same thing," he told her. "Bright light, floating in the air and a..."

"...god awful noise," the dwarf shuddered. "It gives me the willies just thinking about it."

"It seems like we were all brought here," Ethan said and looked pointedly at the fox girl, "against our will. The question I've been wondering is... why?"

They all exchanged glances but none of them had any answers.

"I have been wondering the same thing," came a melodic woman's voice from behind Ethan. Once again, the fox girl seemed to leap straight up into the air and came down on her hands and feet, head darting from Ethan, to the dwarf and then to the new arrival.

A slender, graceful figure stepped into view from behind them and Ethan's breath caught. The newcomer was about the same height as the fox girl. But where the fox girl had an athletic build, the new woman was slender, like a runway model. Despite her slim body, she had full hips and a generous bosom. She was also short for a runway model, just slightly taller than the foxgirl.

Long and willowy, the woman had delicate features and smooth tan skin. Her bright-green eyes were just slightly larger than a human's but it was her long, tapered ears sticking out of her lustrous green hair that gave her away as something other than human.

She was dressed in a simple, if somewhat revealing, high-cut green tunic that was just shy of being indecent but which revealed her long shapely legs and bare feet. He took a moment to *Analyze* her.

> **Yuliana Madeiras**
> **Elf**
> **Commoner**
> **Level 1**
> **Skill increase: Analyze +1%.**

The elf looked at him, a twinkle in her eyes, as if she knew he'd just *Analyzed* her. Could she sense it? Or was she just guessing?

"Who are you?" the dwarf asked, her club at the ready.

"I am Yuliana," she replied with a smile. "And it looks like some of you already know that because of the... what did I hear you call it... the HUD."

"You heard us talking?" the dwarf asked, looking around, a cautious look on her face. "Are there any more of you?"

The elf laughed, a high-pitched sound that reminded Ethan of songbirds. "No, like you, I was brought here by the bright light."

"How long were you listening to us?" scowled Ainslee.

"My kind has exceptional hearing," she told them. "I heard you from the other side of the meadow and came to investigate."

Ethan stood slowly and looked around. His eyes were finally accustomed to the bright light and he glanced around the meadow. It stretched out hundreds of yards and he turned towards the elf, pointing to the far end. "You heard us from way over there."

Yuliana smiled and nodded. "You were very noisy."

"Who is she?" the elf asked, her eyebrows furrowed. "Has she not set her name?"

"How do you know about the HUD?" Ethan asked.

The elf shrugged. "I saw it right away but didn't understand it until I heard you all talking. Once I realized it wasn't some sort of illusion or consequence of dehydration, I was able to manipulate it and enter my name. I do not yet understand some of the options, however.

"Like class," she replied, her eyes going glassy as she must have pulled her own HUD up. "I do not understand what that means."

"It's like a job or profession," Ainslee said dismissively. "You just choose one you like. I'm a knight!"

"Oh," the elf said, her features troubled. "I've never really had a job before. More like a calling."

Ethan was watching the exchange and also casting glances at the fox girl, who seemed ready to bolt at any moment. Still, she stayed and her eyes darted around, her ears and tail twitching. He turned to the elf. "What was your calling?"

"I tended a sacred grove on my world," she replied, her eyes almost tearing. "But I cannot feel the grove any longer."

"You tended trees?" the dwarf asked incredulously. "What's there to tend? They're... trees."

The elf gave the dwarf a scowl. "They are not just trees! They are sentient life!"

The dwarf seemed about to retort but Ethan spoke up first. "You sound like a druid. Someone who is in tune with nature and protects it."

"Druid? That is my... profession?" she asked. "My class?"

"I think it can be whatever you want it to be," he told her. "But usually your statistics help determine your class."

"Statistics?" the elf asked, her head tilted to one side to regard him.

"In your HUD, they're things like Strength, Hardiness, etc.," he told her. "My guess is Intuition is probably a prime attribute for druids."

The dwarf eyed him suspiciously. "You seem to know an awful lot about this HUD, attributes, and classes."

Ethan almost smiled. He wasn't about to tell them his experience came from roleplaying games and online fantasy games. "This is very similar to the way things are in my world."

The dwarf snorted but then shrugged and looked down at the fox girl. "What's her story anyway?" The dwarf talked very slowly, pronouncing each syllable. "Do... you... have... a... name?"

The fox girl hissed. "I have a name!"

"Well then," the dwarf retorted, hands on hips. "Why don't you put it in your HUD. That's Heads... Up... Display."

"I know what it is," the foxgirl spat. Her eyes went unfocused for a long moment and then scowled at the dwarf. "There. I have a name. It is Nia!"

Curiously, Ethan analyzed her.

Nia
Foxling
Acrobat
Level 1

"Nice to meet you, Nia," Ethan smiled at her, then he noticed she had chosen her class too. "What made you choose acrobat?"

"In my tribe, I am a great dancer," she said proudly. "Acrobat is like dancer, yes?"

"Sure," he said. "I guess."

"Very well," the elf said from behind him and he turned to face her. "I have chosen druid as you suggested."

He started to point out that he hadn't actually suggested it but then thought better of it and instead smiled. "Excellent."

The dwarf was looking at him now, her eyes squinting. "So I'm a knight, the foxgirl is a dancer acrobat and the pointy-eared elf is a druid. What about you Mr. human? What is your profession?"

"That is a good question," he replied. "A very good question."

6

"What was your profession back on your world?" Ainslee asked gruffly. She looked him up and down and snickered. "Were you a dancer too?"

Blushing, Ethan shook his head. How could he explain what he had done. He fixed computers, installed software, and did some programming every now and then. None of that really equated to one of the classes he'd seen.

He brought up his statistics.

```
Strength: 10
Agility: 13
Hardiness: 13
Intellect: 17
Intuition: 14
Charisma: 10
```

His *Strength* and *Charisma* were, unsurprisingly, his lowest attributes, followed by his *Agility* and *Hardiness*. Surprisingly, his *Intuition* was his second-highest stat. But then again, a lot of troubleshooting was intuition. His *Intellect* was his highest attribute and he sighed as he realized that probably meant a magic class.

He had never really gone for magic classes, preferring to be in the thick of things. Unfortunately, he didn't seem to have a choice. And then again, he had no idea how magic worked in this alien simulation either.

Ethan brought up the list of classes and focused on the ones that seem to be magical classes.

Channeler

Summoner

Warlock

Wizard

He had a vague idea of what each class should do, in RPG/MMO terms. Did the same apply in this world? It seemed like a stretch but he didn't have any other basis to work from.

If it followed game logic, a *Channeler* would be someone who channeled extradimensional energy for spells. They basically allowed themselves to become conduits for other powers. That presented two issues.

First, he didn't know what sort of "powers" he might be channeling. If magic was real in this game, he didn't want to be beholden to any sort of powerful entity. He'd read too many Faustian stories to be comfortable with that.

Second, he didn't know much more except that in the games he'd played, channelers could end up channeling too much and burning themselves out or even killing themselves. Without knowing if death was real in the game, he wasn't going to risk it.

A *Summoner* would be able to summon creatures to fight for him. He had visions of himself throwing small spheres on the ground and yelling "I choose you!" Then he remembered that in some games, summoners actually summoned demonic creatures. He had no desire to try bargaining with demons - especially if there was any chance they could turn against him.

Warlock held the same issues as summoner. Warlocks gained their powers by making pacts with extradimensional creatures like devils and demon lords. In all the comics and movies, this always ended poorly. No thanks.

The final class was *Wizard*. He didn't know any pitfalls of being a wizard, not unless he had a lightning-shaped scar on his forehead. He thought of wizards like Merlin and couldn't remember any downsides. It definitely seemed like the safest bet, given his other choices.

Gritting his teeth, he chose *Wizard* for his class.

> *You have selected Wizard. Continue (Yes*
> *or No)*
> *Note: Once chosen a class cannot be*
> *changed without retraining.*

Ethan looked at the message and marveled at how similar this simulation was to the MMORPGs he played back home. Had the aliens gotten the idea from them? Or had the developers somehow gotten the ideas from aliens? Were they past abductees? It was an interesting theory but he had no way to prove it at the moment.

He chose Yes to confirm his class and instantly received new messages.

> *New Class: Wizard*
> *Wizards are masters of the arcane arts.*
> *They harness mystical and elemental*
> *energy. While not specialized in any*
> *specific type of magic, they conjure*
> *a wide range of effects.*
> *Intellect +1*

```
Ability gained: Mana Affinity I
Skill gained: Air Magic
Skill gained: Earth Magic
Skill gained: Fire Magic
Skill gained: Water Magic
```

He looked at the messages and brought up his HUD. He thought it was interesting that he had instantly gained a point of *Intellect*. Was he suddenly smarter? He didn't feel any smarter.

He noticed a bent corner in the lower right that seemed to indicate there was another page he could select. Mentally choosing it, he went to a new page that displayed abilities and another for skills. He looked at both.

```
Abilities
Mana Affinity I
Skills
Analyze: 1
Air Magic: 1
Earth Magic: 1
Fire Magic: 1
Mystical Magic: 1
Water Magic: 1
```

The one thing that he immediately saw that was missing were spells. He scrolled back through his messages. It distinctly said Wizards used spells. So where were his spells?

"Seriously!" he grimaced aloud.

"What's wrong?" asked the elf.

"I'm a wizard, Harry," he told them and watched all three women look at him skeptically. "I guess that means I can do magic..."

Nia frowned and looked at him suspiciously. "You mean, real magic?"

"Magic?! Bah!" Ainslee burst out in laughter. "Ha! You going to make some ore appear out of a hat? Or make a pick disappear up your arse?"

Embarrassed, he felt his face growing warm. He'd been embarrassed many times, but this time it was different. This time the warmth from his face spread throughout his body and became a burning.

But something else was different. A new sense of the awareness of the warmth he had previously had. Ethan also felt like he could control the warmth. Tentatively, he focused on the warmth and willed it to gather in his hand. It resisted at first, stubbornly staying where it was. Then he exerted more will and it slowly obeyed.

The warmth gathered in his hand and as it did, his hand grew hotter and hotter until it felt like it was burning. Grimacing, he knew he needed to do something else and his first instinct was to move the warmth outside his body. Even as he thought of it, the warmth seemed to move out of his hand and gather in a ball of flaming energy that hovered just above his hand.

The women gasped and Nia backed up a step. She looked wide-eyed at him. "I thought you just said you didn't know how to cast spells!"

"I don't," he said, looking in awe at the fiery ball in his hand. He grinned like a little boy who had just been given a Christmas present. He glanced over to Nia. "Apparently, I can just do magic."

Even as he spoke, his new sense of awareness could detect something unstable in the ball of fire. His will was keeping the ball together, but it was trying to expand. Ethan tried to force it together but it wasn't working. It wanted to expand. It wanted to explode.

Without hesitation, Ethan threw the ball of flame into the air like a baseball. The ball of flame sailed thirty feet and then exploded into a large fireball about fifteen feet in diameter.

The women dove to the ground as the fireball exploded and Ethan could feel the heat from where he stood. He felt drained but he was still grinning. He'd just created a fireball spell! Just like from one of his tabletop RPG games.

Skill increase: Fire Magic +2%.

Cursing and hissing, the women got to their feet. Ainslee looked into the air and whistled. "I like it."

Nia was crouched down, eying Ethan warily. She glanced between him and where the fireball had gone off repeatedly but said nothing.

The elf shuddered and looked at Ethan with a mix of fear and amazement. "Very... destructive."

A blow on his back nearly knocked him over as Ainslee clapped him on the back with her meaty hand. "Not bad, bean pole! Can you do anything useful, like make mead?"

"I'll work on it." Ethan forced a smile. His brain was still reeling from having just performed real magic. Well, real magic in an alien simulation. He'd also done it mostly by accident. He would need to practice before he could cast spells on demand.

He brought up his HUD and checked out his *Mana* level. His maximum *Mana* was 37 but it was still at its maximum value. It was as if the fireball had cost no mana. That was weird.

He also noticed that his maximum *Mana* had gone up. Was that due to that *Mana Affinity* ability? Or the Intellect gain? Or both?

Maybe spells didn't cost *Mana*, like in the MMORPGs he played. Maybe he could create all the magic he wanted. That would be extremely powerful once he figured out how it worked. Then he noticed his *Stamina*.

Stamina: 17

Ethan frowned. He'd just managed to get his *Stamina* up to 20 by drinking water. Now it was back down to 17. Had casting the fireball drained that much *Stamina* from him? Why *Stamina* and not *Mana*? It felt like wizards should use *Mana* for their spells.

If he was using *Stamina* for every spell, that would be a big limitation. That was especially true if *Stamina* was used for other things. He would need to find a way to raise it.

He realized that he was treating this like a game. He was dropping into his old habits of analyzing game mechanics and naturally trying to get every advantage. It had served him well in MMOs and the tabletop RPGs he played. But was it the best thing to do in this new, bizarre alien simulation.

And he was now convinced this was some sort of alien simulation MMORPG. After all, he'd just done real magic. That simply didn't happen in the normal universe. There were laws of nature. It just wasn't possible.

Ainslee cleared her throat loudly. "Well. It was nice meeting you all, but I think I need to find a way to get home to my clan. And maybe find some mead along the way."

The other two seemed to have similar thoughts and Ethan bristled at the idea. They were literally the perfect MMO party. Normally there was a fighter or tank, that was Ainslee obviously. Then there was a thief, which he supposed Nia was with her Acrobat class. Yuliana was the healer and he was the magical dps. That was too coincidental.

"I think we should stick together," he told them, causing them all to look at him. Yuliana looked neutral. Nia looked like she was about to run away, while Ainslee just scowled.

"And why should we do that?" Ainslee asked, hands on her hips.

"I don't think it was a coincidence that the aliens, or whatever they are, kidnapped the four of us. Each of us has a class that complements the others. Ainslee, you're a knight. Someone who can take a blow and give it back. Yuliana, I'm assuming you can heal with your druid class. Nia, you have stealth. And I have magic."

The women's expressions hadn't changed so he continued. "On my world, there are situations similar to this where teams of people band together. It's nearly always that same general formula. And the one thing you never, ever do... is split the party?"

"Split the party?" Nia asked, her tail twitching.

"Go your separate ways," he clarified. "Together, our classes complement each other."

The women's expressions had softened but they still looked unconvinced. He rolled his eyes. "Plus, there's safety in numbers."

The women exchanged glances with each other before Ainslee rolled her eyes and let out a breath. "Fine. Fine. You all can come with me. But if we find mead, the first bottle goes to me! Got it?"

Yuliana shrugged. "I am willing to stay together... for now. After all, a cluster of trees is stronger than a lone oak."

"I will come for now," Nia looked around and finally nodded, "but only until we find my pack."

Ethan smiled. They had a group. He looked around. Now what? If this was some sort of high tech, virtual reality MMO, then where was the starter quest? And were there monsters, like in normal MMOs that they would have to kill?

"Something is..." the elf started to say but then dove to the ground.

Ethan heard three high-pitched squeals off to his left and a spear sailed past his head, missing him by an inch. They were being attacked!

7

E than dived to the ground, the action shooting waves of pain through his brain. The pain had dulled for the slow movements he had been making but the sudden jarring impact of hitting the earth was excruciating.

Through the haze of pain, Ethan saw three short, lean figures burst into view through the tall grass. The creatures were only about three feet tall, with mottled dark-purple skin that was covered in small scales. They had large, scaled dog-like faces, small beady black eyes and a large mouth full of sharp teeth. They also had lizard-like tails, covered in the same dark-purple scales.

In contrast to their large heads, their bodies were thin, almost emaciated. The things had smaller legs but their arms were disproportionately long, which he guessed would give them nearly the same reach as him.

Almost unbidden, his HUD popped up with a new message as he caught sight of the things bursting out of the grass.

Meadow Clan Raider
Kobold

Warrior
Level 1

Skill increase: Analyze +1%.

Two of the kobold raiders were on the other side of Ainslee. One carried a crude spear, like the one that had almost hit Ethan in the head. The other carried a club, similar to the one the dwarf wielded.

The remaining kobold, who also carried a spear, leveled the weapon at Nia and charged. Glancing over, he saw the foxgirl frozen wide-eyed on the ground. It didn't look like she was frozen in fear. The creature was going to skewer her right through the chest.

Cursing his chivalry, he rolled to put himself in the path of the kobold. Ethan really didn't want to get hit by the spear but he couldn't just lie there and watch it kill Nia.

He raised his hands protectively over his face, hoping the kobold wouldn't hit a vital spot in his chest or abdomen. As he did, he felt a stirring in the air around him as it whirled about him towards his outstretched hands.

The charging kobold reached him in only a couple of seconds. Just as the spear looked ready to go past his hands and be thrust into his chest, it hit something invisible in front of him, deflecting the spear so that it just grazed his left shoulder.

Meadow Clan Raider pierces you with
   crude spear for 1 damage.
Skill increase: Air Magic +2%.

The confused kobold couldn't stop its momentum and slammed into the same invisible barrier, which Ethan guessed was some sort of air shield he must have instinctively created.

The impact sent the kobold sprawling, the spear flying from its fingers.

It also sent Ethan crashing backwards, knocking the air from his lungs. As it did, he sensed whatever invisible shield he had created wink out of existence. He groaned as, once again, he was defenseless. He gasped for air and looked around for the kobold's spear.

Ethan found it to his left, but before he could reach for it, the little kobold recovered and jumped on him. The creature lunged forward with its mouthful of jagged teeth, aiming at his throat. He barely got his left arm up and under the thing's chin, keeping the snapping jaws just out of reach.

With his right hand, he caught the kobold's left forearm but couldn't stop its right hand from raking across his chest with its dirty claws.

Meadow Clan Raider slashes you with claws for 2 damage.

The thing struggled against him. It was much stronger than Ethan expected. Although the kobold was only the size of a human child, he seemed to have nearly the same strength as an adult. Granted, he was a thin, out of shape adult, but he would have thought his size would have given him some advantage.

The creature pressed down, trying to get its jaws around his throat and Ethan felt his arm giving. He also felt the right claws digging into his chest again.

Meadow Clan Raider slashes you with claws for 1 damage.

But he also felt something else. Like he had done when he'd managed to create the fireball, Ethan felt his own heat. Curious, he felt for the kobold's heat. He didn't sense heat, but something else - moving and flowing. Was it water? Experimentally he reached out with his will and touched the water in the struggling creature.

The kobold's eyes went wide for a second then it redoubled its struggles, clawing and snapping at him.

> *Meadow Clan Raider slashes you with*
> *claws for 1 damage.*

It had sensed him reaching out to the water in its body. Unsure what to do, Ethan tried to heat the water, but that didn't work. Remembering his physics, he remembering the faster molecules vibrated, the hotter they were. So, he tried slowing down the water molecules. Effectively, cooling it.

The creature's struggles began to slow and its eyes grew wider. Not only that, but its skin began to turn a bluish color as the water in the creature began to get cooler.

> *You freeze Meadow Clan Raider for 6 cold*
> *damage.*
> *Meadow Clan Raider is frozen.*
> *Skill increase: Water Magic +1%.*

The kobold continued to struggle weakly but its attacks now barely scratched him and did no damage. Ethan continued to will the water in the creature's body to get colder, watching in rapt fascination as frost began to form on the kobold's skin and its breath came out in misty puffs as if it were winter time.

> *You freeze Meadow Clan Raider for 7 cold*
> *damage.*
> *Skill increase: Water Magic +1%.*

The raider's movements continued to slow, even as frost covered its body, until finally it stopped moving completely.

> *You freeze Meadow Clan Raider for 7 cold damage.*
> *Meadow Clan Raider dies.*
> *Skill increase: Water Magic +1%.*
> *You gain 10 experience. Experience to next level 190.*

Ethan looked up into the frost-covered eyes of the kobold who had just been about to kill him and shuddered. Killing monsters in games had never been this real. With an effort, he heaved the small creature off himself and then grabbed the spear.

> *You acquire crude spear.*
> *Crude Spear*
> *Type: Two-handed piercing weapon*
> *Range: 4 ft. / 30 ft.*
> *Damage: 4 points piercing damage*
> *Durability: 3 of 6*
> *Warning: You have no proficiency with this weapon and suffer -1 Strength, -1 Agility when attacking with it.*
> *You have gained: Appraise Skill.*
> *Skill increase: Appraise +1%.*

Standing up, he saw the shirt he had been wearing was shredded and his chest was bleeding from multiple claw marks. Ethan cursed. Then he read the system message and cursed again. The alien simulation used some sort of proficiency system. Without training, he had penalties when using the kobold's spear. But at least it was a weapon.

Ethan also saw that there was some sort of skill involved with examining items, similar to the *Analyze* skill he had used to get information about the enemy. But what did this new *Appraise* skill really do and what would be the advantage of raising it? He had so many questions and no answers.

Looking towards the dwarf, Ethan saw that she had already killed one of the other kobolds, the one who had been carrying the club. But the dwarf hadn't remained unscathed. She was bleeding from a wound on her left thigh and another from her side.

Spear in hand, Ethan circled around the kobold, intending to get behind it. But the last kobold saw him coming and angled its body to keep both he and the dwarf in sight. As he continued to circle, the raider was forced to split its attention between Ethan and Ainslee.

As the kobold's head swiveled from Ainslee to Ethan, the dwarf saw an opening and stepped forward. She brought down the club and the kobold barely got its spear up in a two-handed grip like a quarterstaff to block the powerful blow.

Unfortunately for the little creature, that left its back exposed to Ethan. He stepped forward and thrust his spear into the creature's back.

You pierce Meadow Clan Raider for 3 damage + 5 damage flanking bonus.

The kobold stiffened as the flint tip of the spear punctured its skin. Its arms seem to lose strength and the dwarf took advantage of its lowered guard. With her powerful arm, she swung her club at the creature's head, snapping its head to the side.

Meadow Clan Raider dies.

You gain 5 experience. Experience to next level 185.

The kobold's body staggered a single step to the side and then collapsed to the ground. Ethan and Ainslee looked around to see if there were any other kobolds but none presented themselves.

"What the four moons were those things?" Ainslee demanded, looking down at the little green creatures. Ethan saw her hand clutched at her side where blood still flowed freely. He looked down at his own wounds and saw that for the most part, his bleeding had stopped.

He noticed that both he and the dwarf were breathing heavily from the exertion, which he found interesting for a simulation. Despite the pain in his chest, he had to admit, the simulation the aliens had created was nearly flawless.

If it weren't for the HUD messages and the magic, he might think he was in a real place. He'd literally been scared out of his wits during the combat but somehow he'd been able to cast a spell and stab a kobold. Not bad for a computer tech. Geeky gamers of the world rejoice!

Suddenly the dwarf's face turned red and she spun on Nia and Yuliana. "And where were you two while I was getting skewered by these creatures?"

Nia cowered, still crouched where Ethan had left her. Yuliana, on the other hand, crossed her arms over her chest and glared at the dwarf defiantly. "What was I supposed to do? I am no warrior. I am a tree tender. Plus, I had no weapon."

"Bah," Ainslee muttered. "What good are you?!"

Ethan felt like he needed to intervene. He still felt like there was some reason the four of them ended up in this meadow and that their classes complemented each other. He couldn't have them breaking up and going their separate ways.

"Yuliana," he called out, causing the elf to turn her glare on him. "You chose the druid class, right?"

The elf's face softened slightly and she nodded. "Yes."

"Where I come from," he spoke calmly, trying to defuse the situation. He'd certainly had plenty of experience doing that with irate customers who had gotten their computers infected with malware or left their laptop somewhere where the dog could knock it to the floor.

"In my world, druids can heal wounds," he told her. He gave her a questioning look. "Can you do that?"

"Heal?" she asked. She was no longer glaring but instead looked intrigued. "How would I do that?"

You have gained: Diplomacy Skill.
Skill increase: Diplomacy +1%.

Ethan ignored the skill gain and considered her question. He thought back to how his own powers worked. Then he thought about how a druid's power might work. Druids were nature healers and generally had an affinity towards plants.

"Come over here please," he said, using the same voice he used when he asked customers to show him the malfunctioning computer.

The elf hesitated but then came to stand near him and the angry dwarf. For her part, Ainslee seemed to have calmed down and was watching curiously. Even Nia was watching.

"For me," Ethan started. "I was able to sense the heat in my own body and then channel it to create a fire. Just now, I channeled heat out of the kobold who attacked me and froze it. I think your powers might work the same way - but with plants."

"How?" Yuliana raised an eyebrow.

"See if you can concentrate and sense the plants around you," he told her.

The elf frowned but closed her eyes and seemed to concentrate. Then she snapped them open, a look of surprise on her face. "I feel them!"

"Good," Ethan told her. He wasn't quite sure about the next part but it made sense to him. "Put your hand on Ainslee's wound and then think about channeling the life from the plants into Ainslee."

Both women gave him sharp looks but he held up his hand. "Ainslee, do you want to keep bleeding? And Yuliana, just channel a little bit of life from each plant you sense. It won't hurt them."

At least, Ethan hoped it wouldn't. Considering what had happened when he channeled heat out of the kobold, he wasn't sure.

Yuliana nodded and closed her eyes again. Nothing happened for a long moment. Then, a green glow seemed to surround her hand and spread across Ainslee's wound. The dwarf gasped but then her face relaxed and she grinned.

"Wow!" Ainslee looked at her wide-eyed. "Thank you. That feels heaps better."

Ainslee removed her hand from the wound and through the hole in her tunic, Ethan could see that the flesh had completely mended, leaving just a small scar.

The elf looked from the dwarf to her own hands. "I... I healed her."

"You did." Ethan smiled. Yuliana half-heartedly returned his smile, still staring at the place where the dwarf's wound had been.

"What about that one?!" the dwarf asked sourly, pointing at Nia.

8

N ia shrank back from the dwarf's accusing stare, and then even further as Ethan and Yuliana turned to her.

As he twisted towards Nia, Ethan was suddenly overcome with dizziness and staggered. Now that the fight was over, the adrenaline was wearing off. He became acutely aware of the throbbing pain from his shoulder and chest. But it wasn't just that, his legs felt like jello.

Everything in this simulation felt a little too real. Part of him started to wonder if it really were a simulation. The experience just seemed too real. But then there was magic. And that just didn't fit into the laws of the universe.

Afraid something was terribly wrong, he brought up his character sheet and looked at his statistics.

Name: Ethan
Class: Wizard
Race: Human
Level: 1
Experience: 15

Fame: 0

Strength: 10
Agility: 13
Hardiness: 13
Intellect: 18
Intuition: 14
Charisma: 10

Health: 11
Stamina: 2
Mana: 30
Karma: 28

He frowned as he saw his maximum *Health* had dropped. Was that because of his class change from commoner to *Wizard*? Regardless, it was below half. His *Mana* had changed too, but he'd gotten a point of *Intellect* when he became a *Wizard*. That must affect *Mana*.

Alarmed, he noticed that his *Stamina* was almost completely gone. Using the magic on that kobold had taken a toll. What happened when he ran out of *Stamina*? Would he collapse? Be unable to move? Or just be unable to cast spells?

"Oh," Yuliana said and rushed over to Ethan. "You are hurt as well."

The elf put her hand on the wound on his shoulder and across his chest. She closed her eyes and Ethan gasped as he felt a strange energy flow into him. It was both hot and cold at the same time, as well as painful and itchy. It felt like hundreds of tiny, very hot, ants crawling around the wounds. He imagined he could feel the energy pushing the wound closed and knitting the muscle and flesh back together.

*Yuliana Madeiras heals you for 12
  health.*

She opened her eyes and started to look at her handiwork. Then her eyes became unfocused and rolled into the back of her head and she collapsed. Ethan barely managed to step forward and catch her before she hit the ground.

"What's wrong with her?" Ainslee demanded, stomping over to him.

He scrambled for her wrist and felt for a pulse. Ethan was worried that her anatomy wouldn't give her a pulse but then relaxed as he felt a steady pulse.

You have gained: Healing.
Skill increase: Healing +1%.

He saw the skill gain but didn't have time to think about it. Ethan looked up at the dwarf. "She's alive."

"You can tell that by touchin' her hand?" The dwarf scowled. "So what's wrong with her then?"

"I'm not sure," he replied and began examining her for any wounds. Then he remembered how low his *Stamina* had gotten from using his own magic. Was that her issue? Had she completely depleted her *Stamina*? "She might be out of stamina."

"Stamina?" The dwarf furrowed her brow. "That's one of the items in the HUD, right?"

"Yes," he replied. "Using my magic depleted mine. Healing us might have used up all of hers."

"So what do we do for her?" the dwarf asked. "I owe her. We can't just leave her like this."

"The water," came Nia's voice from behind them. "It restored stamina. It might restore hers."

Ethan and Ainslee both looked back at her and then at each

other. He shrugged. "It did restore stamina. It's worth a shot."

Leaning the prone elf against the dwarf, Ethan walked over to the stream and gathered some water in his cupped hands. Walking back over to the elf, he tried to pour some water into her mouth, but it just spilled over her face. "Lean her head back and open her mouth."

The dwarf did so and he allowed a little of the water at a time to drop into the elf's open mouth. He kept drizzling the water into her mouth for almost a minute before she began coughing and her eyes fluttered open. She looked around wide-eyed for a moment before appearing to realize where she was - and who they were. "Wha- What happened?"

"I think you used up too much of your stamina," Ethan replied. "Can you check your HUD and see what your current Stamina is?"

"My stamina?" she asked groggily. She blinked several times before seeming to understand what he had asked. "Oh, right. The writing."

The elf's eyes went unfocused for a moment before she tilted her head. "It says 1."

Nodding, he stood up and held out his hand to help her to her feet. She looked at his hand for a moment before taking it and he pulled her to her feet. "Try drinking some of the water. It restores stamina." He glanced at Nia. "As Nia reminded us."

The foxgirl gave a slight smile, still maintaining her distance. Yuliana turned and gave her a smile too. "Good thing you have a sharp memory."

Yuliana walked over to the stream and began to drink water. She nodded after a few handfuls. "Yes, that's working."

"Now," said the dwarf, turning back towards Nia. "Why didn't you help us?"

Nia dropped her eyes to the ground, her tail puffy and twitching. After a long moment, she raised her head. "I am Cha'to'mir'ta. I am not permitted to kill enemies."

Ainslee screwed up her face. "You're a what?!"

"I am Cha'to'mir'ta," Nia said, letting out an exasperated breath. "I am not permitted to kill enemies unless commanded by my alpha."

Ethan touched his neck, where the claws had left marks earlier. "You didn't seem to have a problem with me?"

Nia's look turned sheepish. "I was disoriented. Plus, I would not have killed you. I only wanted answers."

"Could have fooled me," Ethan muttered under his breath. She'd done nearly as much damage to him as the kobold.

Ainslee threw up her hands and rolled her eyes. "Have you looked up at that planet there?! I don't think this is your home anymore! So the rules of your tribe don't apply here!"

"I am Fire-Storm pack wherever I go. The rules apply whenever I am!" Nia growled.

"Well, then, you're useless if any more of the green beasties come to get us," the dwarf said, waving a hand dismissively. "Aren't you?"

"Wait a minute," Ethan said. He had a bad feeling that leaving the foxgirl behind would be a mistake. Too much of this was like the games he played. He couldn't help but wonder if the aliens who had put them here had modeled it after the MMOs of Earth somehow. If that were the case, then breaking up the party was a bad idea. And he didn't think they were all dropped in the middle of this meadow by coincidence.

Ainslee looked at him but put her hands on her hips, setting her jaw. Nia looked his way too, her gaze both angry and hopeful.

"This whole thing is very similar to..." he almost said game, but he wasn't sure if they would understand the concept of what an MMO was. "... a battle simulation my people would do. In these simulations, there was always a squad of people who had unique skills and worked together."

Glancing at them, he saw that they all seemed to be listening, even Yuliana. "This world is extremely similar, right down to the HUD, to my world's simulations. And if that's the case, the aliens - or whatever brought us here - might be testing us in a similar fashion. If that's the case, then we each possess some skill or talent that will help the group in certain situations."

Yuliana and Nia looked intrigued but the dwarf just scowled. She opened her mouth to say something but Ethan beat her.

"Ainslee, you are strong and sturdy. On my world, they would call you a tank. You would be the backbone of the group," he told the dwarf. She puffed out her chest and nodded.

He looked at the elf. "Yuliana, you would be the healer. Your healing would keep us alive and you may find that you can do magic that actually helps us, which we refer to as buffs. Also a very important role."

"Nia," he said, turning to the foxgirl. "I have a feeling that in addition to your acrobatics, you're probably pretty stealthy. Maybe you've even done some scouting? Is that right?"

The foxgirl looked at him suspiciously. "How would you know that?"

"Because you fill the role of scout," he said. "Do the other tribes you war against set traps? Have you learned how to spot and disarm them?"

Nia's eyes narrowed even more. "Yes, but how would you..."

"Because we have people who do the same thing," he replied. He just didn't mention that they were real people playing virtual characters in a MMO. Probably best to leave that part out.

"And what about you, magic boy," Ainslee smirked. "What's your role?"

"Magic," he replied. And then remembered the other role that wizards and magic-users typically filled in tabletop role-playing games. "And knowledge?"

The dwarf snorted. "Knowledge? You're new to this place

too. What knowledge do you have?"

Ethan smiled. "If the aliens did design this after the Earth simulations, then I have years of experience."

"And if they didn't design these after your war games?" the dwarf asked, crossing her arms.

"Then." Ethan smiled bigger. "This place is probably even more dangerous than I think and you're going to need every person you can find watching your back. Because these kobolds are probably the weakest thing we're going to encounter here."

The women looked thoughtful for a long time, even Ainslee. The dwarf muttered to herself but at least she wasn't leaving.

"If you know about these... simulations," Yuliana said quietly. "Then why were we brought here? What is the purpose?"

Ethan frowned. That would seem to be the million-dollar question. Along with, why them? And why him? "I don't know. But I think it's significant that they just dropped us all in this meadow at the same time and said absolutely nothing."

All three women shot him confused looks. He quickly continued. "I think they dropped us all here because we're supposed to work together."

At that, the women nodded, Ainslee somewhat begrudgingly. He gestured around. "And the fact that they didn't tell us anything specific, probably means they want us to discover it ourselves. It's what we call a sandbox or open-world."

He paused and looked around, then looked up. "But whatever we do, I have a feeling whoever brought us here will be watching us."

Skill increase: Diplomacy +1%.

"All the time?!" Ainslee screwed up her face and looked up at the sky. "That's creepy."

9

It took several more minutes, and two more skill gains in *Diplomacy*, before he convinced all of them that they should stay together. While Ethan was talking, the group took turns drinking water. They had all been very low on *Stamina* and the cool, refreshing water of the stream restored them. To a point.

He noticed that his *Stamina* could only be raised to 50% of his maximum by drinking water. When he asked the others, they experienced the same thing. He wasn't sure what would cause them to restore the remainder, but they'd gotten all they could from the stream.

Ethan also insisted they search the bodies for anything useful. It was then he discovered that looting was not the same as in the MMOs. In the MMOs he had played back on Earth, he had simply clicked on a corpse. Once he did, all of the items the creature carried were either deposited in his inventory, or he was presented with a menu to select which items he wanted to take.

No manner of poking, prodding, or selecting them in his HUD caused a loot screen to appear. Instead, he'd finally gotten bent down and physically examined the bodies. Neither Ainslee nor Yuliana seemed comfortable with looting the bodies.

"You should leave the dead lie," the dwarf argued. "Nothing good ever came of desecrating the dead."

"We should leave the bodies so that nature may take its course," Yuliana told him.

"The spoils of the vanquished are our trophies," Nia protested and crouched down next to one of the other bodies.

Ethan took a more pragmatic direction. "Right now, we don't have any equipment or weapons. Let's take whatever we can from them in case we're attacked again."

Despite his words, neither the elf nor the dwarf took anything from the bodies. He retrieved the other two spears and the cudgel that the kobolds had been using as weapons. The items were crude, but usable and much better than being unarmed.

Other than their weapons, the kobolds had nothing but loincloths and some crude beads on leather thongs they wore wrapped around their necks and wrists. If this were a MMO back on Earth, they would have dropped coins and maybe some armor. Was this some sort of noob area?

With Ethan's t-shirt shredded by the kobold's claws, he had been hoping he'd find a replacement. No such luck. For now, he'd have to either continue wearing the shredded t-shirt or go shirtless. He decided to keep the shredded t-shirt. With the double suns, it might at least prevent sunburn.

Another thing he noticed was that, unlike the Earth MMOs, the items dropped didn't seem to scale to fit the player. It was something common to most MMOs he had played. Whenever he found an item, no matter if it came from a small race, like kobolds, or a large race, like giants, it always shrank or grew to fit his avatar. Given that the weapons didn't enlarge themselves at all to fit his larger size, the kobolds' "long spears" became shortspears to them.

Unfortunately, neither Yuliana and Nia had proficiency with the spears, but Ainslee did. With a little persuading, Ethan managed to convince her to use one of the spears, giving her club to the elf, while he kept the one the kobold dropped. And then there was Nia.

The foxgirl took a look at the spears but remained adamant that she could not kill enemies. None of them were happy about it, but Ainslee in particular didn't like the fact that Nia would not be helping in any fights.

Then Ethan came up with an idea. The flint spear tip was only held to the spear by leather wrappings and he took the time to unwind them and remove the tip. He then took strips of leather from the kobolds' loincloths and wound them around the shaft of the former spear. When he was done, he examined it.

You have fashioned crude staff.
You have gained: Woodcraft.
Skill increase: Woodcraft +1%.
Crude Staff
Type: Two-handed crushing weapon
Range: 4 ft.
Damage: 4 damage (crushing)
Durability: 3 of 6
Skill increase: Appraise +1%.

He smiled at his handiwork and noticed that he had no proficiency penalty. Did that mean he could use staves without any penalty? He offered the staff to the foxgirl.

Nia eyed the weapon and then looked at him with a raised eyebrow.

"Is there anything that says you can't pummel an enemy into unconsciousness?" he asked her.

Tilting her head, the foxgirl shrugged but Ethan saw a slight smile play across her lips. "As long as I do not kill them, there is nothing forbidden. It will be like sparring matches."

"Do you know how to use a staff?" Ethan asked.

In answer, Nia snatched the staff from him, twirling it around in an arc before passing it behind her back to the other hand. Finally, she snapped it under her armpit while dropping into some sort of fighting stance, with her other arm extended. She looked indignant. "I am Fire-Storm pack!"

"Okay then." He grinned.

"Fine! Fine! The kitty can hit things with a stick," the dwarf huffed, looking at Ethan. "You claim to know so much about this world. So where do we go?"

Ethan frowned at the irritable dwarf. "I never claimed to know specifically about the world. Just about the gaming aspect of it."

"Whatever," the dwarf scowled. "Where does your gamey knowledge tell us we should go?"

All the women looked to Ethan and he resisted the urge to rub his forehead. Somehow he'd become the defacto leader. Normally, he wouldn't have been uncomfortable in the role. After all, he'd been the leader of most of his groups. But that had mostly been because the others were lazy and he actually had plans.

Now it was different. This wasn't like the games he'd played. There was real pain in this game. Possibly even real consequences. After all, if he died in the alien "matrix", did his body die wherever the aliens were keeping it? He didn't want to find out.

Ethan looked around the meadow and beyond. To the west were tall, ice-covered mountains. They looked like pictures of the Rocky Mountains he'd seen or possibly even the Himalayas. It seemed foolish to go near them without proper equipment.

Looking east, there was more forest, with large trees sticking out of the normal canopy. If this was Earth, he might have thought they were redwoods. To the north was more forest, though without the larger redwood trees. The south looked like flatlands and hills.

Checking the stream, he noted that it flowed south, towards the flatlands. Would it empty into a large river? Perhaps there was a settlement of some sort along the river. In medieval times, he remembered reading that towns usually sprung up around natural resources - and that included water.

"We can try south," he said.

"Any idiot can see that's the easiest path." Ainslee smirked. "I could have chosen that way with me eyes closed."

"Would you prefer to go a different way?" Ethan asked, trying not to let the frustration show in his voice.

The dwarf shrugged. "Not really. That way's as good as any."

After looking around at Nia and Yuliana to see if the other women had any objections, Ethan started south along the stream. He breathed a soft sigh of relief when he heard the other women fall into line behind him. At least they were following him.

As they began walking, Ethan took the time to fashion himself a staff from one of the other spears. He had no idea what the real effect of the spear's non-proficiency penalties were, but he'd rather not find out the hard way - during combat. As he finished, he received another skill increase.

Skill increase: Woodcraft +1%.

Happy with his staff and the skill increase, he smiled and walked on. But he didn't get far. The group walked only a few hundred yards down the stream before coming across an area where the wall grass had been flattened. In the middle of the area was the face-down body of what looked to Ethan to be a small human male, but with dark-purple hair.

The others quickly gathered around the body, Yuliana gasping in surprise. "A dead child! Who would do such a thing?!"

Motioning them to stay back, Ethan bent down and looked at the scene. The child's body had several puncture wounds that looked like they had been made by spears. He compared his own spear head to some of the wounds. "I think the kobolds who attacked us did this."

You have gained: Forensics.
Skill increase: Forensics +1%.

He raised an eyebrow at the skill gain. Forensics didn't really seem like a skill that fit this setting, but who knew how aliens thought.

"What?" Nia asked, seeing his expression.

"I just received a skill, Forensics," he replied.

"What is four-in-sicks?" the elf asked, her own eyebrow raised.

The dwarf huffed. "It's for telling how people were killed. That's what our sheriffs call it when they investigate a killing that doesn't seem clan-related."

"You can't smell the person who did it?" Nia asked.

"Hah!" the dwarf snorted. "Some dwarves you CAN smell from a few feet away. But we cannot smell them once they've left the scene."

Nia sniffed. "The kobolds who attacked us are the ones. I can smell them. I have never smelled anything like the child." Nia moved up and pointed to the ground. "There, you can see their footprints on the..."

The foxgirl stopped and tilted her head back and forth. "I have gained a skill. Tracking. It is as you said. It is on the hood."

"HUD," Ethan corrected and Nia glared at him. He just smiled back. "That's good. Generally, the more skills we have, the better."

"You want to see skill," the dwarf chuckled. "You put me at a forge and give me a hammer and some metal. I'll show you some skill!"

"I have considerable skills in husbandry," the elf told them proudly. "I tend a very prestigious grove."

"Husbandry," Ethan repeated. It was a word he hadn't heard often. In fact, he thought maybe he'd only ever read about it in passing. "Does it seem strange to any of you that we're all speaking the same language?"

The women looked at him and then at each other. The dwarf screwed up her face. "Now that you mention it, I had thought it a bit peculiar. I only really speak Clanspeak. And the only ones who know it are the other members of my clan. There's the common dwarf tongue but I never needed to know it. Oh, and the tradespeak. The merchants use that when they're trading with the gnomes and giants."

"Giants?" Nia looked wide-eyed. "How large are giants?"

Ainslee shrugged. "I'm not entirely sure. I've always stayed in the village. I've never actually seen one in person. But they say anywhere from fourteen to twenty feet."

The foxgirl's eyes grew as wide as saucers and she looked up in the air, probably trying to gauge how tall a twenty-foot-tall giant would be. "How do you defeat them?"

The dwarf looked aghast. "Defeat them? They are kind, gentle creatures. At times, my clan has come out to protect them from the trolls, who like to raid their villages."

"Gentle?" the foxgirl muttered in disbelief.

"Aye." Ainslee nodded.

Ethan had only been half-heartedly listening. He'd been

scanning the entire area around the child's body for footprints but hadn't received any *Tracking* skill. Was it tied to her class? Or perhaps an attribute. In any case, it didn't seem like he would be receiving it.

Figuring he would probably regret it, he reached out and turned the child over. To his surprise, it was not a child at all. The face was more weathered than a child's and the small person had thick mutton chops that reached to the corners of his mouth. If he had to give the race a name, he would say it was a halfling. An adult halfling.

Standing up he looked at the girls. "And this would be us if we had been alone."

Ainslee snorted but said nothing. The other two women just nodded. The dead halfling raised questions. Had it been a NPC, or non-player character, like the kobolds? Or had the halfling been another player, abducted from his home world and dropped into the game by the aliens?

But the question that was really nagging Ethan was about the halfling's fate. Was he really dead? Or had he respawned somewhere and this was just his corpse. They had no way of knowing but until it was proven otherwise, he had to go on the assumption that if any of them died in this simulation, they'd die in real life.

10

His group found three more bodies that Ethan thought of as "player" bodies. The first body was a curvy female with dark-brown skin, and small goat-like horns. The woman's legs were goat-like as well and covered in shaggy brown and white fur. If he had to put a name to her race, he would have said satyr, like from the old Greek myths.

The body of a kobold was lying near the satyr with two puncture holes in its chest that matched the satyr's horns, leaving no doubt to what had killed her. Nevertheless, Ethan examined the wounds on the body to get another skill increase.

Skill increase: Forensics +1%.

"Is that a... demon?" Yuliana gasped.

Ethan started to shake his head but stopped and shrugged. For all he knew, it was a demon. "I guess it could be, but I suspect it was another race abducted by the aliens and plopped down here. It's similar to a race from our old legends called satyrs."

"At least she took one of those suckers with her," the dwarf commented.

The satyr wore a leather strap-like outfit similar to what Nia wore on her body, only much more worked and tooled. When Ethan looked closely, he could see patterns in the leather but it looked like nothing he had ever seen before.

"Anyone want the outfit?" he asked. All three women gave him looks of disgust but he shrugged. "She's dead. We are alone and have no supplies. If we don't want to end up like her, we need to use any resource at our disposal, no matter how distasteful."

"No, thank you," Yuliana said and turned away.

"You call that an outfit?" The dwarf shook her head and gestured to her buxom bosom. "Won't fit me and I wouldn't wear it if it did. Too much skin showing for my taste."

He saw Nia eying the demoness' strap-like outfit but then glanced down at her own modest chest and then at the dead woman's much larger chest and sighed. "I don't think it will fit me either."

Ethan found another kobold spear nearby and took it with him. It was better to have too many weapons than not enough. Since he had to carry all of his weapons, he began to miss Earth MMOs' inventory system.

After leaving the satyr woman, they came across two other bodies, both male. And both appeared to have been killed by the kobolds.

One looked roughly like a human except for a ridged nose and forehead and deep green-blue skin. The body was dressed in a sleeveless mustard tunic and dark-brown pants. Although both were bloody, both seemed better than his own clothes and he stripped them off the dead man. Unfortunately, the pants were too large for him, but he could wear the tunic over his ripped t-shirt after washing out the blood in the stream.

The last body was very odd. It was humanoid, but had the

head of a crow, or possibly a raven. Its head and body were completely covered in black feathers and it wore no clothes except for a bandolier of pouches and a leather belt, which Ethan took.

"That is a strange one," Nia muttered, looking at the crow man. "I've never even heard of a being such as this."

"Me either. Why are there so many bodies?" Yuliana asked.

"Yeah." Ainslee scratched her chin. "These kills look fresh."

"I think," Ethan started. "That we all arrived at the same time."

He gestured the way they were going. "I suspect the kobolds came from this direction. They killed the crow guy first, then onto the blue-skinned guy and so on. We were lucky. We were at the end of the line and we were together."

Strapping the bandolier over his shoulders and buckling the belt around his waist, they started following the stream again.

"If the kobolds came from this direction," the elf said as they began walking again. "Is it wise to keep going this direction?"

Ethan considered her question as he scanned the area in front of them. She was right. It didn't make sense to retrace the steps of the kobolds. That would lead them to more kobolds, possibly even a village of kobolds. But that assumed the kobolds had been coming from this direction. Perhaps they were heading back to their village.

"There could be more kobolds ahead of us, but there could be more kobolds behind us," he replied, still looking forward. "We'll need to keep an eye out either way."

"In other words," Ainslee said to Yuliana, but loud enough so that Ethan could hear. "He's pulling this all out of his arse."

They continued following the stream through the meadow. After what he guessed was a mile, the meadow dipped into a large valley. The stream led down the middle of the valley and merged into a river on the far end of the valley. On the opposite side of the river was what appeared to be a dirt road that ran adjacent to a forest.

Ethan pointed it out. "Is that what I think it is?"

"Looks like a road to me. Guess I owe you an apology." The dwarf smirked. "I'll get you an I.O.U for that apology, as soon as I can find a paper and quill."

Ethan ignored her and headed down the meadow towards the river. The women followed him and they quickly made their way through the meadow, to the bank of the river. The river was only fifteen feet wide and didn't look particularly deep. But it was fast moving.

Walking up and down the river, they found a number of large rocks and boulders that seemed to make a path across the river. They started down the embankment to the rocks when Nia hissed behind him.

"Kobolds!" she growled.

The group looked around, weapons coming to the ready. Ethan glanced up and down the river, his adrenaline already getting him ready for a fight. "Where?!"

Nia sniffed. "Not here. Not now. But they were here. They use this passage across the river often. I see footprints and I smell them."

"How long?" Ethan asked, peering into the forest.

"Two, maybe three hours," Nia sniffed again.

The group relaxed and Ainslee muttered under her breath. "Could have said that to begin with instead of getting me all riled up."

"Do you think you are smelling the ones who attacked us?" Yuliana asked the foxgirl.

"I think so," Nia said. "Their scent is the same. But... maybe more."

"More?" Ethan asked. "More kobolds than the ones we faced?"

Nia nodded. "There are smells I do not recognize, but they are definitely kobolds."

"Do you know how many or which way they went?" the dwarf asked sourly. "You know... something useful?"

The foxgirl bit her lip and shook her head. "I cannot tell exactly how many. But if we cross the river I might be able to tell if the scent is stronger on the other side."

"Of course," the dwarf muttered. "Cross the river first."

And they did cross the river. One by one, hopping from rock to rock, all four of them made it across the river and up the embankment on the other side. Once they were there, Nia stopped and sniffed the air. She walked around the area, sniffing the entire time before rejoining the group.

"The other kobolds crossed the river with the group who attacked us," she told them. "The scents on this side of the river are fainter, though just by a little. But there are many kobolds' scents here. Some days old, some yesterday. I see many overlapping tracks too. They use this way often."

"This must be a common ford," Ethan stated as he looked up and down the river. There didn't seem to be another place to cross it easily within eyeshot. This could be the only easy ford for miles.

"What does this mean for us?" the elf asked, clearly worried.

"It means we're probably going to get our arses handed to us by a pack of kobolds," the dwarf answered.

"Not necessarily," Ethan said, stooping down to examine the road. Despite not being able to gain the *Tracking* skill, he could clearly make out the hoof prints of horses and the straight tracks of wagon wheels. "This road is used by someone who has domesticated horses - or what passes as horses on this planet. And, they have carts too. See here." He pointed out the wagon tracks. "Someone other than kobolds are using this road."

"How do you know it ain't the kobolds?" the dwarf asked.

Holding up one of the spears, he gestured to the flint spear head. "The kobolds are using crude weapons like this. I don't think they're the kind to domesticate horses and build carts. Besides, the carts look too big for kobolds."

The dwarf crunched up her face as she regarded the tracks. In the meantime, Nia came over to examine the tracks. She traced several different outlines, moving around the road before looking off to their right, towards some mountains in the distance. "The most recent tracks go that way."

"Then perhaps we should go the opposite direction," the elf said, looking down the long road to the left.

"If we wish to find a settlement and possibly get some answers," Ethan said. "I think we should follow the most recent set of tracks."

"We have no idea whether the creatures who made those tracks are friendly," Yuliana said. "Do we want to take that chance?"

"The elf has a point there," the dwarf agreed. "The kobolds were tough enough with their crude weapons. If we run into something with real weapons, we're going to be a bit outclassed."

"True," Ethan replied and looked the way the tracks led. "But I think we all want some answers and that might be our best bet to find some."

Nia sighed but nodded. Ainslee grumbled but nodded too. That just left the elf. The woman stared down the road in one direction before looking down the other direction. She did it several times before sighing and nodding. "Very well, I will follow you."

"Let's get going," he told them as he looked into the sky. "I have no idea when the sun will set - or if it will set - but if we can find a settlement of some friendly race, I'd rather not spend the night outdoors with the kobolds."

Muttering their agreements, the women fell in behind him and the group began marching down the road. As they walked,

Ethan wondered what other indigenous life might be on this planet. And more importantly, would the life they found be friendly.

Whoever or whatever had made those tracks obviously had mastered the wheel, in order to make the cart. That probably meant some degree of metalsmithing to make nails and such. He wasn't sure exactly how to construct a medieval-style cart, but he assumed it wasn't just tied together with leather cord or twine. Plus, there were some sort of hoofed animals pulling the cart, so that meant whoever they were had mastered animal domestication.

Then again, just because they reached a certain level of medieval technology, it didn't mean they would be friendly. Careful to hide his expression from the others, he frowned as he realized they could be hopping out of the frying pan and into the fire.

His group walked along the road for an hour. During that time, they noticed that more of the ringed planet was becoming visible. Ethan wasn't an astronomy expert, but he guessed that they were on a moon of the enormous ringed planet and they were revolving around it. At some point, the moon would pass behind the planet and be hidden from the sun. How dark would it become at that point, he wondered.

Towards the end of the hour, they came upon a stone bridge that looked like it could be from Earth. They stopped just before the bridge, looking it over. It was crude but well made. Just stones and mortar. It reminded Ethan of some of the historic bridges from the 1700's he'd seen in some of the historic parks he'd visited.

He was about to comment about how it looked like an old bridge from his world, when he sensed movement from the forest to their left.

You have gained: Perception.
Skill increase: Perception +1%.

He looked at the skill in his HUD as his head turned towards the forest.

"I hear something moving in the forest," the elf stated and then tilted her head. "Several somethings."

Nia dropped to a crouch, readying her staff and sniffing the air. She made a low growl. "Kobolds!"

As if they had been waiting for that cue, two arrows whistled out of the trees towards them. One appeared to have been aimed at Ainslee, but struck the ground in front of her. The other had been aimed at him but missed by at least a foot.

At the same time, two spear-wielding kobolds came charging out from underneath the bridge. His mind immediately went into gaming mode and he evaluated the situation.

"Ainslee," he yelled, pointing at the charging kobolds. "You and Nia charge the archers. I'll take care of these two. Yuliana, stay here in case what I'm planning doesn't work."

Ainslee grumbled but charged off into the woods, along with Nia. Ethan turned towards the quickly approaching kobolds and reached into himself. His previous fireball had been an accident. Now he was trying to consciously do it, while under pressure.

The kobolds came closer and Ethan felt the heat within himself. He pushed it to his hand and then formed it into a small ball. The flaming ball appeared and he hurled it right into the path of the incoming kobolds.

As it reached them, it exploded with a boom. The resulting fireball was much smaller than his previous one, but it was still large enough to engulf the two kobolds.

You burn Meadow Clan Raider for 13 fire damage.

You burn Meadow Clan Raider for 22 fire damage.

Meadow Clan Raider dies.

Skill increase: Fire Magic +1%.
You gain 10 experience. Experience to
*   next level 175.*

The kobolds barked in pain as the fire enveloped them, the concussion of the fireball tossing both creatures to the ground. One didn't get up and his HUD showed that it was dead. The remaining kobold howled in pain and staggered to its feet.

Ethan rushed forward, his staff in a two-handed grip, and brought the weapon down on the creature's head.

You crush Meadow Clan Raider for 4
*   damage.*
You have gained: Two-handed crushing
*   weapons.*
Skill increase: Two-handed crushing
*   weapons +1%.*

The creature staggered, its eyes going unfocused for a second. Taking advantage of the kobold's dazed look, he pulled back the staff for another strike.

Whether the kobold recovered at that moment or the kobold had been faking being stunned, it shook its head and hopped out of his range just as Ethan brought the staff down. Off balance from his swing, he was unable to avoid the spear thrust of the kobold.

Meadow Clan Raider pierces you with
*   crude spear for 1 damage.*

Luckily, it was a glancing blow but the spear tip still drew a line of blood across his forearm, pain lancing up from the wound. He grimaced and stumbled back from the raider. Despite its small size, Ethan had no doubt that the creature was a more experienced combatant than him. He needed to put some space between them so he could cast another spell.

The kobold followed him, jabbing at him with the spear but Ethan was able to bat the tip away with his staff. He kept retreating and the raider kept advancing, not giving him a chance to cast another spell.

But, Ethan hadn't just been retreating. He'd been purposefully keeping the kobold's attention on him. And away from Yuliana. The elf had gotten behind the kobold and brought her club down on the creature's head.

> *Yuliana crushes Meadow Clan Raider for 1*
> *damage + 3 damage flanking bonus.*

The kobold yelped and spun around to face the new threat, leaving its flank unguarded. Ethan surged forward and brought his staff down on the creature's neck.

> *You crush Meadow Clan Raider for 2*
> *damage + 3 damage flanking bonus.*
> *Meadow Clan Raider dies.*
> *Skill increase: Two-handed crushing*
> *weapons +1%.*
> *You gain 5 experience. Experience to*
> *next level 170.*

He heard a crack as the kobold's neck snapped. The raider's body went limp and it dropped bonelessly to the group, its head at an unnatural angle.

"Good job," he told the elf, whose face bore a deer-in-the-headlights look. She seemed like she might turn and run at any moment.

"Yuliana," he said, getting her attention. "You did good. Let's check on the others."

The woman looked at him without really seeing him for a moment and then blinked, her eyes coming into focus. She nodded and together they ran for the edge of the woods where the sounds of fighting could still be heard.

When they arrived, it was just in time to see Nia bash one of the kobolds on the side of the head. The agile foxgirl then swept around with the other side of the staff and hooked it under the kobold's ankle, sending the creature sprawling. As it struggled to get up, she hit it again, forcing it back down.

"Kill this one!" she snarled as she caught sight of them. "I am not permitted!"

Rushing forward, he reached the kobold just as Nia stepped to the side. The creature's eyes followed the foxgirl as she side-stepped and it never even saw his two-handed overhand strike as it came down.

> *You crush Meadow Clan Raider for 3 damage.*
> *Meadow Clan Raider dies.*
> *Skill increase: Two-handed crushing weapons +1%.*
> *You gain 5 experience. Experience to next level 165.*

The kobold let out a soft whine and then dropped to the ground, unmoving. Ethan immediately turned to the left, watching as the dwarf skewered the remaining kobold with her spear.

"Ha! Take that you little varmint!" Ainslee barked. The dwarf turned towards them and saw the other dead kobold. She glanced from the corpse to the foxgirl. "You kill it?"

Nia looked at the dwarf defiantly and shook her head. "I do not kill!"

"Bah," the dwarf scoffed. Ainslee's eyes darted to the dead

kobold and then back to the foxgirl. "At least you kept it from shooting me in the back."

"We killed the other two," Ethan said. His mind reverted to game mode and he immediately wanted to loot the bodies. "Let's search them."

They recovered the archer's bows, rough hide quivers, and 23 arrows. One of the archers also had a small pouch containing some dried leaves. He took out one of the leaves and examined it.

You have gained: Herbalism.
Skill increase: Herbalism +1%.

Gwara Root
Type: Herb
Duration: Instant
Effect: Heals 4 points of damage over 1
    minute.
Other: Raw leaves heal 4 points of
    damage but may be refined and
    concentrated into a potion. Requires
    Alchemy, rank 1.

"What is it?" Nia asked. "Poison?"

Ethan shook his head. "The opposite. Some sort of healing herb called gwara root. Have any of you heard of it?"

He was met by blank looks and shakes of the head and he wondered if this was created just for this simulation. He held out the herb. "When I looked at it, I received the herbalism skill. Anyone else want to try to get the skills?"

"I do not understand what all of these skills and experience mean," Yuliana said. "But I continue to get messages on the HUD."

"In the war games on Earth," he said, after no one else spoke up. "They quantify things into skills and ranks. Generally, you must have a skill to use it or do things related to it. Or having the skill gives you additional uh... things you can do.

"For example, this herb description tells me if I have the Alchemy skill, I can make this herb into a potion," he said. "Which probably means it will be more potent or faster acting or both. Without that skill, I may not be able to do that."

"That is confusing," Yuliana said and Nia and Ainslee both nodded.

"I think," he told them, trying to phrase things in non-game terminology, "that this alien world operates differently than our worlds. Things here are more exact. For instance, back home, if I hit someone with a staff, I don't know whether it really hurt them except by watching their reaction. Here, when I hit one of the kobolds, it tells me precisely how much damage I inflicted."

"So," the dwarf grumbled. "The more of these 'skills' we have, the better."

"Basically," he admitted. "We should try to learn as many skills as we can."

"Fine," Ainslee said and held out her meaty hand. "Give me the plant and let me see if I can get this herbal skill."

They all took turns and all received the skill. In game terms, he guessed *Herbalism* was a general skill anyone could learn, whereas the *Tracking* skill he'd tried to learn earlier must be related to class, race, ability or something else.

"So now what?" Nia asked.

"We keep going and hope we reach whatever's down this road before nightfall," he replied. "Do any of you know how to use a bow?"

"I do." Nia frowned. "But I will not shoot enemies."

"Actually," he smiled. "I was thinking more of using the bow to shoot some game. I don't know about the rest of you, but I'm actually starting to get hungry."

There was a general murmur of agreement and Nia held

out her hand for the bow. "I know how to use the bow. And I am allowed to hunt food."

"Good," he said and handed her one of the bows and quivers. "As we walk, maybe you can keep your eyes open for some small animals we can cook."

Nia nodded and they moved back down to the bridge to examine the other kobolds. The spears of the other two raiders were charred and not worth taking and they carried nothing else of any value. Leaving the bodies where they lay, the group walked over the bridge and continued down the road.

12

They walked for three more hours before the light began to fade. The planet moved in front of the suns, blocking them from viewing and letting darkness fall across the area. The dark revealed a total of six other moons of varying sizes but all looked three to four times the size of Earth's moon.

He found that unlike dwarves and elves of MMOs or tabletop games, neither Ainslee nor Yuliana could see any better than he could. Unsurprising, given her fox-like appearance, Nia had excellent night vision.

They found a clearing that seemed to have been used as a campsite for other travelers and decided to stay there for the night - after Ethan insisted on scouting it out. He didn't want another ambush.

Nia turned out to be an excellent hunter and a crack shot with the bow. She killed several creatures that passed as rabbits in this world. At least, they looked like rabbits to him, only leaner and with wider ears. Also, their coloring was different than any rabbit he'd seen. Their fur was shades of brown and gray with subtle tiger stripes across their backs and sides.

Starting a fire was no problem. With a little effort, he was able to conjure a small flame that caught things on fire but did not hurt him. He knew he needed to experiment with this new power, but he also needed to conserve his *Stamina* in the case of another ambush.

Nia was able to find two sticks that had a "Y" on one end and rig up a simple spit to cook the meat. She had rolled her eyes when she had received a notification about gaining the Cooking skill. "I already know how to cook. I do not need a HUD to tell me!"

After cooking the rabbits over the fire, they all took a portion and began eating them. The meat was gamey and greasy but he was so hungry, Ethan didn't care. He was starving and it was food.

He did start to wonder about this game or simulation the aliens had constructed. It seemed exacting in the amount of detail they had included. His muscles ached. He was hungry. He could taste the different flavors and textures of the meat.

It seemed an enormous undertaking to create such an elaborate world. And to what purpose? Why had Ethan and the others been abducted? Was this some sort of social experiment? See how the species got along? If so, then why the monsters who killed the others?

He wondered briefly about his friends back on Earth. None of his online friends had ever been to his house. In fact, they all lived in different states. They'd send him IMs and emails, but that would be it. They might even think his computer had been fried by a storm. That had happened before.

What about the rest of the world? He didn't really have any friends in the area. His nearest neighbor was two fields over. Would anyone even miss him until he stopped showing up at work enough times?

"This sure ain't my world," Ainslee muttered, mouth full.

The dwarf was staring up at the various moons. "I ain't even heard of nothing like this."

"Me either," Yuliana said. "This doesn't not feel like my world. I cannot hear any of the plants."

They all looked at the elf who shifted uncomfortably. "What?"

"You... hear plants?" Ethan asked.

"Of course," the elf said. "I am a grove tender. I hear the plants. I know what they need and I give it to them. Do your people not listen to the plants?"

Nia, Ainslee and Ethan all exchanged glances. He shook his head. "I don't think our plants speak. And if they do, no one on my planet can understand them. We've learned what makes plants grow, we grow certain edible plants and then harvest and eat them."

"Yah." The dwarf nodded, taking another bite of her rabbit. "We grow different mushrooms but mostly the edible type, but some for medicines."

"Prey eat plants." Nia smirked. "We eat prey."

"Okay then," Ethan said.

"Do any of you have any idea why we might have been abducted?" he asked them. "And thrown on this... world?"

Ethan had almost said game, but had caught himself just in time. Given the level of technology the others had on their worlds, he wasn't sure how he could explain, let alone convince them, that he thought they were in a game.

A very realistic game, but a game nonetheless. The real universe didn't have HUDs or magic. So this couldn't be real. And if it wasn't real, and assuming he wasn't just dreaming or hallucinating all of this, then it had to be some extremely sophisticated game.

"I don't know," the dwarf said. "I feel like I should be more concerned and want to get back to my world more... but I don't. It's weird."

"I have thought as much also," Yuliana said. "I should be missing my grove much more than I am. I should be wanting to get back and yet it's almost as if I no longer feel a connection to the grove."

"I too feel no compulsion to want to get back to my... world... or my mate," Nia said.

"Roo mate?" the dwarf asked, teeth ripping another mouthful of meat off the rabbit carcass.

"You are bound?" the elf asked, her eyebrows raised.

Ethan couldn't be sure in the firelight but he thought Nia might be blushing. "I am my alpha's newest wife."

"Newest? You mean he has more than one?" the dwarf asked.

Nia's face scrunched in confusion. "Of course. Do not your strongest males take their pick of the females?"

"Uh, no," the dwarf snorted. "One male. One female. The females do the picking cause the males just think with that pickaxe between their legs. Another two years and I'll be seventy. Might think about finding me a man then. Well, assuming I get back home."

Ethan coughed, tried to swallow and then coughed again. "You...you're seventy years old?"

"Are ya daff?" the dwarf retorted. "I'm sixty-eight. I'll be seventy in two years."

"Seventy?" Nia said with wide eyes. "That's... that's not possible."

"I know I look young for my age," the dwarf said, smiling. "But I really am sixty-eight. How old are you?"

"Six," Nia replied, still appearing to be unable to process the dwarf's age.

This time it was the dwarf's turn to cough. She sputtered and coughed before finally being able to speak. "You're six... as in... six years old?"

"Yes," Nia snapped back. "I am six as of last winter!"

"You're a child!" the dwarf boomed. "Just a babe!"

"I am no baby!" growled Nia. "I am a full member of the tribe!"

"Nia," Ethan said, trying to defuse the tension that had suddenly sprung up. "How long do members of your tribe live?"

Still glaring at the laughing dwarf, she took a moment to answer. "Twenty, if they are not killed in battle."

Ainslee stopped laughing and looked over at the foxgirl. "Your people only live twenty years?"

"My people only live about eighty," he said and turned to the dwarf. "I'm guessing your people have a much longer lifespan."

The dwarf looked between Nia and Ethan. "You're joking, right?"

Ethan shook his head and Nia continued to glare.

"Oh," Ainslee muttered. "I'd say the average lifespan is about two hundred and fifty or so, though a few of the elders are over three hundred."

"So proportionate to lifespan," Ethan said, doing some quick calculations. "Ainslee, you are about a fourth of your maximum life, Nia, you are just under a third and I'm about... uh... around a third."

He was actually going to be thirty this year, so he was probably over a third of his way through his lifespan. But he wasn't going to mention that to the women. He looked at Yuliana, who had remained quiet during their conversation. "What about you?"

The elf remained quiet for a long moment before answering. "I do not think we measure things the same way your peoples do."

"Ah, come on now," the dwarf chided. "You don't have to be shy about your age. We all told ours."

The elf shook her head. "You do not understand. My people do not have a lifespan. We do not... die. Well, that is to say, we do not die unless something happens to us - a forest fire, a lightning strike, I remember one of us was even killed by a falling tree that had grown old."

The others all looked around at each other. Nia spoke up first. "You do not grow old?"

Yuliana nodded. "We are small at birth and grow into mature adults. This takes a few hundred years. But once we reach our mature forms, we no longer age. I am the same now as I was when I was when I was two hundred."

Ainslee swallowed loudly. "Just how old are you?"

"As the rest of you," she replied, smiling. "By my people's standards, I am only newly matured. I am three hundred and sixty-four."

Ethan whistled without realizing he had done it. "So, you're the oldest. You have hundreds of years more experience than the rest of us."

The elf blushed and Ethan realized how that sounded and felt the heat in his face. "Sorry, I didn't mean..."

Yuliana just smiled. "I sense that my people do not look at age the same as your people do. And as far as experience, the only experience I have is with my grove. And the plants here are very different... and silent."

There was silence for several minutes until Ethan began to feel uncomfortable. Eager to break it, he finished off the last of his rabbit and looked to Nia. "Thanks for the meal, Nia. It was good."

"I could probably eat two more," the dwarf said but nodded at the foxgirl. "But that at least took the edge off my hunger."

Yuliana looked around and blushed. He noticed that she hadn't really eaten any of her rabbit. Ethan cursed himself for not noticing sooner. "Do you not like it?"

Still blushing, the elf forced a smile. "I do not eat the flesh of other living creatures. The grove has always supplied my needs. Nuts, berries, herbs. Please do not think me ungrateful, but I cannot eat this."

He was about to open his mouth when the dwarf reached over and unceremoniously grabbed her rabbit and began to eat. Ainslee saw the others staring at her. Her mouth was full but she managed to get out a few words. "Wah? M' hungry! She not eatin it."

"It's okay." Yuliana smiled. "I would not have eaten it."

"Are there berries or nuts around here you can eat?" he asked.

The elf shook her head. "I have been looking all day but I have seen nothing familiar."

"Tomorrow," Ethan said, "we will all keep an eye out."

Nia nodded but the dwarf just continued eating.

"Thank you." The elf smiled.

They were all tired and sore and decided to go to bed, though without bedrolls, he didn't think the ground would make for a very comfortable sleeping area.

"We should set a watch," he told them.

"A watch?" Yuliana asked, tilting her head.

"We should take turns staying up and keeping an eye out for enemies," he clarified. "Like kobolds. We don't want a group of them sneaking up and killing us in our sleep."

"That's a cheerful thought." The dwarf grimaced.

"It is what I would do," Nia said. They all looked at her. "Sneak up on the enemy and attack them when they are vulnerable. There is no shame in that!"

"Right," said Ainslee, eying the foxgirl. "Maybe we should have two of us staying up at a time."

Nia glared back at the dwarf. "You are not my enemy. I would not harm you while you slept!"

"And," Ethan pointed out. "Two people will mean only two shifts. That's less sleep."

"Bah." The dwarf waved her hand at them. "I sleep with one eye open. So no one better try and sneak up on me!"

"I can take first watch," he volunteered. "I don't think I can sleep right away anyway."

Nia glanced up at the moons and grimaced. "How do we know how long the watches should be or how to measure the passage of time? These stars and moons are strange to me."

Frowning, he looked up in the night sky. Nia was right. He could see the various moons and they had been the focus of his attention earlier. But looking around at the sky, he saw no familiar star clusters. No Big Dipper. No Little Dipper. Nothing at all that looked familiar.

He chuckled to himself. Of course the sky didn't look like his sky. This was a simulation. The entire sky was probably made up by the aliens. Perhaps they'd even purposefully made the stars different. Who knew with these aliens.

"How about we stay up as long as we can," Ethan offered. "And then wake the next person. If the last person feels sleepy, they can wake me. And we can just keep going around in a circle until it's day."

They all agreed and the women settled down at various spots, trying to get some rest. Ethan took the few minutes while they were getting comfortable to gather more wood for the fire. When he returned, Ainslee was already snoring loudly.

He smiled as he walked back into their camp. At least one of them would get some sleep.

than wasn't sure how long he stayed up before waking Nia for the next shift on watch. The moons had moved in the sky but he didn't know how to measure time by them. But as the night went on, he had become more and more tired. When he began to feel himself nodding off, he woke Nia to take her shift.

The fox girl started awake, claws coming out. Wide-eyed, she seemed to recognize him just before slashing him across the chest. Her hand stopped and her eyes darted around the camp. Nia seemed to remember where she was and her claw retracted back into her fingers.

"My turn?" she asked groggily.

"Yeah," he told her and grinned. "Your turn to listen to the dwarf."

Nia cringed as Ainslee let loose with another deep snore and she turned to the sleeping dwarf.

"At least it might scare off the animals," Ethan offered and the foxgirl gave him a half-hearted smile before yawning.

"I wake Yuliana?" she asked.

"Yeah," he replied and moved over to his sleeping spot.

Taking off his tunic, he bunched it up and used it as a pillow. He looked up into the night sky, seeing the different moons and the alien stars. It seemed like as soon as he closed his eyes, he was asleep.

He woke up the next morning by himself. He'd half-expected to wake up this morning in his familiar bed, maybe hung over from a night of drinking and gaming. No such luck. He was still in that alien simulation - or whatever it was.

A snore cut through the silence of the morning and Ethan looked to his left. The dwarf was leaning against a log, snoring. Ethan frowned as he looked at the fire. Ainslee must have fallen asleep and had let it go out. Shaking his head, he got up. At least, he tried to get up.

He was sore. He was sore in muscles he hadn't even known he had. Wincing, Ethan stopped moving in the middle of standing up. His arms, legs, and neck were all painfully sore. Why was everything so sore? He couldn't ever remember feeling this sore. Slowly, because that was the only way he could, he got to his feet. He winced and grunted softly as he stood.

Finally standing up, he realized something else. He had to relieve himself. Now. Making sure the women were still asleep, Ethan hurried into the trees and found some bushes that obscured him from the camp. He quickly, and painfully, took care of business.

Afterwards, he walked slowly back to the camp, trying to stretch out the sore muscles. As he did, he wondered why the aliens would put normal bodily functions into their simulation. He'd never played an MMO that included any sort of bodily functions. It just wasn't done.

And then there was the sore muscles. He could understand the pain from wounds but sore muscles? What was heroic about sore muscles? Nothing! You didn't see Beowulf or Hercules complaining about sore muscles. Of course, both

Beowulf and Hercules were in great shape. His game avatar was his normal, computer-tech body.

For a moment, he wondered if this really was a simulation at all. Was it possible this was all real? His body looked, felt and acted just like his regular body. Ethan shook his head to clear it of the crazy idea. He had done magic. He'd made a fireball. That was impossible in the real universe. Magic didn't exist. Not real magic. It defied the laws of physics.

So why did the aliens include muscle aches and embarrassing bodily functions? It didn't really make any sense. But then again. These were aliens with the technology to travel between the stars. How could he assume they would think the same as he did. Maybe to them, a simulation had to be exact, right down to having to take a piss.

Walking back into the camp, he nudged the dwarf lightly on the foot. Ainslee snorted, muttered something and then went back to snoring. He nudged her several more times, each one slightly harder, before the dwarf came awake with a start.

"I'll get to the smithy, Da!" she muttered loud enough to wake the others. Ainslee looked around disoriented before slumping back down and sighing heavily. "I thought I'd wake up back in me bed and find this was also some dream."

"Sorry," Ethan told her. "I'm afraid not."

Nia and Yuliana were stirring now too, stretching and groaning. It appeared none of them had slept well. He noticed the women glancing around at the woods and bit his lip to hide a smirk. It looked like he wasn't the only one who woke up needing to relieve himself.

"I must go," Nia said first and wandered off into the woods.

Ainslee and Yuliana exchanged embarrassed looks but nodded. "Me too."

Turning his back to the woods, Ethan continued to stretch his stiff and aching muscles. While he stretched, he brought up his HUD and checked out his stats:

```
Name: Ethan
Class: Wizard
Race: Human
Level: 1
Experience: 35
Fame: 0
Strength: 10
Agility: 13
Hardiness: 13
Intellect: 17
Intuition: 14
Charisma: 10
Health: 21
Stamina: 26
Mana: 28
Karma: 26
```

Ethan frowned as he read the display. His *Health* wasn't back at full and his *Stamina* hadn't regenerated beyond 50%. Worse, he now had less *Mana* and *Karma* than he had last night before going to bed. Why was he losing stats?

That didn't make sense. In most MMOs, you slowly regained your health and other things. Certainly resting should have healed him up to full. And yet, he wasn't full. Not even close. It made no sense. Unless.

Looking at the campground and the lack of blankets and pillows, he doubted any of them had enjoyed a good sleep. Was that the reason? Did he and the others need a good night's sleep to restore their stats to full?

"That feels better! I thought I was going to burst!" muttered the dwarf gruffly as she walked back into camp. She stopped and bent to the side, stretching her torso. "I feel like I spent all day working my arse off at the smithy. And all we did was walk!"

"And fight!" came Nia's voice behind them. The foxgirl

strode into camp, apparently unbothered by fatigue or sore muscles. She bent down easily and picked up her weapons. "I will go see if I can find us breakfast."

Nia began walking away but looked over her shoulder. "You should make sure there is a fire going when I return."

A half hour later, the foxgirl returned to a roaring fire. In her hand, she carried a pheasant. At least, it looked like a pheasant, except for the fact that it had no feathers. Instead, the creature had scales of various colors that decorated its entire body.

"What is it?" Ainslee asked, her face screwed up in a mask of disgust. "A lizard?"

Nia shrugged. "It is breakfast."

While the foxgirl cooked the lizard pheasant on their makeshift spit, Ethan went with Yuliana to try and find something edible. He felt bad for the elf. She hadn't eaten at all since she arrived.

"Do you have the herbalism skill?" he asked as they walked into the forest.

"The herbalism skill?" she replied.

"Check your HUD," he said. "I think it allows you to identify plants and herbs."

The woman's eyes went glassy for several seconds before coming back into focus. Yuliana shook her head. "I do not have that on the HUD."

Remembering how he had gained the skill, he brought out the pouch of herbs and handed them to her. "Try examining the leaves."

The elf did so and smiled. Her eyes went glassy for only a second and then she handed the pouch back to him. "I have gained the herbalism skill. Thank you!"

"You're welcome," he said. "The more of us who have it, the better. I'll have to show it to Nia and Ainslee when I return."

The two of them walked in silence for several minutes

before finding a berry bush. Taking one of the berries, he examined it.

```
Neryiak Berry
Type: Herb
Duration: 1 day
Effect: Causes 1 point of poison damage
    per hour for 24 hours.
Other: None
```

"Poison," she sighed and her stomach chose that moment to growl. She looked down and then back up, her cheeks flushing. "Sorry."

"No need to apologize," he said, flashing her a smile. "The rest of us were at least able to eat last night. You haven't had anything since you got here I'm guessing."

She nodded, cheeks still flushed. They looked for another twenty minutes before heading back to the camp. Like when they searched, the two of them walked in silence. It made Ethan uncomfortable but he resisted the urge to try and start idle chatter. Besides, he wasn't very good at talking with members of the opposite sex.

When they reached the camp, they found Nia scolding the dwarf, who was holding a very empty-looking pheasant carcass.

"I tried to stop her," Nia said in an exasperated tone. Her ears were back and her tail was puffy. She put her hands on her hips as she glared at the dwarf. "But she ate both of your portions."

"You ate my portion too?" he asked, anger swelling up. Ethan was hungry too. He'd tried to help the elf find her own food and now he was going to go hungry.

The dwarf turned to him and gestured at him with what remained of the pheasant carcass in her hand, using it to punctuate her words. "I was hungry! I'm this... what did you call me?

Oh yeah... tank. Well, the tank needs food! Foxy can go get you another one!"

Ethan seethed but held his tongue. He could feel fire. In him. In the firepit. He knew he could call it. Shape it. He knew he could burn the dwarf to ash. He felt the fire gathering in his hands. Waiting for him to command it.

Blinking, he saw both Ainslee and Nia backing away, fear on their faces. He took a deep breath and consciously willed the fire to leave him, pushing the heat away. It took a long moment, but he felt his temperature returning to normal.

He took several more deep breaths. Nothing he said now would bring back his food. Despite her shorter stature, the dwarf probably outweighed him. It was very likely that she naturally ate more, in which case she'd probably gone to bed hungry. But that still didn't give her the right to eat his share.

"Fine," he said through gritted teeth. "I'll look for some berries while we walk. Grab your stuff! We're leaving."

The women just stared at him for a moment. Frustrated and angry, Ethan snatched up the handful of weapons and stalked off down the road. After a minute, he heard the footsteps of the women following him.

Part of him felt relieved. But the rest of him was appalled at what he had felt earlier. What he had been thinking about doing. He wasn't a violent person. He wasn't even a person who got angry easily.

But a minute ago, he had been ready to unleash a torrent of fire down on the dwarf. What was wrong with him? Why was he feeling this way? And most importantly, how could he stop it from happening again?

14

The group walked in silence for over an hour before a squeal of delight from Yuliana broke the morning calm.

"Berries!" she exclaimed and ran off the road towards the trees.

Ethan, who'd been too caught up in his own thoughts to look for food, glanced over at her. The elf scrambled at the small hill up to a patch of bushes just in front of the treeline. She plucked some off and looked at them.

She smiled at Ethan, waving the berries in her hand before unceremoniously tossing them into her mouth. As if in response, his stomach growled loudly. That was all the encouragement he needed. He quickly joined her by the berry bushes.

Once he reached the bushes, he paused. He looked at the bush and the berries closely. It looked familiar. Very familiar. He plucked one of the small, bluish-purple round berries and examined it.

Blueberry
Type: Fruit

Duration: N/A
Effect: 1 serving of 80 blueberries
   provides 0.1 of your nutritional
   needs.
Other: None.

Blueberries? It was an actual blueberry. Like the blueberries of Earth? Tentatively, he tasted it. It tasted just like an blueberry! How was that possible? How had the aliens incorporated an Earth blueberry plant into their simulation?

He plucked another blueberry and held it up. "Has anyone seen this berry before?"

"No...It...is... boo...berry," Yuliana said, her mouth full. "It is not poison. It... says... provides nutrition."

"Yes," he nodded. "But has anyone seen this berry before?"

She shook her head. Ainslee, who had come over to the bushes, was shoveling berries into her mouth as fast as her meaty hands could rip them from the bush. She looked over at him and shrugged. "Not... seen... them."

He turned back toward the road, where Nia stood with crossed arms. He gave her a questioning look. "Ever see this?"

The foxgirl squinted and shook her head. "A berry. It is prey food. One berry looks like another."

He frowned. So no one else had ever seen a blueberry. That meant the aliens definitely took it from Earth. But how? And why?

Ethan noticed Nia hadn't come to join them in the berry eating. "Not eating berries?"

The foxgirl scoffed. "I do not eat prey food. I eat prey!"

Sighing, Ethan turned back around. They had one person who wouldn't eat meat. Another who would only eat meat. He snickered as he cast a sideways glance at the dwarf. And one who ate twice the food as everyone else. Just great.

Seeing how fast the other two were cleaning off the bushes,

Ethan began to stuff his own mouth full of berries. In short order, the berry bushes were picked clean.

"We should not have eaten all of the berries," Yuliana said, her face guilt-stricken. "We should only have taken what we needed."

"Oh," the dwarf said, pointing to herself with her thumb. "I needed that. Trust me! It ain't meat, but it'll do in a pinch."

"In this case," Ethan agreed. "I think Ainslee's right. We do need it. We may not find another berry bush for some time."

Yuliana looked back to the now-bare blueberry bushes and nodded slowly. "Perhaps you are right."

The group continued on for three more hours. Just before they were going to call a break for lunch, they spotted a dark cloud of smoke rising off in the distance. They paused, looking at the column of smoke.

"That seems like it's a big fire," Ainslee said. "Too much smoke for a campfire."

Nodding, Ethan thought back to the house fires he'd come across on Earth. They created smoke like that. Or maybe a large bonfire. Either way, it took something intelligent to build a house or create a bonfire large enough to make a smoke cloud like that.

"We should check it out," he told them. "It could be people."

The women looked at him. Ethan shrugged. "Some sort of intelligent life."

"Perhaps it is a wildfire," Nia said.

Ethan looked at the smoke again and shook his head. "I don't think so. See how the smoke is all coming from one place. If it were a forest fire, it would spread. You would have a larger area smoking."

"Well," huffed the dwarf. "Let's go check it out. If they're intelligent, they may have figured out how to make mead or ale!"

Ethan shook his head. The dwarf seemed highly motivated

by food and drink. He made a mental note in case that information came in handy later. He glanced at the other women. "Come on, let's go check it out."

They all fell in behind Ainslee at a slow run, which didn't last long for Ethan. Out of shape, he quickly became winded and slowed to a walk. And he wasn't the only one. Apparently, Yuliana was not accustomed to running either. Which made sense when he thought about it. She tended a grove. How big was a grove and how often did you have to go running in a grove?

Holding his side, Ethan motioned for Ainslee and Nia to continue.

"Neither... am I," the elf breathed. "The grove... does not... need... fast... attention."

In only a few minutes, Nia and Ainslee were out of sight around a curve in the road. Ethan and Yuliana walked until they had caught their breath, then jogged a little while before being forced to slow down again.

It took them fifteen minutes for them to reach the other two. They found the dwarf and foxgirl hiding behind part of a large fallen tree, just outside a clearing. Nia heard them approach and motioned for them to come to her. She made a patting motion in the air which Ethan took to mean they should stay low.

He and Yuliana crouched down and made their way to the fallen tree. As soon as he reached the thicket, the dwarf turned to him. "More of the kobold things. They burned down one building. Now they're lighting a second one on fire."

Shocked, Ethan started to stand but Nia put a hand on his shoulder. "Slowly. So you do not attract attention."

Nodding, he slowly stood up where he could see the clearing. Poking just his head and eyes above the trunk of the tree, he saw that they were right. In the far end of the clearing was what was clearly some sort of barn, though instead of walls, the sides looked more like a fence. Not that it mattered since the entire thing was engulfed in flames.

Closer was what looked like a simple house with a thatched roof, which kobolds were throwing burning sticks onto. Even as he watched, parts of the roof began to burn, sending up more smoke. He could hear multiple screams from inside the building. The kobolds just barked in their guttural language. Ethan couldn't understand it, but the tone told him they were enjoying it.

Anger surged inside him and he quickly counted the number of kobolds. Eight. He cursed silently and ducked back down. He looked at the others. "There are people in that house. We have to help them."

The dwarf gave him a disbelieving look. "Are you mad? There's twice as many of them as there are us."

Gritting his teeth, he poked his head up. Four of the kobolds were in the same area. If he could take them out with a fireball, that would even the odds. Ethan grimaced. He'd have to channel a lot of heat. It would take a lot of his Stamina. But what choice did he have? He couldn't just let them burn to death - simulation or no.

Ducking back down, he motioned them towards him. "Four of them are close together. I can take them out with a fireball."

The dwarf gave him a doubtful look. "You didn't even kill two last time. Just one."

"I'll channel more energy this time," he growled. He took a breath and tried to speak slowly and articulately like he did with annoying customers. He checked his Stamina and was unsurprised to see it was low given all the jogging he'd just done.

What would happen if he channeled more Stamina than he had. Would he pass out like Yuliana had? Another scream came from inside the house and he knew he didn't have a choice. "I will channel more energy. But, if I do that, I might fall unconscious. So someone please make sure they don't kill me."

Looking at each other, Nia and Yuliana both nodded. Ainslee still looked dubious but nodded too. "Fine. But if you don't kill four of them, we're probably going to die."

Ethan nodded curtly. He knew the stakes and accepted them. He couldn't just let people burn to death. He looked around. "Get ready."

The women nodded, their grips tightening on their weapons. They all looked at each other grimly but their faces were resolute.

Closing his eyes, Ethan tried to find the fire inside himself again. He could feel it, though not nearly as strong as when he'd been angry at the dwarf. He started to reach for it when he sensed more heat.

He sensed the heat in the women around him, each of them a different level and different amount. Ethan thought he could actually tell who was who by their heat pattern. Then something else caught his attention.

He reached out further and thought he felt the fire on the house. It was a sharp, burning heat. Much hotter than the women's heat. He reached for it and felt it slip away from him. It wanted to keep doing what it was doing.

Exerting his will, he reached out hard this time. Not with mental fingers, trying to pick it up. This time he pictured using a mental hand or shovel and scooped it up. It came along reluctantly and he began to squeeze and compress it.

Once more the fire resisted. It didn't want to be compressed. It wanted to burn. It wanted to expand. He pushed down harder and felt it give. He also felt his strength going but knew he had to keep going. Ethan kept pushing it into a ball. Compressing it. He opened his eyes and looked at the house.

The fire from the roof was gone. Hovering over the roof as a small ball of bright light. The kobolds had stopped moving.

They were all standing there, staring at the light. They were completely entranced by it.

He felt his strength leaving him and saw blackness on the edges of his vision. Just before the darkness overtook him, he willed the ball into the group of kobolds. Then he felt himself falling, slipping into darkness.

Far away, he heard thunder. Or maybe it was fireworks. And then... nothing.

15

The first thing Ethan became aware of was the smell of charred wood. The second thing was how much his head hurt. He hesitated on opening his eyes. Part of him wanted to believe that he would open up his eyes and find himself in his bedroom, but he knew that wouldn't be the case.

"I think he's awake," a woman's voice said. It didn't sound familiar. "Go get his women."

Hearing the woman mention "his" women, Ethan forced his eyes open. The first thing he saw was a ceiling of uneven sticks that held back what appeared to be straw. The straw was loose in places and he could see through it to the thatch roof above.

He realized he was lying on something that was both soft and firm at the same time, like a lumpy bed. He glanced to his right and saw the wall of the room, a rough wall that looked like it was made of layers of packed dirt or possibly clay. Glancing to his left, he saw a human woman he didn't recognize.

At first glance, the woman looked old. But as he focused, he could see that the lines in her leathery skin were mostly from sun damage, instead of age. This was a woman who had led a tough life.

The woman looked at him with a mixture of emotions, but put on a smile. Ethan had seen that kind of smile and knew it was forced. "Glad to see you are awake, Sir Wizard."

"What?" Ethan blinked. He sat up slowly, feeling drained and exhausted. Without really thinking about it, he brought up his HUD and looked at his stats.

```
Name: Ethan
Class: Wizard
Race: Human
Level: 1
Experience: 75
Fame: 1

Strength: 10
Agility: 13
Hardiness: 13
Intellect: 17
Intuition: 14
Charisma: 10

Health: 21
Stamina: 1
Mana: 20
Karma: 28
```

His *Stamina* was at 1! Had he dropped into negative *Stamina*? Was that even possible? He remembered what had happened to Yuliana when she had done too many healing spells. She'd dropped unconscious until they'd raised her *Stamina* with the water from the stream. Is that what they'd done?

He realized the woman had said something else and went to dismiss his HUD, before remembering to analyze her.

Margery

Human

Farmer

Level 3

Skill increase: Analyze +1%.

He learned her name was Margery and that she was a Farmer. Ethan was surprised to see that she was a level 3 farmer. And was Farmer a class or a profession? Was she a real person? Maybe a "player" like him? Or was she some sort of simulation-controlled construct, like the non-player characters, or NPCs, from MMORPGs?

He realized Margery was looking at him expectantly. He dismissed his HUD and gave her an apologetic look. "I'm sorry, what was that?"

"I asked if you would like some ale," she asked.

Ethan was about to ask for water but then took another look around. He guessed he was inside the house that the kobolds had been trying to burn down. He remembered that it was somewhat crude and looked like a simple medieval home with a packed dirt floor.

Could he trust the water? So far, the alien simulation had been extremely detailed and he wouldn't put it past them to include parasites, bacteria and worse in the water. At least with ale, the alcohol would kill most things. He hoped.

"I would love some." He smiled.

The woman nodded and took a clay mug from the floor and handed it to him.

"Thank you," he told the woman, remembering at the last second not to use her name since she hadn't offered it. He had no idea how she would react to him knowing her name and if it would spook her any more than she already was.

Bringing the beverage to his lips, he smelled it. It smelt hoppy and some other scents he couldn't quite place. He took a tentative sip and had to immediately fight the urge to spit it out. It wasn't just hoppy, it was very yeasty. It was like drinking liquid bread dough. And it was warm. Having always drank his beer cold, warm ale was strange to him.

He forced himself to swallow it and hoped the ale wouldn't make him sick. As it went down, he realized that the ale was also extremely weak and lacked any real carbonation. He looked at the woman and nodded.

Realizing it was a good time to ask for names, he offered his own. "I'm Ethan. What's your name?"

The woman seemed taken back by the question and she hesitated before answering. "Margery, milord."

"Just Ethan," he chuckled. "Not milord or lord wizard."

She smiled slightly. "Yes mi... Ethan."

He heard a door open and then the bustle of people. Then, his companions crowded into the room. They all looked concerned.

"We were worried," Yuliana said as the three women pressed into the small room.

Ainslee snorted. "Bah! I told ya he would wake up. Used up all his stamina with that there fireball! But you sure did fry those kobolds!"

"It worked?" he asked. He realized that he was much lower than he should be and looked around to see that he was on more of a pallet instead of a bed. Pushing himself up, he stood up. As he got to his feet, he felt the room spinning and he might have fallen if Nia hadn't pushed her way past the others and caught him with her quick reflexes.

He gave the foxgirl a weak smile. "Thanks."

"Easy," Margery said. "From what I saw you used a whole bunch of magic. You're lucky you're still alive."

He looked down at Margery curiously but it was Yuliana who answered. "We have been talking with Margery and Hamond while you were unconscious. Apparently, it is common knowledge that using too much magic can kill you."

"What?" he asked, suddenly feeling sick to his stomach. He'd almost died? And those other times he'd used magic, he could have died? That put a new twist to things. Falling unconscious was one thing. If he could actually die, that was something else.

"How much is too much?" he asked, looking from woman to woman.

"Sorry, milor... I mean, sorry, Ethan," Margery replied, her eyes fearful. "I don't know."

"Maybe we should talk outside," the dwarf said, giving a meaningful look at Margery. "I think the fresh air would do you good."

Yuliana and Nia both nodded and gestured towards the door with their heads. He rolled his eyes when Margery wasn't looking. "Yes, fresh air sounds good."

Ethan started towards the door and almost collapsed. Only Nia's strong arms kept him up.

"Maybe he should rest a little longer," Margery said but then immediately bit her lip.

"It's okay, Margery." The dwarf smiled. "I think a good dose of fresh air will liven him back up."

Nodding, and supported by Nia on one side and Ainslee on the other side, he went outside with the women. They walked past a man, which his HUD identified as Hamond. Near the man were six children of varying ages. The two tallest, and presumably oldest were girls. His HUD identified the older girl as Jade and the younger was named Emma. The boys were Hunter, Braydin, Gage and Wiatt.

It was a strange mix of names. If it were Earth, he would have guessed the names had come from different ethnic backgrounds. What kind of cultures did this world have?

Glancing backwards, he caught sight of the house. From the outside, the home looked like something he'd see in an old English or Irish countryside. At least, that's what he envisioned from the British TV shows and movies he'd seen.

He didn't have much time to consider it as his companions stopped just out of earshot of the man and his children. Leaning against a tree, he looked around at the somber faces of the women and frowned. "What?"

"We were talking with the people here," Yuliana started. "They told us quite a bit about this place. And they might have mentioned one or two things about wizards."

"Oh," Ethan replied, his eyebrow raised. "Like what?"

"Like how there aren't any wizards," Ainslee burst out, punctuating her words with a meaty finger pointed at him. "Cause something or someone killed them all!"

Ethan gave them a confused look. "Wait... what?! Who killed them all?"

"Something they won't mention," the dwarf retorted, lowering her voice. "But apparently, whatever it is has been killing wizards. And some of the other magic people, or whatever she called them."

"Arcanes," Nia supplied.

"Right." Ainslee bobbed her head. "Arcanes."

"But no druids." Yuliana smiled and then gave him an apologetic look.

"So wait," he said, still trying to process their words. "Something or someone is killing wizards and other arcane casters, but they won't tell us what?"

Nia shook her head. "I don't think they know. I'm not sure if anyone does."

"Right!" the dwarf cut in, a dark grin on her face. "They

said that. No one knows what's killing them. Only that it's been going on for about the last year or so and that it's gruesome."

"Gruesome?" Ethan asked, swallowing involuntarily.

"Yes," Yuliana interrupted, giving the dwarf a hard look. "They were all killed a particular way."

Ethan motioned for her to continue but the women exchanged looks. He let out an exasperated breath. "Just tell me already."

"Brains! They ate their brains! Sucked out of their heads," the dwarf said, making a slurping sound.

"What?" Ethan asked again, not sure he'd heard them correctly. Were there zombies in this simulation? Zombies that ate brains? He'd been thinking he was in some sort of MMORPG simulation. Was he in a zombie survivor game instead?

"Apparently, the news reached every corner of the kingdom that these people live in," Yuliana explained. "Wizards and the arcanes are being found dead. One of their eyes is punctured and it looks like their brain is... sucked out through the eye socket."

"At least," Nia said, "that's what these people have heard. Who knows how much is true and how much is just rumor."

He looked between the women's faces. It was clear none of them believed it was all just rumor.

"That's why they are afraid of you," Yuliana explained. "Not because of who you are, but what you are. They know you're a wizard and they're afraid whatever is killing wizards will show up and kill you - and them too."

"Suck their brains right out of their eye," said the dwarf, gesturing at her eye and making a slurping sound with her mouth again.

"Geez," Ethan breathed. As if being in an alien simulation that played like an MMORPG wasn't bad enough. He had inadvertently picked a class that was apparently being murdered by having their brains sucked out. Just wonderful.

He shook his head, trying to get a grip on the situation. He frowned as he looked up at his companions. "Since we have no idea whether or not those rumors are actually true, we should leave these people."

Biting his lip, he looked from face to face. "If you're worried, I'll go my own way from here on out."

The women looked at each other, a knowing look passing between them. He got the impression that they had already talked about it. Just great.

"We'll stick with you," the dwarf said. "For now. After all, you seem to know the most about this place."

Ethan was about to object and point out that he didn't really know any more than they did, but stayed quiet. He needed their help. That was especially true if there was something coming for him that wanted to eat his brain.

"Oh," Nia said. "And we learned something else."

Bracing himself for more bad news, he looked at Nia. "What else?"

"There's a village called Hawkshead a day's walk down the road," she replied, smiling. "Near the mountains."

"We should check it out and see if we can find more answers," Yuliana told him. "About why we are here."

"And see if they have better ale," the dwarf said with a sour face. "The stuff these people have tastes like drinking stale bread!"

Sighing, Ethan nodded. Any thoughts of more rest were gone. They needed to get to the village and find out more information about the wizard slayings. Otherwise, he could be next.

16

A n hour later, the family assembled in front of the house as Ethan and his group prepared to leave. Despite being thankful, they were obviously relieved to see them go. This seemed especially true for Ethan, who the children pointed at and whispered.

"We won't say nothing about you being a wizard," Margery told them, giving a stern look to the assembled children.

"But you best be on your guard," Hamond said. He gave the group an apologetic look and nodded to the burned-out barn. "Sorry we can't offer you no supplies. But with so much of the livestock lost, we don't have nothing to spare."

"It's okay. Thanks for letting me rest up." Ethan smiled.

Although it had been obvious that they were nervous about having him stay, Hamond and Margery had allowed him to stay and rest. It had been good because the women insisted that he go back inside and lie down after eating some of Margery's stew.

He'd still felt weak and had done as they asked. And while he didn't sleep, he had been able to determine that his *Stamina* would regenerate while he rested. As close as he could tell, as long as he lay down and did nothing, he regenerated 1 *Stamina* and 1 *Mana* every minute or so. Since he had no watch, he calculated it using the time-honored "One Mississippi... Two Mississippi" method, but it seemed fairly accurate.

But like before, his *Stamina* never went above half though his *Mana* regenerated to full. He wasn't sure why *Stamina* stopped regenerating at half, but it was annoying. Especially when casting spells seemed to use so much of it.

He didn't understand why casting spells took *Mana* and *Stamina*. That, at least, was very different from the MMOs. In every MMO he ever played, magic used up one stat, and it wasn't a physical stat like *Stamina*. Maybe this was something the aliens had gotten wrong.

"Good luck to ya," Margery said and waved to them. Ethan wasn't the most socially adept person, but he did recognize a dismissal when he saw one.

"Good bye," he said and turned towards the women. "Shall we?"

A few minutes later they were walking down the road towards the village of Hawkshead. According to the farmers, Hawkshead was a tiny town consisting mostly of dwarves and humans now.

Once, it had been a thriving silver mine, but the silver had run out and the miners had eventually left for other mines. Now, it was mostly abandoned now. There were independent farmers around Hawkshead, but they didn't consider themselves part of the village. Margery said that only a couple dozen people lived in the village now. And those that stayed were there because they had families or had no other place to go.

"So you really think there are dwarves like me in this village?" Ainslee asked as they moved past some fields.

All eyes turned to him and Ethan was reminded that they seemed to think he had some hidden knowledge about this place. He shrugged. "I don't know. They might be dwarves. But not like the dwarves you're used to."

Furrowing her brow, Ainslee looked at Ethan. "What do you mean?"

"The humans we just met were like humans on my planet," he explained. "But many hundreds of years ago. They didn't really resemble humans alive today on my planet."

"Yah," the dwarf responded, looking thoughtful. "But didn't you say your people only live like 80 years or something."

He nodded.

"So a few hundred years is many generations." She smiled. "For a dwarf, that's one or two generations."

Ethan considered her words and then nodded. "That's a good point. I hadn't considered that."

In honesty, he had forgotten how old the dwarf was. He was still having a hard time wrapping his head around how old Ainslee, and especially Yuliana, were in comparison to him. It was hard to imagine Yuliana, who looked like she could be in her early twenties but was actually well over ten times his age.

"If the other elves have been here for one or two generations, they may remember how we got to this world," Yuliana said hopefully.

"And how we can get home." Nia nodded.

He kept quiet. While it was possible that someone might know a way to "logout" of this simulation, he doubted it. And even if they did, what then? They'd wake up in some alien mothership or base? He looked up at the ringed planet they orbited. For all he knew, they really were on some moon of that giant planet, only in some base, connected to a bunch of wires that fed them impulses.

A terrifying thought struck him. What if there was nothing left of their bodies? What if they were just a brain with a bunch of wires and nutrient tubes running to it? There would be nothing to wake up to and nothing to go back to.

He shook his head to clear the idea but he couldn't shake it. His mind replayed every horror and science fiction movie where people were abducted or mutilated. Each scene became worse than the next until he finally had to quit and force himself to pay attention to his surroundings to keep his mind off of his possible fate.

As the group walked towards the village and the mountains in the distance, they found several more wild blueberry bushes and ate their fill. Ethan made sure he kept a few extra handfuls for Yuliana, since she would not be able to eat with them later.

The elf refused at first. Yet once he pointed out that the others would be eating meat tonight, she'd changed her mind and accepted them gratefully. When they realized she had nothing to store them in, Ethan stored them in the bandolier he'd taken the day before.

They traveled on until dusk, passing several more farms along the way. During the afternoon, storm clouds had started to gather, causing the skies to grow prematurely dark. By the time they were ready to stop for the night, a torrential downpour had begun. With no cloaks and no raingear of any kind, the group was drenched to the bone in no time.

"Blasted rain!" the dwarf shouted, her curse punctuated with the roar of thunder.

"It is not so bad." Yuliana smiled and stretched her arms out to the rain.

Nia said nothing, but her expression was not happy. The foxgirl was drenched and her normally fluffy foxtail was waterlogged and dragging on the ground.

"Do we find shelter," he yelled over the sound of the deluge, "or keep walking and hope we reach Hawkshead?"

"Are ya crazy?" The dwarf scowled. "There's no shelter around! How are we supposed to find some?"

"Keep moving," Nia growled. It was the most she'd said since it started raining. "Let's find the village and get inside."

"I am fine in the rain," Yuliana said and twirled around. "But it would be difficult to sleep in. Perhaps we should press on, especially since this area will flood tonight."

Turning, they all stared at the elf.

She shrugged and gestured around. "The ground here is low and you can see that the river is already rising. This road and the low areas here will flood before daybreak."

"Then we better get moving!" shouted the dwarf. "Because I don't swim!"

They kept marching in the dark, a soaked and unhappy Nia leading the way. Her fox-like eyes were able to see well in the dark and keep them on the road. The rain intensified at one point and they were forced to hold hands to prevent them from losing each other.

Unfortunately, the rain had also made hunting impossible and there wasn't enough visibility to look for berry bushes. Instead, they all went hungry. All except Yuliana, who he quietly passed the leftover berries from his bandolier. He made sure not to let the dwarf see them, lest an argument erupt over the small amount of berries.

Drenched and miserable, his small group kept walking through most of the night. Once the suns' warmth was gone, the rain was no longer as refreshing as it was chilling. Several times, Ethan checked his HUD and saw that his *Stamina* was gradually going down. Worse, he and the others had received a debuff.

Chilled
Effect: You are unable to regenerate
Stamina. Lose 1 Stamina per hour.
Movement slowed by 10%.
Duration: Until cured or dried.

They were all concerned by the condition and even

Yuliana's healing could not cure it. He guessed there was some other version of her healing ability that removed conditions. Like a Cure Disease spell in one of the tabletop RPGs he played.

That meant either Yuliana didn't know how to cure the condition or the ability was out of her level range. After all, they were all still only 1st level.

The group walked on late into the night. They had just crested a hill when Nia let out a whoop. "The town!"

Ethan squinted into the darkness but saw nothing. "You sure?"

"Through that narrow pass," she said, pointing into the darkness. "I can see buildings."

Unable to see, Ethan nodded and accepted the foxgirl's word. "Let's go then!"

The ground was slick and the pass was narrow, so once again they all joined hands and carefully made their way down the hill and through a narrow pass. When they reached the start of the buildings, they immediately began searching for an inn. They passed what appeared to be a shop on one side and a smithy on the other.

Then they entered into some sort of town square or just an open area and found a large, two-story building that looked like it had seen better days. Just before they knocked on the door, Ethan stopped them.

"What?!" the surly dwarf demanded. "I want to get out of this rain!"

"This is an inn," he said.

"I know what it is," Ainslee shot back angrily. "Why do you think I want to go in?!"

"I'm not sure how it is in your world," Ethan responded, trying not to get angry himself. He remembered the last time he'd gotten angry at the dwarf. "But in my world inns cost money."

The dwarf stepped back as if slapped. Her countenance fell. "You're right. And we have no money."

"What do we do?" Nia asked. She looked even more miserable than the dwarf.

Ethan thought quickly. They were in a town. A medieval town. Inns cost money. What didn't cost money? They could break into the inn and demand shelter, but that would surely cause issues. He had no desire to end up in jail or stocks or whatever these people did as punishment.

Breaking into a house posed a similar problem. Just then he heard a horse whinny from behind the inn. Did they have a stable? Maybe one with a roof?

"Follow me!" he said and led the group behind the inn. As he had suspected, there was a stable. And it had a roof. There was only one animal in the stall, an old mule that looked as if it could have been from Earth.

They quickly checked the other stalls and found an empty one that was clear of horse manure. The bottom of the stall was lined with hay. While the hay closer to the entrance was wet, the hay towards the back was mostly dry. Tired and desperate to get out of the rain, they all crowded in and closed the stall door.

Still wet and cold, they all huddled together for warmth and before he even knew it, Ethan had drifted into an exhausted sleep. Even the dwarf's snoring didn't wake him.

17

Ethan woke to screaming and the stench of manure of animals. At least those were the first two things that he noticed. He opened his eyes and blinked at the morning light streaming into the stall. He looked down to see Nia raising her head from his lap. She had been curled up next to his legs but now looked around and blinked as well.

Moving her head off his left shoulder, Yuliana was looking around as well. She looked like she was in a daze and he doubted any of them had gotten more than a few hours sleep. Eyes blinking, she looked at Ethan. "What is the yelling?"

Ethan was still partially in a daze from having just awakened but looked around to find the source. He listened again.

"Da! Strangers in the stables!" a voice was yelling. It sounded like a child. Probably a boy's voice.

"I think we've been discovered," he groaned. "I'm not sure if it's illegal or if the innkeeper might try to charge us, but we'd better get moving."

Turning, he nudged the dwarf on his right shoulder. "Ainslee, wake up!"

A loud snore was the dwarf's only answer. Ethan nudged

her again harder, and her eyes popped up, a wild expression on her face. "Wha?! Huh?"

"I think we may have worn out our welcome," he told the dwarf, who barely seemed to acknowledge him.

Trying to get up, Ethan grimaced as it felt like every muscle in his body was sore. He heard similar groans from everyone except Nia. They all struggled to their feet just in time to see a squat portly male dwarf and dwarf child appear at the door of the stall.

The portly dwarf had ebony skin like Ainslee, with long white hair pulled back in a ponytail. He had a long, thick white beard that was split and braided. For clothes, he wore a simple but serviceable outfit, a cream shirt under a brown leather vest and blue trousers tucked into leather boots. The child was a male and wore only pants with no shirt and no shoes. He was hiding partially behind the older dwarf, who Ethan guessed was his father.

"Hey, you vagrants!" he yelled. "What do you think you're..."

The dwarf stopped talking as his eyes moved over Ainslee. His brow furrowed and he huffed out a breath. He looked down at the boy behind him and back to Ainslee. "My wife will be having a fit if she finds out I let one of the kin sleep out in the stable."

The dwarf scowled at the rest of them before turning back towards the inn. "Better come in and let us feed ya. Otherwise the wife'll have a fit. Not many dwarves left. Especially womenfolk..."

The dwarf stopped and turned back around, noticing none of them had moved. "What are you waiting for? An engraved invitation?"

Ethan lightly nudged Ainslee. She looked up at him and he nodded his head to the dwarf and mouthed the words "no gold."

Ainslee looked disappointed but nodded, understanding

his meaning. "Sorry, kind sir. We have no money to pay for breakfast."

"Of course you don't have money!" the male dwarf barked, rolling his eyes. He gestured at the stall. "If you had money, you wouldn't be sleeping in the stables, now would ya?" The dwarf sighed. "Name's Fearghas and the lad be Sawney. Do not worry. We'll give you a meal and my wife'll likely talk yer ear off! We haven't had much news since the caravans stopped coming."

Fearghas turned around and resumed walking down the alley that led to the front of the inn. He looked back over his shoulder. "Come along. Quickly now!"

The group looked at each other and then looked at Ethan expectantly. He sighed. He wished they'd stop looking to him for all the answers. He was just as lost in this new world as they were.

Looking at the retreating dwarf, he shrugged. "I don't know about the rest of you, but I could use a good meal."

That was all the encouragement they needed. Ignoring stiff and sore muscles, they all jogged after the dwarf and quickly caught up with him.

"Good choice," Fearghas said, not looking back. Sawney glanced at them and reached over and took his father's hand. "We need to get inside before..."

The group was just about to clear the alley when two large figures stepped into the entrance of the alley, blocking their way.

"Loki's Balls," the dwarf swore as the figures appeared.

"Behind us," hissed Nia.

Ethan glanced behind them to see two more figures block their escape. The figures were all human but ranged in size and girth. Each wore weathered and stained leather armor and equally rough-looking gray cloaks. But what immediately caught his attention were the short swords and daggers sheathed at their sides.

He briefly wondered if they were town militia or guardsmen who had come to arrest them for sleeping in the stall. But judging by their demeanor, he suspected a more sinister purpose.

"I told you I heard yelling," one of the men in front of them said to the larger man next to him.

Focusing, he examined all four men in his HUD to see what they were dealing with. He also took the time to size up the dwarf and his child. He received an increase in *Analyze* for each

Gamel
Human
Brigand
Level 2
Fulk
Human
Brigand
Level 1
Warin
Human
Brigand
Level 1
Rojor
Human
Brigand
Level 1
Fearghas
Dwarf
Innkeeper
Level 3
Sawney
Dwarf
Level 0

He frowned as he saw that the big man was level 2. He had no idea what levels meant in this simulation and what the power difference was between levels. Gamel could be twice as powerful as them or only a fraction more powerful. There was no way of knowing. Not for the first time, he wished there was a tutorial or help menu.

"Gamel," the innkeeper said with a frown. "We're paid up. Why are you bothering us?"

"Shut your mouth, Fearghas." The big man scowled. "You might be paid up, but they ain't."

"Yeah, boss," chuckled the man next to Gamel, who his HUD had identified as Fulk. "They ain't!"

"You see," Gamel explained. "We're the local militia. And there's a tax to be paid by all citizens and visitors to support the militia so you nice people can stay safe."

"Militia, my arse," Fearghas snorted softly. "They're bandits."

"Now," Gamel said, "I think 1 gold per head should do, what do you think?"

"Yeah," chuckled Fulk, "one gold a head."

"They don't have any money, Gamel," Fearghas pleaded. "They were sleeping in the stables. Just let them go."

"No money?" Gamel frowned and looked them up and down, making a disgusted face. Then a twisted grin spread across his face. "Well, we'll need to confirm that. We'll have to search them. Especially the women."

"Yah," giggled Fulk, who Ethan realized was an idiot. "Search the women real good."

"You will not touch us," Nia growled, her face contorting into a snarl.

"The fox's feisty," said one of the men behind them. "I like them feisty."

Realizing what the men intended, Ethan felt his blood boil. He felt the heat rising up in him, just like before when he was angry. But this time it was even more intense. He remembered the farmers' warning about something killing wizards. If he used fire, he'd mark himself as a wizard to these men. If word got out, would someone, or something, come for him?

He didn't want to take that chance. If he used magic, he'd have to be very subtle about it.

"Why don't we take them back to the stables and... search them proper," Gamel grinned mirthlessly.

"Gamel, please don't...." the innkeeper started but Gamel glared at him and moved his hand to his shortsword.

"I think you should go take care of your family," the brigand said between clenched teeth. "You wouldn't want anything to happen to them after we get done... searching."

Fearghas looked down at his terrified son and then back at them. His father was a mask of guilt, concern and anger. Finally, he hung his head. When he spoke, his voice was hoarse with suppressed anger. "I'm sorry, I can't risk..."

"Go," Ethan said between gritted teeth. His anger somehow fueled whatever fire magic he possessed, and it was getting increasingly difficult to contain it. "Go."

Pulling Sawney after him, the innkeeper hurried past Gamel, who let him pass, and then stopped. Fearghas glanced back at them apologetically and then disappeared around the corner.

"If I use my magic," he whispered. "There can't be any witnesses."

Ainslee snorted. "Considerin' what they have planned for us, I'm fine with that."

"Me too," Nia growled.

"That is acceptable to me as well," Yuliana whispered.

"Ethan," Nia said, wide-eyed. "The air around you is wavering, like in the desert heat."

"And you're throwing off heat like a forge," the dwarf nodded.

Ethan frowned. He was holding back the fire, but it must be

heating up the air around him. That might give away his power. He paused. Air. He had air magic too. And the air was invisible. Could he use air instead of fire to mask his powers?

He'd only used air once before to block a blow from one of the kobolds. He wasn't sure what he'd done but it was worth a try. And, he had an idea of how to disguise any air magic he used.

"Ainslee and Yuliana," he whispered as the men started towards them. "Take the ones behind us. Nia and I will take the ones in front."

"With pleasure," Ainslee growled and turned to face the oncoming bandits.

Fulk cackled and started to draw his shortsword and dagger. "The girlies want to play."

"Put those away," Gamel ordered and nodded at the group. "We don't want to damage the goods."

"Yeah," Fulk giggled. "Don't want to damage the goods."

"Leave," Ethan said loudly, the force of his anger and fire raging inside him giving him strength. "Just turn around and walk away."

You have gained: Intimidate.
Skill increase: Intimidate +4%.

The men paused briefly, looking at Ethan, seeming to size him up again. After a long moment, Gamel laughed. "This one's got a set. I'll give him that."

"He must," snickered one of the men behind them Ethan had identified as Rojor, "to have 3 women."

"Or maybe he's their pet," chuckled Warin, the brigand next to him.

"Okay." Gamel smirked. "Cut the loudmouth and then we search the women."

"Yah," Fulk parroted with a wicked grin. "Cut the loudmouth."

Ethan balled his hands into fists, barely able to keep the power contained. He nodded at Nia. "So be it."

18

As the words left his lips, Nia leapt into action - literally. The foxgirl leapt up to head level and covered the distance between her and the brigands in the blink of an eye. She lashed out with her quarterstaff at Gamel's face.

Just as her staff impacted, Ethan focused his will. Before the air magic had responded to what he wanted, which was to block the enemy's blow. Now, he wanted to attack. He willed the air to strike the man in the face with as much force as possible.

The result was more than he had hoped for. Through his magic "sense" he felt the gathered air strike the brigand in the face with the force of a sledgehammer.

> *Critical Strike!*
> *You pummel Gamel for 37 critical air damage.*
> *Gamel dies.*
> *Skill increase: Air Magic +1%.*
> *You gain 10 experience. Experience to next level 115.*

Gamel's head snapped back and the man staggered back a step before falling backwards, head back at an impossible angle. At the same time, Ethan felt his own strength drain away. A quick look at his *Stamina* showed it had dropped by nearly a third. His *Mana* on the other hand, had only dropped a point.

Nia in the meantime looked down at her staff and then to Ethan. Her face was anguished, and he realized she thought she had killed the man. He gestured at the dead brigand and then at himself and wiggled his fingers.

She gave him a curious look and then nodded, seeming to understand. She turned back around just as Fulk cackled and stabbed out with his shortsword. Nia tried to dance away, but the blade sliced her across the abdomen. One of her hands went to the wound as she tried to backpedal away from the brigand.

Seeing her hurt, anger flared up again and he barely suppressed the fire. Instead, he willed the air to something he wasn't sure would work. He reached out with a hand of air, snatched the lower tip of Nia's quarterstaff and brought it slamming up between Fulk's legs.

Critical Strike!
You pummel Fulk for 19 critical air damage.
Skill increase: Air Magic +1%.

The blow had been unexpected, by both Fulk and Nia. The brigand's mouth fell open and his eyes went wide. At the same time, the strength seemed to leave his arms and his blades dipped.

Nia took advantage of his momentary weakness and hit him twice more between the legs. The brigand's weapons clattered to the dirt as the man's hands went between his legs, a strangled gasp escaping his lips. He collapsed to the ground, writhing in agony.

Walking over, anger and fire still coursing through his veins, he reached down and picked up the man's discarded dagger. Knowing what they had intended to do to the women, Ethan had no remorse as he stabbed the man in the back of the head.

Critical Strike!
You pierce Fulk for 12 damage.
Fulk dies.
You gain 5 experience. Experience to next level 110.

You have gained: Short Blades.
Skill increase: Short Blades +1%.

Fulk spasmed and then went still. Nia looked up at him, a questioning look on his face.

"That was me." He nodded to the dead form of Gamel. "You didn't kill him."

Forcing a smile, Nia nodded; her hand still covered the gash and Ethan could see blood trickling through her fingers.

"We need to get you healed," he said and looked to the end of the alley.

Ainslee was bleeding from several gashes, the red blood bright against her ebony skin. One of the brigands was on the ground and the other was running away.

The fire inside wanted to burn down the man and he knew he could, but he resisted. He couldn't use fire without revealing himself as a wizard. Sighing, he let the man go and called out to Yuliana. "Nia needs help."

Yuliana healed both women but then looked exhausted. Checking his own *Stamina*, he saw that it was down to 5. He shook his head at how much *Stamina* the magic took from him.

"What do we do with the bodies," Nia asked, nodding at the three dead brigands.

"Personally," Ethan said, reverting back to his gaming experience, "I think we should strip them down, take their gear and any money they have. Considering they just tried to rob us... and worse... I have no compunctions."

Ainslee shrugged, still bleeding from a gash across the forehead. "I'm okay with that."

They dragged the bodies to the back of the alley and proceeded to strip them. As they did, Ethan examined each item.

Leather Cuirass
Type: Chest armor
Armor: 3 of 4
Durability: 8 of 10

Leather Breeches
Type: Leg armor
Armor: 2 of 4
Durability: 4 of 10

Leather Bracers
Type: Arm armor
Armor: 2 of 2
Durability: 8 of 10

Leather Boots
Type: Foot armor
Armor: 2 of 2
Durability: 9 of 10

Iron Dagger
Type: One piercing weapon

```
Range: 3 ft. / 30 ft.
Damage: 4 points piercing damage
Durability: 4 of 6
```

```
Iron Shortsword
Type: One piercing weapon
Range: 3 ft.
Damage: 6 points piercing damage
Durability: 3 of 6
Warning: You have no proficiency with
    this weapon and suffer -1 Strength,
    -1 Agility when attacking with it.
```

They also recovered pouches of coins from each of the bandits, with Gamel's pouch having the most coins. Examining all of the equipment got them each almost 20% in the *Appraise* skill. He smiled. At least the skill was easy to rank up, even if he wasn't sure what ranking up would actually do for him.

Ethan also found an iron key on a leather cord around the leader's neck. He wondered if it went to a building or maybe a room at the inn. Or maybe a chest or storage area. But where?

Fulk seemed to be about the same size and build as Ethan and he took the man's clothes and armor and put them on, replacing his own torn t-shirt and dirty sweatpants. He kept his socks and managed to fit the man's boots on, even if they were a bit tight.

Gamel's larger chest armor, boots and bracers fit Ainslee, but the leggings were much too large to fit her stubby dwarven legs.

The other man was larger and bulkier than either Yuliana or Nia, though Nia did manage to get his bracers to fit.

Ethan handed the short swords to Ainslee, who gave them a few practice swings. Satisfied, she belted on the scabbards for them. "They're not axes or hammers, but they'll do better than that kobold spear."

Since the dwarf had two of the short swords, Ethan, Yuliana and Nia each took one of the daggers. And rather than leave the shortsword behind, Ethan added it on his belt. After all, he had just gained the *Short Blades* skill.

He quickly checked the weapon in his HUD. Apparently, *Short Blades* didn't apply to short swords, as it showed he was not proficient.

"So now we have money to get a proper meal?" Ainslee asked hopefully.

"I'd say so," Ethan commented, jingling the pouch at his hip. "I'm guessing these guys had a protection racket going on and we have the proceeds."

The girls looked at him with confused looks and he sighed. "They were forcing the local businesses to pay for protection - from them. Basically, the merchants paid or these brigands roughed them up or damaged their business."

"Why would they do such a thing?" Yuliana asked in confusion.

"Money," Ethan replied.

"And power." Ainslee nodded. "Those scum probably loved beating up on weaker folk."

"They are cowards," Nia spat.

"Thor's Hammer! What in blazes have you done?!" came a familiar voice from behind them.

Ethan turned to see Fearghas, brows furrowed, looking at the naked brigands. The innkeeper let out an exasperated breath. "You are all dead."

It was Ethan's turn to furrow his brow. "What do you mean?"

Fearghas looked up and down the alley, as if making sure no one else was watching. Then he sighed. "Those are the Graycloaks. And they won't let stand what you've done."

"You know what they were going to do," Nia hissed, eyes narrowed and tail still puffy.

The dwarf nodded. "I do, lass, and I'm sorry. But that was only four of them. There be more of them. Twice that number yet. And it looks like you let one get away, so no doubt he'll be running back to the others to report what happened."

"What will happen then?" Yuliana asked, her face showing her innocence. Ethan guessed she hadn't had much experience with brigands if all she did was tend a grove of trees.

"They'll be back for revenge," Ethan answered. "Right?"

Fearghas nodded. His face was pained. "I'm sorry, lad, lasses, I can't help you. No one can. If we do, they'll take it out on our families. I can't... I just can't lose them."

Ethan reached out and put a hand on the dwarf's shoulder. It was obvious the dwarf wanted to help them but was afraid for his family. Ethan guessed he would do the same in the dwarf's situation. "It's okay, Fearghas. Do you know where the Graycloaks call home? What's their base of operations?"

The innkeeper once again looked up and down the alley before answering. "It's common knowledge they took over the old silver mine headquarters, just north of town. They've been a scourge on this town since they arrived. If you could somehow run them off or...well... kill them, I know the townsfolk would be happy."

Fearghas Stormaxe has offered you the quest "Stop the Graycloak Brigands I"

A group of bandits known as the Graycloak Brigands have been terrorizing the village of Hawkshead.

Eliminate the remaining brigands (0 / 8)

Reward: 100 experience, +250 reputation

with Residents of Hawkshead, +250 reputation with Fearghas Stormaxe

Accept quest (yes or no)?

Ethan could see the others had received the quest too, as their eyes had gone suddenly glassy. He read the quest again. It was much like the quests in MMORPGs that he played online. There were even rewards.

He accepted the quest and then looked around at the confused looks from the women. Clearly the idea of questing was foreign to them. Ethan found it interesting that he seemed to be the only one familiar with the MMO-style mechanics. He wondered why that was.

"Thank you, Fearghas," Ethan said. "We'll take care of them. Go back to your family."

The dwarf nodded and turned to leave. He stopped but didn't turn around. "I don't really think my wife's porridge turned out so good today. I think I might have her throw it out in a few minutes. Probably just set it out on the back porch and let the crows eat it."

Understanding the dwarf's words, Ethan smiled. "I think the crows would appreciate that."

"Aye," said the dwarf and disappeared around the corner of the alley.

A few minutes later, the backdoor to the inn was opened and a pot set out. Then several wooden spoons. After that, the door was shut and Ethan thought he heard the door being locked again.

"What is porridge?" Yuliana asked suspiciously as she looked at the pot.

The stuff looked like runny oatmeal, but to be sure he took one of the wooden spoons and tried it. It tasted like oatmeal, maybe with a touch of honey. "It's chopped grain, probably boiled with a bit of honey, I think."

Nia sniffed it and shook her head so the rest of them finished up the porridge in record time. After eating, he checked his *Stamina* again and saw that between the food and the time doing nothing, it was almost back to half. If only he knew how to get it back to full.

"What did you do during the fight?" Nia asked. "I did not see anything."

"Air magic," Ethan replied. "I figured air would be hard to see. And if they don't see me do anything, they won't know I'm a wizard."

Nia nodded soberly. "I thought I had killed that man."

"Sorry," he apologized. "I didn't have time to go over the plan."

Nia nodded and lapsed into silence. Ethan took the opportunity to explain the questing mechanics to them the best he could. Yuliana seemed to have the hardest concept with it, as she had nothing like it in her experience. The other two women found analogies from their previous lives.

"It's like an order ticket, right?" Ainslee said. "Someone orders a tool or a weapon and they give you specific instructions. Right?"

"Or like a scouting mission," Nia offered. "You are told by the alpha to go scout an enemy camp and return with a report."

"Similar to both those things," Ethan replied. "It's got aspects of both, but it's much more... specific and rigid. At least, from my experience."

The women looked thoughtful for long moments. Finally, Ainslee stood up and patted her short swords. "Let's go teach the other thugs a lesson and do this quest-thingy."

19

"**A**re we sure we want to do this?" Yuliana asked as they walked through the village. The elf had been quiet since they left the inn. "If I read the 'quest' correctly, there are eight brigands left."

She looked at Ethan for confirmation and he nodded. "That's what it looks like. We have to kill eight bandits."

"Is that really what we want to do?" Yuliana asked, her forehead wrinkled in concern. "After all, it is one thing to defend ourselves. It is another to attack others unprovoked."

"We have a quest," Ainslee pointed out.

"None of us really understands what that even means," Yuliana shot back. She looked at Ethan. "Except Ethan. Does having a quest make it right?"

All heads turned to Ethan, as if he magically had the answers. He sighed. Morality was never really an issue in MMOs. In the MMORPGs he'd played, there had been all sorts of quests. Occasionally, the writers made them morally dubious, but in the end, the players knew it was just a game and nothing they did really mattered. Was it any different in this simulation?

His mind went back to the dead "players" they'd found when they'd first arrived. Those had probably been real people and now they were dead. What about the people he thought of as NPCs? Could they be real? Would they be killing real people?

Ethan remembered what the brigands, real or not, had been ready to do to the girls and he set his jaw. "No, just having a quest doesn't make something right."

The elf nodded, getting the confirmation she was seeking.

"However," he continued and the wrinkles on the elf's forehead reappeared, "having a quest doesn't make it wrong either. From what I gather, these people are terrorizing the town through numbers and violence. Look how quickly they were about to take advantage of you three."

The women nodded, even Yuliana.

"And I doubt that was the first time," he told them. "They were too quick and willing. The other reason has more to do with our own self-preservation. If we don't go after the brigands, they will come after us."

Pausing to let that sink in, Ethan continued. "We killed three of their number. They cannot let that go unchallenged. They rule through fear and intimidation. They have to kill us now - probably publically - to reassert their dominance.

"It's kill or be killed," he said. "And I'd rather fight them on our terms rather than theirs. Otherwise, I have a feeling they will do something to us and it will be very public and very painful, as a lesson to the villagers."

The elf shuddered and wrapped her arms around herself. Nia looked pale and even Ainslee looked uncomfortable.

"We could leave," Yuliana offered.

"And go where?" he asked. "And would they follow us? I'd rather face them head on than have them ambush us somewhere. Remember, they know this area much better than we do."

The elf bit her lip. "But so much death."

"It's them or us, honey," Ainslee muttered. "Personally, I choose us."

Ethan remembered that she had tended trees, or a grove or something. He thought back to one of the summers when his parents had a garden and an idea came to him. "Yuliana, if there are one or more diseased plants but the others are healthy, what do you do with the diseased plants?"

"You would..." she started to reply and then seemed to understand where he was going. Her voice became very small. "You would remove them."

"These men have become diseased," he told her. "And we are going to remove them so the rest of the people, those in the village, can thrive."

The elf didn't say anything for a long time. Finally, she nodded. He could tell she wasn't convinced but at least she was still coming with them.

After that, the group walked on in silence, leaving the cluster of buildings that made up the village and heading north.

Fearghas had pointed out north to them after Ethan asked the direction. The dwarf had said something about how the mountains can mess with people's sense of direction. Ethan had nodded and pretended that was it but the reality was, this was the first time someone had pointed out a direction to him in this world. Now that he had it and could compare it to the position of the suns and the ringed planet, he thought he'd be able to find it again.

Glancing to make sure no one was around to overhear here, Ainslee turned to him. "So, mister wizard, any idea how we can take on eight of these thugs?"

Ethan shrugged. "Not yet. We need to see their base of operations and look for weaknesses. Figure out a way to lure some of them out so we're not fighting them all at once."

"Yes," Nia agreed. "We must separate the weak from the herd. A herd is dangerous. But a single prey is weak. It is easily overcome."

"Divide and conquer," Ethan agreed and Nia looked at him and tilted her head. Then she nodded.

"Yes, divide and conquer," she repeated and then smiled. "I like that."

"Um," the dwarf broke in, stopping in her tracks. "If that's our plan, maybe we shouldn't be walking down the main road out of the village."

Ethan stopped and looked around. He wanted to facepalm himself. Of course. He'd been thinking like the MMOs he played. Get quest. Go to place. Kill bad guy. Return and get reward.

But this wasn't an Earth MMO. Whatever this simulation was, it was much more like real life. The people, or NPCs or whatever they were, thought like real people. They might set traps or ambushes or have scouts.

He nodded to himself. Yes, this was more like a tabletop RPG, where the gamemaster was out to challenge the party. That's how Ethan needed to think of this. Not as him against a computer game, but him against another living, breathing, thinking person.

"You're right," he told the dwarf, who nodded smugly in acknowledgement. "We need to get off this road and approach them from the side, or better yet, circle around and approach from the north, where they won't be expecting it."

Nia and Ainslee nodded while Yuliana just bit her lip. Ethan guessed the elf still wasn't happy about them aggressively going after the brigands. He turned to her. "Yuliana, if you aren't comfortable with this, you can go back to the village and wait for us."

All eyes turned to the elf, who seemed embarrassed by the sudden scrutiny. She continued to bite her lip for what seemed like minutes before blowing out a breath. "No, I will go with you. You are right. They started it and now we must finish it. They are a diseased branch and must be pruned from the tree."

Ethan nodded and gestured into the forest to their left. "That's a good example. Let's duck into the forest and see about scouting this place out and then circling around."

The group followed him into the forest as he cut in just far enough that they could see the road through the trees. He had Nia watching the road, making sure they didn't miss the Graycloaks if the brigands marched in force on the village.

If that happened, he knew there would be no way to get around using his fire magic. The air magic seemed potent for one opponent at a time, but he needed what the MMOs called area-of-effect spells. And that meant a fireball. At least, that was the only way he knew to affect more than one enemy at a time.

He needed to practice with this magic. In RPGs and MMOs, magic classes weren't his favorite. Ethan liked combat classes. But he'd played magic classes before and there was always a system. Once you learned the system, it was straightforward.

The problem in this simulation was that he didn't know how the magic worked. And there was no wiki, FAQ or forums to help him figure it out. Based on the people they'd talked to earlier, it sounded like the only people who would have been able to help him, other wizards, had been systematically killed off.

An idea hit him then. Spellbooks! Or just books in general on wizardry. Was it possible he could find some and they might shed some light on how to best use his powers? He made a mental note to ask about any libraries or book collections when they went back to the village.

Twenty minutes later, the forest opened into a large clearing. In the middle of the clearing was a two-story structure. The building looked rundown but still serviceable and the smoke from the chimney told him that someone inhabited it.

"Is that the building?" Ainslee whispered.

Squinting, Ethan shrugged. "I can't tell."

"It is," Nia said with conviction. The foxgirl pointed to the right side of the building where two men came around the corner. Both wore similar gray cloaks.

"Good eyes," he murmured as he watched the men walking casually around the front of the building and then turn around the corner. They were obviously patrolling.

"They have bows," Nia added.

Squinting, Ethan tried to see the bows but failed. "Are you sure?"

The foxgirl just sniffed and didn't bother responding.

"Fine," he whispered. "You're sure. If those two have bows, we have to assume the others have them as well. Or at least, they have access to them."

"So no rushing them," the dwarf smirked.

"Probably wouldn't be a good idea," he agreed.

"Can you just... you know, make the place explode?" Ainslee asked. "I mean, I know someone is killing wizards but who's going to know?"

Ethan had been thinking along those same lines. Provided they killed all the brigands, there would be no one to say the house was hit by a fireball, as opposed to them setting the house on fire and it burning down.

The major problem was his *Stamina*. He might be able to get one good fireball off, like he had at the farm, but then he might be unconscious. And without knowing which room they were in and how many were in the room he targeted, he could end up wasting it or just getting one or two Graycloaks. That would leave the bulk of the brigands for the three women.

"I doubt I could blow up the entire building," he replied finally. "And sending a fireball through one window would be a gamble unless we know we could get most of them."

Ainslee grunted and turned back to watching the building.

He could hear her muttering under her breath. "What good is magic if you can't blow up buildings..."

With the patrol, there was no guarantee that attacking from the north would buy them anything. The patrol would see them and raise the alarm. Once it was raised, the rest of the bandits would take up positions and pelt them with arrows. Or they'd all rush out and overwhelm them with sheer numbers.

They could try to wait for nightfall, then try to sneak closer. But that assumed that the brigands didn't march on the town before then. Somehow, he couldn't see the brigands waiting an entire day to get retribution.

Ethan watched the sentries go around the building again in their tell-tale cloaks and similar leather armor. Yup, they looked like cookie cutters of the brigands they'd killed, as if they'd bought the same outfit at some renaissance faire.

He grinned as an idea came to him. It was risky but it might just allow them to get the first attack in. But, he'd need to time it just right or the whole would blow up in their faces. Possibly literally.

Turning to the others, he gestured them away from the clearing's edge. "I've got an idea."

20

"Help," Ethan rasped, limping down the path towards the building. His eyes were wide, his face and head were covered in blood. His left arm hung limply at his side, the sleeve of his shirt bloody. His right leg was bloody from the thigh down and looked like it might collapse at any time. He tried to limp faster and nearly stumbled before rasping again. "Help me!"

The sentries came around the corner of the building and saw him coming. The larger man, Ethan was close enough for *Analyze* to reveal his name as Rhett, pointed at Ethan and said something to the smaller man. The smaller man, Ethan's HUD identified him as Handor, gasped and ran into the house yelling.

Rhett, sword and dagger still sheathed and bow strapped to his back, hurried over to where Ethan struggled to walk. Ethan watched him come, resisting the urge to smile. It was all part of his plan.

Having seen that the sentries wore the same basic clothes, armor and cloaks as the group of brigands they had killed, Ethan had quickly come up with a plan. He was wearing Fulk's clothes and armor because he had been the same size as the man.

After explaining the plan to the women, Nia had killed two rabbits and Ethan had covered his face and hair in the blood, as well as smeared more blood on his arm and leg. With the blood obscuring his face, Nia said he could pass for the now-dead Fulk unless someone was right on top of him.

Dressed in his Fulk costume, he had circled back around to the road. He had limped down the road and then cut down the path that led to the building that served as the bandits' lair. So far, things were going according to his plan. So long as the brigands came out before the sentry recognized him, his plan would work. If not, well, he didn't want to think about that.

Rhett was getting closer and still no one else had come out of the building. Ethan cursed under his breath. If they didn't come out soon, the whole plan would go up in smoke. The bandit came within six feet of him and Ethan was forced to use plan B.

Falling onto his hands and knees, he did his best impression of hacking up a lung. At the same time, he slammed his hand against a rabbit's bladder hidden just under the top of his shirt, causing blood and other fluid to shoot out in front of him. To someone looking at him, it appeared as if he just coughed it up.

Rhett came to a halt as the blood splattered. The man backed up a step. "Three moons, Fulk! Hang in there!"

His face hidden, Ethan smiled. The bladder had been a last-minute addition when Ainslee had accidentally stepped on the first rabbit's and sent blood and other fluids spraying all over Yuliana's leg. The elf had been horrified and spent ten minutes cleaning herself.

He hadn't been sure that it would work, but the fear of having blood coughed up on him was keeping the brigand at bay for now. Just a little longer. He just needed the brigands to come outside. What was keeping them?

As if in answer to his silent pleading, five brigands rushed out of the building. Together with Rhett, that made six. There were supposed to be eight of them. He silently cursed. He had hoped to get all eight at once but realized he couldn't wait any longer.

He reached down once more and focused his heat. He focused into his right hand but kept inside. He brought up his HUD and saw his Stamina dropping quickly. Still, he kept focusing, drawing more heat. Then he pushed off with his left hand and brought up his right, aiming into the middle of the brigands.

With a cry he forced the fire out and it shot from his hand in a small white-hot ball. The ball traveled the ten feet to the center of the surprised brigands and then exploded into a fireball that threw Ethan hard against the ground.

> *You burn Rhett for 37 fire damage.*
> *Rhett dies.*
> *You burn Irwin for 21 fire damage.*
> *You burn Handor for 42 fire damage.*
> *Handor dies.*
> *You burn Cranley for 39 fire damage.*
> *Cranley dies.*
> *You burn Macon for 27 fire damage.*
> *You burn Warin for 41 fire damage.*
> *Warin dies.*
> *Skill increase: Fire Magic +6%.*
> *You gain 40 experience. Experience to*
> *   next level 70.*
> *Quest updated.*
> *Stop the Graycloak Brigands I*
> *Eliminate the remaining brigands (4 / 8)*

Lying on his back, ears ringing from the fireball's explosion, Ethan struggled to push himself up. His HUD was still active and he could see that he hadn't killed all six of the bandits. Two were still alive. And two more were unaccounted for, probably still in the building. But they'd halved their numbers.

Flipping himself around, he pushed himself up and struggled weakly to his feet. His hand fell to his waist, fingers closing over the hilt of the knife on his belt. Pulling the blade free of the sheath, he looked around at the charred bodies of the brigands.

Two of the bodies were groaning and moving, starting to get up. Each of them had someone atop them, which Ethan guessed was what had saved them from the full blast of the fireball. He started to stagger towards the nearest when a twang sounded as something struck him in his left shoulder, causing him to fall over.

Eldon pierces you with pine crossbow for 11 damage.

Pain exploded from his shoulder as he fell. Looking at the shoulder, he saw a small arrow sticking out of his shoulder. No, not an arrow. It was a crossbow bolt. Reading the message in the HUD, he confirmed it. One of the brigands had just shot him.

There was another twang and the ground next to his head erupted as another bolt embedded itself in the ground a few inches from him. If he remembered, crossbows had to be cranked and then reloaded. That took some time.

Summoning up his strength, Ethan pushed himself off the ground, pain shooting through his left arm. He stumbled to the building and slipped around the corner, out of sight of the brigand crossbowmen.

He heard some scuffling from inside the building, followed

by grunts of pain. Wincing from the pain in his arm, he smiled. The women had arrived. He had sent them to circle around and come in from the north. While the brigands' attention had been on him, they had crept up from the north undetected. He loved it when a plan came together.

Ethan started to let himself sag against the wall when one of the scorched bandits who had survived the fireball came stumbling around the corner of the building. The man, the HUD showed him as Macon, looked to be in bad shape, with the left side of his face blackened and most of his hair burned away. The entire left side of his body was charred as well and the smell of burnt flesh permeated the area.

The brigand held a shortsword in his hand and growled the moment he saw Ethan. Despite the fatigue he felt and the pain pulsating in his left shoulder, Ethan threw himself at Macon. The brigand got his shortsword up and Ethan felt the blade slide across his hip, just below his leather armor.

Macon pierces you with iron shortsword for 7 damage.

But now Ethan was inside his guard. He stabbed the long knife once into his chest, pulled it out and then stabbed it in again.

You pierce Macon for 5 damage.
You pierce Macon for 4 damage.
Macon dies.
Skill increase: Short Blades +2%.
You gain 10 experience. Experience to next level 60.
Quest updated.
Stop the Graycloak Brigands I
Eliminate the remaining brigands (5 / 8)

Macon's eyes glazed over and his body fell back with Ethan on top of him. The crash pushed the crossbow bolt further into his shoulder and he let out a cry of pain.

Pine crossbow bolt pierces you for 2 damage.

Carefully rolling himself over with his right hand, Ethan landed on his back, staring up. A burned and battered figure, which his HUD told him was Irwin, appeared over him with a shortsword held in a blackened hand.

"I'll... kill... you," Irwin rasped as he took another step towards Ethan.

Ethan saw that his Health was down to 6 and went to reach for his magic but saw his *Stamina* was only at 7. He probably only had enough *Stamina* for a single spell. And casting it would render him unconscious again.

Irwin took another step towards him and Ethan realized he didn't have a choice. He prepared to focus air into a thin attack against the man's throat when a staff smashed down on the man's hand, causing him to drop the shortsword. The other end of the staff then swept down, taking out the man's legs.

The man toppled backwards, slamming hard into the ground. Standing just behind where Irwin had been was Nia. She gestured down to him. "Hurry, kill him. You know I cannot!"

With a supreme effort of will, he pushed himself up and crawled over to the prone brigand as he struggled with the staff pressed down on his groin.

Lurching up with the dagger in his right hand, he crashed into Irwin and drove the dagger deep into the man's chest. The brigand's eyes went wide and then he coughed up blood once before going still.

You pierce Irwin for 5 damage.
Irwin dies.
Skill increase: Short Blades +1%.
You gain 5 experience. Experience to
*   next level 55.*
Quest updated.
Stop the Graycloak Brigands I
Eliminate the remaining brigands (8 / 8)
Quest updated.
Stop the Graycloak Brigands I
You have eliminated all of the brigands
*   who have been terrorizing Hawkshead.*
*   Return to Fearghas in Hawkshead for*
*   your reward.*
New Quest: Stop the Graycloak
*   Brigands II*
One of the brigands mentioned a boss.
*   Someone may have hired or organized*
*   the brigands. Investigate the*
*   brigands' headquarters for signs they*
*   were working with anyone. Find*
*   evidence of any affiliations and*
*   bring to the villagers.*
Evidence: (0/1)
Reward: 100 experience, +250 reputation
*   with Residents of Hawkshead*
Accept quest (yes or no)?

In his HUD, he saw that the original quest had been completed. Ethan guessed the women had already taken care of the other two brigands. But now there was a new quest. It was known in MMOs as a quest chain, where one quest led to another. He accepted the quest and then just lay there, breathing hard.

A minute later, Ainslee and Yuliana appeared. Ainslee knelt down and took hold of the crossbow bolt. "Sorry, wizard-boy. The bolt's got to come out. I'll count to three. One..."

On one, the dwarf yanked the crossbow bolt out of his shoulder, causing him to jerk and scream. Almost immediately he felt the ice-cold healing as Yuliana's magic healed him up.

Yuliana Madeiras heals you for 13 health.

He could feel muscles healing, causing his shoulder to spasm. It felt like thousands of ice-cold ants running up and down his arm. And then it was gone and his shoulder felt better but was still sore.

"That's all I can do," the elf told him.

"Yeah, sorry." Ainslee shrugged. "She healed me earlier. One of the brigands got a lucky shot."

The dwarf reached down and, grabbing his hand, hoisted him to his feet. She looked at all the bodies. "So now what? One of the brigands in the house told the other to go tell the boss. He tried to run out the side but Nia took care of him. Now I got a new quest-thingy. Something about evidence."

Ethan nodded, rotating his sore shoulder. "I got the same quest. I guess we loot the bodies, then search the house and see if we find whatever evidence the quest is talking about."

21

They gathered the bodies outside the front door and took all of the worthwhile loot. In the MMOs he used to play, the games always had some sort of inventory system. Items you collected went into an endless backpack that allowed you to carry far more than a real person ever could. Looking at all of the items arrayed on the ground, he found he missed that feature.

At Ethan's insistence, each of them took turns using their *Appraise* skill on the items, which earned them all rank 2 in the skill.

You have reached Rank 2 in Appraisal.
+1 Intellect.

He looked at his HUD, surprised he had received a bonus to his *Intellect*. He again wondered what, if any, effect that had on him. Thus far, Ethan had received two bonuses to his *Intellect* and he didn't feel any smarter. Perhaps it simply governed certain game mechanics? He had noticed that his maximum

Mana had increased along with the *Intellect* boost. Too bad his spells didn't seem to actually care about *Mana*.

He realized the women were all looking at him and he blinked, dismissing the HUD. "I'm sorry. What?"

"What do we do with all of this stuff?" Ainslee huffed. "And what's with the Intellect boost? What does that mean?"

"I think it's just a measurement of how the ... world," Ethan caught himself wanting to say game or simulation but knew that would be too difficult to explain to them. "Knows how to calculate success on certain things. For me, it also increased my mana - not that it seems to do anything for casting spells."

"So, in other words," Ainslee snickered. "It's useless."

Ethan shrugged. In most MMORPGs, there were what were referred to as "dump" stats. They were stats that didn't matter to the class a person was playing and thus, they didn't have to invest any points into. For a tank like Ainslee, *Intellect* would be considered a dump stat. To him, normally *Strength* would be that dump stat.

But this world was different. Who knew what uses the stats would have. *Strength* might have something to do with carrying capacity. If that were the case, given the lack of a "virtual" inventory, *Strength* might play a larger role.

Hardiness certainly played a big role. It affected not only his *Health*, but his *Stamina* too. He had found both to be vitally important so far. For now, it was best not to treat any stat as a dump stat.

He gestured to the equipment they had salvaged. "I suggest we each find whatever fits and is comfortable wearing, then leave the rest. At least for now. If the village has a general store of some sort that buys used gear, maybe we can sell it later."

"That seems morbid," Yuliana said, looking at the items, "selling the items of the dead for profit."

Ethan was about to retort but Nia beat him to it. "These

men were enemies. When you vanquish an enemy, their lands and possessions become yours. That is the way."

Yuliana bit her lip and ran her hand through her green hair. The elf's wrinkled brow showed she was not convinced. Finally, and convincingly, she nodded.

The group spent the next half an hour picking through the items to see what each wanted. His fireball had blackened some of the armor and burned away parts of clothing. The gear that survived had very low durability.

He frowned as he looked through the various equipment. It did seem to be a drawback to using his fireball. It did great damage in an area, but damaged the equipment too. That was something he never had to worry about in MMORPGs or tabletop RPGs. The loot was always like new when you took it off a corpse.

In the end, they were each able to find suitable armor. One of the men had been particularly skinny and his items fit Yuliana. Of course, "fit" was a relative term. It was extremely snug around her large chest and a bit loose around her slim waist. Still, it would offer her some protection.

For weapons, he'd had them all systematically tell him what their *Appraise* revealed so he could see which items each of them could best use. The process had taken time, but he felt it was important. They should each be armed with the weapons they could use best.

Unsurprisingly, as the *Knight*, Ainslee had proficiency with all of the weapons they had found. That made sense to him, since in most RPGs, fighter classes had all the weapon proficiencies. She grumbled about not having an axe or hammer but picked out the two best shortswords.

Nia, who Ethan still thought of as a thief class, had proficiency with the majority of them, the lone exception being the crossbow. He wasn't sure why she had proficiency with the bow but not the crossbow.

It didn't make sense to him, but there was no gamemaster to argue with. When he asked her about the crossbow, she admitted that on her world, her people hadn't made anything like a crossbow. Could that be why she didn't have proficiency? Or was the *Acrobat* class just not proficient with it?

Of course, even if Nia could use them, didn't mean the foxgirl would use them. Other than the bow to hunt and the staff in battle, she adamantly refused other weapons. The only exception was a well-made dagger she took for skinning animals.

This was frustrating for Ethan. He had never been a metagamer, but he had tried to optimize his build in MMORPGs and even the tabletop games to fit his game style. Sometimes, that meant taking weapons or skills that didn't look sexy, but which gave him better survivability.

Watching Nia purposefully hamstring herself rubbed him the wrong way. Not that it was his place to say anything, but he suspected that if she were dual-wielding short swords, she could make quick work of their enemies. Sighing inwardly, he moved on to the elf.

As a druid, he wasn't sure what to expect with Yuliana, but she appeared to not be able to use items made mostly of metal. She had proficiency with the club, the bow, the staff and even the crossbow. In her case, she had no experience in either combat or weapons, so giving her something like a crossbow would probably end in disaster.

And then there was Ethan, the wizard. He could use daggers and staffs, and the crossbow, but nothing else without penalty. His fantasy of being a dual-wielding wizard with a sword in one hand and staff in the other seemed to be just that, a fantasy. Then again, if he faced down a fiery demon on a narrow bridge in some underground mine, he'd probably wet his pants.

Each of the brigands had also been wearing a coin purse,

though the amount of coins in each varied wildly. After taking all of the coins and adding them up, he saw that they had 4 golden coins, which he guessed were the most valuable. Each of them had a crown on one side and the portrait of a fierce but regal man on the other side. Ethan guessed that was the king. But king of what land?

They had 7 coins that were gold and silver. The outer circle of the coin was silver with an inner circle of gold. This one had a different crown on one side and a portrait of a regal-looking woman on the opposite side. The queen maybe?

The last two coins were pure silver and copper coins. The silver coins held the image of a castle on one side and what Ethan guessed might be a griffon on the other side. The copper coins were the smallest coins and had the image of crossed swords on both sides. They had 12 of the silver coins and 23 of the copper.

Ainslee's eyes gleamed as she looked at the coins. "Hopefully this means we can buy a good meal and some ale."

Ethan nodded but was thinking more of a decent room with a decent bed. He was bone weary and his entire body ached. What he wouldn't give for his old bed and about a day of sleep. And coffee! Definitely coffee!

Not for the first time, he thought the aliens' simulation was just a little too realistic. If this was like Earth MMORPGs, they were supposed to be the heroes. And heroes didn't wake up with aching backs and feet. At least, he certainly didn't remember reading about Hercules, Jason or Perseus waking up and needing an hour to work the kinks out of their back.

"You exchange goods for these... coins?" Nia asked. She had been silent as they had counted the coins. But as he looked over to her, he wondered if her world used any form of currency, or at least, did they use coins? Then he noticed Yuliana perk up at the question too, her eyes looking at the pile of shiny coins.

Glancing between the elf and the foxgirl, he held up one of

the coins. "Yes. Each of the coins represents a certain value. The goods are priced based on that value and you exchange the goods for the coins."

"Why not exchange them directly?" Nia asked, her brow wrinkled. "Why an extra step?"

"Some goods are too big or bulky to exchange," he responded. "So a man can take a herd to the market, exchange it for some coins, walk back to his village and use the coins to buy the supplies he needs locally.

"I take it neither of your worlds use coins?" he asked.

Both Nia and Yuliana shook their heads. Yuliana looked wistful. "The grove gave me everything I needed. There was really no need for trade. Sometimes, a blight would wipe out a species and I would need to ask for seeds to replace the plants that died."

Ainslee rolled her eyes, obviously not impressed with the druid's world and customs but he shot the dwarf a hard look before she could open her mouth and criticize them.

"We do not use currency either," Nia said. "Everything is owned by the Alpha. He distributes the goods based on need."

"What about resources you don't have?" Ethan asked.

"If the pack does not have something it needs, we take it," Nia stated simply.

"That's one way to do it." The dwarf shrugged. "Personally, I want to take some of these coins and turn them into mead."

Ainslee insisted they divide up the coins but Ethan shook his head. "Let's hold on to them until we know their values, then we can split them up."

The dwarf narrowed her eyes at Ethan. "And who gets to hold onto them until then?"

"Yuliana," he said, surprising the elf.

"Me?" she asked. "Why me?"

"I'm guessing of all of us here," he replied. "You have the least interest in them."

The elf shrugged. "I do not know if I fully understand the concept of these coins."

"Which makes her perfect to carry them," Ethan said.

"Fine. Let her carry them," Ainslee grumbled. "Can we go search the house so we can get back to town and get some mead?"

Ethan couldn't help but agree. The sooner they finished searching the house, the sooner they could return and maybe get a hot meal and a good night's rest.

22

Geared up and coins safely with Yuliana, the group moved inside the building. The two-story structure was similar to the buildings they'd walked by in the village. It was made from some material he wasn't familiar with but its roughness suggested some sort of straw or clay-based bricks. Like all the buildings he'd encountered so far, this one had a thatch roof, although this roof was in a sad state of disrepair judging by the holes he could see.

Inside the building might have once been offices, but anything of worth had been taken or burned for heat or cooking. It was obvious that the downstairs rooms had been used by the bandits for sleeping since only tattered blankets and empty wooden kegs littered the dirt floor now.

"Bah," Ainslee muttered as she finished checking the kegs. "The miserable brigands drank it all! There's nothing left!"

"Let's keep checking," Ethan said. "I noticed one of those brigands was level 2. Maybe he was the leader. He might have a separate room."

"If he was the leader, then why would the HUD ask us to find the leader?" Yuliana asked.

"Maybe he was a boss, but not THE boss," Ethan said, remembering various RPG quests, book plots and movies. "Maybe that 2nd-level guy, Gamel, was their leader but someone else hired them."

"That is cowardly!" Nia screwed up her face. "To have another fight your battles!"

"Maybe." Ethan nodded. "If we find this evidence, maybe it will shed some light. Let's keep looking."

There were no doors, they'd probably been taken or burned for firewood. Stepping through the walkway, they moved into the adjoining room. Like the previous room, it also had several blankets strewn around the floor and nothing else.

Moving onto the third room, they found the remnants of a wooden staircase. Like the other wood in the building, it had been scavenged for firewood.

"I guess we won't be searching the top floor," Ethan observed. He frowned, remembering some particularly sadistic game masters. "Unless we don't find the evidence down here."

"You had better come here," said Yuliana, who had ventured into the next room. "Is this evidence?"

The rest of the group looked into the final room. There was only a single bedroll in this room and it was an actual bedroll, not just a couple of tattered blankets. But the odd thing was the mining picks in the corner, some of which looked recently used.

"Are the picks evidence?" Nia asked.

Ethan scanned the room again. If Gamel had been their leader, then this was most likely his room. He suddenly remembered the key he'd taken from Gamel's corpse and excitedly retrieved it from around his neck.

"Look around for a chest or something with a lock," he told them, brandishing the key so everyone could see. "I'm guessing this key goes to something here."

Yuliana looked from the key to the room. "There are only the picks and the sleeping blanket."

Scanning the room, he had to agree. There were only the stack of picks and the bedroll. Was it somewhere else? Or was it hiding in plain sight? Someplace the other brigands wouldn't go. Walking over to the bedroll, Ethan pulled it back.

Like the farmer's home, the floor of the building was hard-packed earth. Pulling back the bedroll revealed an area that had been dug out and then covered over with sticks so Gamel could still sleep over it.

Bending down, Ethan hurriedly pulled out the sticks, exposing a shallow hole with a rusty metal chest. He started to reach into the hole to get it but stopped. Did this simulation have traps? He'd triggered his share of traps in tabletop RPGs and more than once ended up killing the entire party. He didn't want to make that mistake here.

"Get it!" Ainslee said eagerly. "Let's see what's in it!"

"Hold on," he replied, still studying the chest and the surrounding hole.

The women watched him, curious. Yuliana leaned close. "What are you looking at?"

"Trying to see if there are any traps," he replied, wishing he had a flashlight. He rubbed his forehead with his fingers. He didn't have a flashlight but he was a wizard. He quickly brought up his HUD and checked his *Stamina*.

Stamina: 18

The time they'd taken to collect the items and go through them had allowed him to regenerate a chunk of his *Stamina*. He thought he could risk a little experimentation. After all, in most games wizards had a certain amount of utility and didn't just blow things up.

He focused on what he wanted, feeling the heat within him

but only taking a small bit. He imagined it forming itself into a ball around head height and hovering there. He pushed on a bit of the heat and envisioned what he wanted it to do. No sooner had he envisioned it when a ball of yellow light appeared just in front of his head, shedding light in the room and down into the hole.

Skill increase: Fire Magic +1%.

The women all scrambled back, eyes wide. Ainslee dove out through the door, thudding into the floor with a grunt. He sighed as he realized they probably thought he'd conjured a fireball. He narrowed his eyes and looked at the ball of light, growing worried. He hadn't, had he?

Cringing, he watched the light for several seconds. When it didn't explode, he smiled and looked around. The women, including Ainslee who had peeked into the room, were all glaring at him.

"You should have warned us!" Nia told him.

"That was very reckless," Yuliana chided.

"Hah," Ainslee chuckled. "You had me going! I thought for sure you were going to blow yourself up."

She came in and clapped him hard on the back. "But don't do that again without warning us!"

"Sorry," he said apologizing. "I didn't think about it looking like a fireball."

"Just warn us before you use your magic," Yuliana said. "Please."

"Sorry about that. I'll warn you next time," he told them. He brought up his HUD again to check his *Stamina* and *Mana*.

Stamina: 17
Mana: 38

He stared at the numbers. He'd only used a point of each. Why? Was it the effort involved? Ethan desperately wished he knew the rules of this magic system!

"So it's just a ball of light?" Yuliana asked. The elf cautiously moved her hand towards it. "It gives off heat."

"It is like a torch?" Nia asked, squatting down to look at it. She moved her hand above it and beneath it, as if testing for strings.

He smiled at the catgirl's amazement and then turned back to the task at hand. Ethan peered into the hole, trying to see any wires or mechanisms. The light made it easier to see but he couldn't spot anything.

A thought occurred to him. Would he be able to spot traps? Normally a thief or rogue-type class had that ability, not wizards. Was this like the *Tracking* skill? Would he not be able to see them no matter how hard he tried?

"Nia," he said and motioned her over. "Can you look in the hole and see if you see anything unusual? Any wires or something that doesn't look like part of the chest or dirt?"

The foxgirl glanced away from the floating ball of fire and down into the hole. "You want me to look for the traps?"

"Yes." He nodded. "I'm wondering if this is like the *Tracking* skill you acquired earlier. You might be able to see something I can't."

Nia shrugged and bent over, peering into the hole. She tilted her head several times before sitting up. "I don't see any traps and I have not received a new skill."

"Thor's Hammer!" Ainslee huffed and pushed her way through. With no caution or warning, the dwarf bent down, grabbed the small chest and pulled it out. "There. See. No traps. Can we get on with this so we can get back to the inn and get some mead!"

Ethan looked from the chest in the dwarf's hands to the hole and back. He wanted to say something. He wanted to yell and explain how they all could have died if there had been a trap. Instead, he just sighed. It wouldn't do any good if he did.

"Fine," he said. "Put it down and we can open it up."

The dwarf practically dropped the chest in front of him. She moved behind him and crossed her arms over her chest. Her booted foot started tapping impatiently.

Unwilling to argue, he took the key from around his neck and put it into the lock on the chest. It fit. He turned it clockwise and heard a click. He smiled up at the women peering down at the chest. "It worked."

He let go of the key and reached out to the lid, pulling it open. The moment he did, he heard three fast clicks. Ethan swore. Out of reflex, he erected an air shield in front of them, feeling the energy drain out of him. Even as it did, the ball of light winked out of existence.

Skill increase: Air Magic +1%.

Three small darts shot from the back of the chest. They hit his air shield and dropped to the ground, their momentum spent.

"Thor's Hammer! What were those?" the dwarf exclaimed.

"Was that the trap?" Nia asked from across the room. Ethan hadn't even seen the foxgirl move but she must have leaped away.

Instead of answering, Ethan checked his stats.

Stamina: 9
Mana: 38

The air shield had cost him almost half his *Stamina*. Frustrated, he dismissed his HUD and looked around at the women, leveling a pointed look on the dwarf. "That was a trap.

A dart trap. And they might even be poisoned. That's why we search for traps first!"

Ainslee rolled her eyes and slapped him hard on the back. "Bah! You took care of it! Just do your magic stuff when you open chests."

Ethan took a deep breath, trying to maintain his cool. "That was the simplest trap. It could have sprayed acid, triggered something in the room, sprayed poison gas or any number of things my air shield couldn't have blocked!"

"Fine, fine," the dwarf said, making a dismissive gesture. "Just look in the chest already."

He let out an exasperated breath and summoned back the ball of light.

Skill increase: Fire Magic +1%.

Ethan peered into the chest. The first thing he saw was a small leather pouch. Cautiously he pulled it out, hearing it jingle. More coins. Setting it aside, he looked in and found several pieces of folded parchment, a few pieces of crumpled parchment and an inkwell and quill.

Pulling out the parchment, he opened up the first. It was a letter written in careful, measured handwriting. He read the letter aloud.

Gamel,

I received your note. Are you sure
 you've found it? Do not enter the
 tomb without me! I will meet you at
 the mine entrance at noon on Starday.
 Remember, we can't be seen together!
C.

"A tomb?" Yuliana asked.

"What tomb?" Nia echoed.

"Who is C?" Ainslee breathed at his shoulder, her warm breath tickling his ear.

"No idea. But there's more," he replied and opened up the next letter.

> *Gamel,*
>
> *Tell your men that I don't pay them to come into town every day. The villagers are cowed. I want them searching for the tomb. We're on a time schedule here. I'm not sure that I trust the kobolds to keep strangers out of the village for much longer and any more attacks could compromise the caravans permanently.*
>
> *C.*

"What is Starday?" Yuliana asked.

"A day of the week maybe? Or a holiday?" Ethan ventured.

"This letter must be from before the first," Nia said. "In the first they had found the tomb. This one says he wants them searching for it."

"So this guy C hired the kobolds too?" Ainslee asked.

Nodding, he opened the last note. "It looks that way."

> *Gamel,*
>
> *Yesterday was good but next time you should pull your punches a little more. I can barely see out of my right eye. But the others are no longer suspicious. Good work.*
>
> *C.*

"I don't understand," Yuliana said.

"This C person hired the brigands but it looks like they didn't hit up his shop and people were probably talking," Ethan replied, folding the papers back up and putting them on the floor. He looked at the crumbled parchment. Had those been other letters? Or replies?

Pulling one of the crumbled notes, and smoothed it out. The writing was obviously a different person, crude and shaky but readable.

> **Cuthbert,**
> **We broke through the wall you told us**
> **about. It looks like you were right.**
> **We found a...**

There was a large blotch of ink after the last word and he guessed the quill must have dripped ink onto the paper and he crumpled up the draft and threw it into the box.

> *Quest updated.*
> *Stop the Graycloak Brigands II*
> *Evidence: (1/1)*
> *Quest updated.*
> *Stop the Graycloak Brigands I*
> *You have found evidence that Cuthbert,*
> *the village general store owner, has*
> *hired the brigands and the kobolds.*
> *Return to Fearghas in Hawkshead for*
> *your reward.*
> *New Quest: Stop the Graycloak Brigands*
> *III*
> *You have learned that Cuthbert, the*
> *village general store owner, has*
> *found a tomb inside the abandoned*

> *silver mine. Confront him and bring*
> *him to justice.*
> *Confront Cuthbert: (0/1)*
> *Reward: 200 experience, +500 reputation*
> *with Residents of Hawkshead*
> *Accept quest (yes or no)?*

Ethan accepted the quest and looked around at the others. Their eyes were glassy, which meant they had gotten it too.

"Can we at least go back and get a pint of mead before we confront this Cuthbert?" Ainslee begged.

23

The group walked quickly back to Hawkshead. Without directions to the silver mine or even knowing if it were Starday, they had no way of confronting or intercepting Cuthbert at the mine. Their only other clue was the letter that mentioned his shop in the village. Ethan guessed Fearghas would know the man, and where to find him.

Before they left the brigands' headquarters, Ethan had gone over to the river and washed off as much of the blood off his head as he could. It was sticky and starting to smell, and he looked like someone who should be dead.

This close to the mountains, the river water was freezing and his face had nearly gone numb before he'd been able to wash all the rabbit's blood off. When he was done, he no longer looked half dead. Now he looked like a hobo. Yup, that was Ethan, the murdering hobo.

Once he was cleaned up, they walked down the mountain into Hawkshead. Approaching the village in daylight, they could see how small the village actually was. It was barely a dozen buildings and given its isolated nature, he wondered why anyone would still live out here with brigands and kobolds.

From the high elevation, he could also see the forest and occasional farm that stretched out to the south of the village. Ethan couldn't imagine those few farms provided all the food for the village, but then again, he knew next to nothing about farming.

On Earth, he'd lived in an old farmhouse in the middle of nowhere, surrounded by corn fields that his neighbors tended. Despite this, he still knew nothing about farming, other than once or twice a year, big machines ran through the fields and did something. Then corn grew. Then in the fall, other big machines came and harvested the corn. He was guessing that wasn't how things worked in this world.

Entering the village, they went straight to the inn. In the daylight, he could see a sign on the outside of the front of the two-story building. It was a picture of a crow perched on a pick. Faded words named it as "The Crow and Pick".

"I can't wait to get some mead or ale!" Ainslee said excitedly as they walked through the doorway of the inn.

They stopped just inside the entrance. Ethan wasn't sure what he had been expecting, but this wasn't it. The main room of the inn looked like it was a tavern, but one which hadn't seen use in some time. There were a half dozen wood tables littering the main area to the left, but they were dusty and chairs and stools had been stacked on top of them. To the right was a wooden bar, but it too was dusty and had bar stools stacked on top of it.

He saw Ainslee's face visibly fall as she took in the dusty bar. "I'm thinkin' there's no mead in this town."

"Mead?" Fearghas said, walking into the main room. "Other than what I make for the brigands, this town's as dry as a bone."

The dwarf looked them up and down, obviously noticing

that they all wore brigand gear. A hopeful expression crept onto his face. "Were you... were you able to stop them?"

"Yes," Ethan said. "We killed them all. They won't be bothering you again."

```
Quest Complete.
Stop the Graycloak Brigands I
A group of bandits known as the
    Graycloak Brigands have been
    terrorizing the village of Hawkshead.
You put an end to their reign of terror
    by slaying all of the brigands.
You gain 100 experience.
You gain +250 reputation with Residents
    of Hawkshead.
You gain +250 reputation with Fearghas
    Stormaxe.
Congratulations!
You have reached level 2. Experience to
    next level: 155.
+1 Attribute Point.
+1 Mana.
New ability: Summon Minor Elemental.
```

Several emotions played over Fearghas' face but finally a large grin split the dwarf's face. "I cannot even begin to tell you what this means for us! Between those kobolds to the south and the brigands, we've been bled dry."

"No mead?" Ainslee muttered pitifully.

"Well now." The dwarf grinned. "Since you put an end to those scoundrels, they won't be taking the mead I have brewing down in the cellar."

"Mead?!" Ainslee's face brightened.

Fearghas gave her an apologetic shrug. "Sorry, lass, I just

gave a batch to those miserable graycloaks. The next batch won't be done until next Starday."

Ethan's ears perked up at the mention of Starday. "Fearghas, what day of the week is it today. We've been on the road so long, we've lost track."

The dwarf snorted. "It's Starday, of course. And tomorrow's Sunsday."

The women looked to Ethan. They understood the significance too. He nodded to them and turned back to Fearghas. "What time is it now?"

The dwarf looked out the window and then shrugged. "About an hour after midday."

Ethan cursed under his breath. They probably missed Cuthbert. He pulled out the letters and held them out to the innkeeper. "You should look at these."

"Eh?" The dwarf arched an eyebrow. "What's this?"

"Someone named Cuthbert hired the brigands and the kobolds," Ethan told him. "Those are letters."

"Wha?!" The dwarf's eyes went wide, his face a mask of disbelief. "The mayor? It can't be!"

"The mayor?!" Ainslee snorted. "Ha! He's been bleeding you all dry! Worst mayor ever!"

His face flushing with anger, Fearghas snatched the papers and began to read them. As his eyes darted across the words, his face grew more and more red. Finally he threw them to the ground. "That slimy piece of worm-ridden...."

Quest Complete.
Stop the Graycloak Brigands II
One of the brigands mentioned a boss.
　　Someone may have hired or organized
　　the brigands. Investigate the
　　brigands' headquarters for signs they
　　were working with anyone. Find

*evidence of any affiliations and
bring to the villagers.*
*You have given the evidence to the
villagers of Hawkshead.*
You gain 100 experience.
*You gain +250 reputation with Residents
of Hawkshead.*

"Where is his shop?" Ethan cut in after reading the new messages on his HUD. "He might still be there."

"Oh, I'll show you where his shop is," the innkeeper growled. The stocky dwarf stalked behind the bar and emerged with a cudgel that looked suspiciously like the leg of a table. "Follow me!"

They left the inn, following the angry dwarf as he walked west. Ethan took the opportunity to really look at the buildings this time. Next to the Crow and Pick was a large, two-story building. A weathered sign identified it as the Riverside Inn but it looked to have been abandoned for years.

To his left there were several smaller buildings. They also appeared to be abandoned. The larger of the two was made of stone and appeared to be some sort of small temple or church. The second had a faded sign with a picture of a loaf of bread. A baker, perhaps?

They came to the intersection where the road split north and south. North was the bridge over the river and the road that led back to the brigand's headquarters. To the south were the farms. It was the way they'd come in yesterday during the rain storm.

From the south, another dwarf came bolting out of his house. He had a leather apron on that held several tools in various loops and the dwarf had a layer of sawdust that created a cloud behind him as he ran.

His hair was long and dark red, streaked with gray and

matched his beard. Both were loose and unkempt, a contrast to Fearghas' braided beard. At the moment, the dwarf's face was as red as his beard as he ran towards them with a hammer in hand.

Ethan quickly scanned the newcomer in his HUD.

Hamish
Dwarf
Cooper
Level 4

"Is this them, Fearghas?!" the dwarf yelled. "The ones that'll get us all killed!"

"It's okay, Hamish." The innkeeper stopped and stepped protectively in front of them.

"Thor's hammer, Fearghas! How is it okay?" the red-headed dwarf demanded. "Those scoundrels aren't going to let pass someone killing three of their members!"

"They took care of the others," Fearghas said calmly, reaching out and putting a hand on the man's shoulder. "It's over. They're all dead!"

"What? They killed them?" Hamish rocked back on his heels. He looked between Ethan and the women and Fearghas. "You lot? Killed all of them?"

"They did," Fearghas said, anger coming back in his voice now. "And that treacherous little coward Cuthbert hired them."

Hamish backed up a step as if shoved. "The mayor?! Hired them?! No!"

"I saw it in his own handwriting!" Fearghas countered angrily. "The wretch has been playing all of us, looking for that tomb!"

"The tomb?!" Hamish scoffed. "That was just a rumor those miners told."

"Apparently not," the innkeeper snorted. "Cuthbert had the

graycloaks searching for it in the mines when they weren't too busy roughing us up and taking our mead!"

"I still find it hard to believe that the mayor would do that," the dwarf said. "I mean, who cares if he finds a tomb."

"Did you forget? We all still have a stake in the mine," Fearghas said. "And anything that comes out of there."

"Oh." The red-headed dwarf scratched his head. "I guess that's right. But why the brigands?!"

"I'm not sure." Fearghas frowned. "Maybe to prevent us from knowing what he was doing. Maybe after he got whatever treasure is in the tomb, he was going to have them kill us all."

"That rotten son of a troll," Hamish swore and brandished his hammer menacingly. "Where is he now?! I'm going to give him a piece of my mind and quite possibly a piece of my hammer!"

"We're checking his store now," the innkeeper replied. "Come with us."

The six of them walked to the far side of the road to a medium-sized, one-story building. The building's sign just said Cuthbert with a faded crest. Fearghas stomped up to the door and slammed his meaty fist against it. "CUTHBERT! We want a word with you!"

They waited for what seemed like only a few seconds before Hamish did the same, pounding several times and yelling Cuthbert's name.

They two dwarves alternated pounding on the door and yelling his name for several minutes.

"I do not think he is home," Yuliana said quietly.

"We'll see about that," said Hamish and he leaned back and kicked the door. The red-headed dwarf shoved himself against the door and the door swung open with a spray of splinters near where the latch had been.

Hamish looked at the broken lock and snorted. "He can bill me for it! If I don't pound him into mutton first! CUTHBERT!"

The group moved into the front room which Ethan immediately recognized as some sort of general store or supply store. At least, it had been once. Like the inn and the abandoned buildings he'd passed, it didn't appear that he'd done much business in the recent past.

One noticeable exception was a shelf that was covered with dust except for the outlines of picks. Ethan smirked. He knew where the missing picks were. Cuthbert had given them to the graycloaks to find the tomb.

Hamish and Fearghas moved through the store area and into the back. He stayed in the store with the women, but he could hear them clattering into the things.

"He's not here," Nia said. "His scent is old."

Ethan nodded. "It's after noon, he's probably still waiting for the brigands at the mine entrance."

"Do we have to go after him," Ainslee groaned. The dwarf was still in a foul mood after learning there was no mead.

"I think Fearghas would be mighty grateful," Ethan told her. Remembering her near obsession with mead, he added. "And he'd probably give you all of the mead he has brewing."

Skill increase: Diplomacy +1%.

The dwarf brightened and she licked her lips. "You think so?"

"I think these people will be grateful to see justice done." He nodded.

The two dwarves returned, their expressions sour. Fearghas leveled his gaze on them. "That slimy piece of sheep dung isn't here! According to that note, it stands to reason he's at the mine already. We'd be much obliged if you bring that dirty rotten scoundrel back here to face justice."

Fearghas Stormaxe has offered you the
quest "Bring Cuthbert to Justice"
Mayor Cuthbert has been paying brigands
and kobolds to terrorize the village.
Fearghas wants you to bring the mayor
back to Hawkshead to face justice.
Retrieve mayor (0 / 1)
Reward: 100 experience, +250 reputation
with Residents of Hawkshead, +250
reputation with Fearghas Stormaxe
Accept quest (yes or no)?

Ethan looked to the women who either nodded or shrugged. He accepted the quest and turned back towards the dwarves. "We'd be happy to!"

24

After getting directions to the mine from Fearghas, Ethan and the women headed north, back over the river for the second time that day. This time, as they walked, the women began quizzing him about the messages they had received.

"I'm a level 2 knight now," Ainslee said as they walked. "What does that even mean?"

"I'm not 100% sure in this world," Ethan replied. "But generally, it means you are more powerful."

Ainslee frowned at him. "More powerful? How?"

"Did you receive some additional health and maybe a new ability?" he asked.

The dwarf's eyes went unfocused for a moment. When they came back into focus she was frowning. "Something called minor war cry. What's that supposed to do?"

"Can you examine the skill itself?" Ethan asked.

Ainslee huffed but her eyes went glassy. She read the description to him.

Minor War Cry

```
Type: Knight
Cost: 5 Karma / 5 Stamina
Range: 20 ft.
Duration: 1 minutes
Description: Caster and all allies
    within 20 feet gain +2 to Attack, +2
    Defense
```

She stared at Ethan. "What does that even mean?"

"I think it means that when you use that ability we all do more damage to enemies and take less damage from enemies for one minute," he replied. "A good ability."

The dwarf made a face. "Doesn't seem that good. I'd prefer a fireball or an ability that summons a keg of mead!"

Rolling his eyes at Ainslee, Ethan turned to Nia and Yuliana. He asked the other two women about their new abilities and they relayed the description to him.

```
Grasping Plants
Type: Druid
Cost: 5 Karma / 5 Stamina
Range: 30 ft.
Duration: 2 minutes
Description: Caster can summon nearby
    roots or plants to hold a creature in
    place. Creature may escape by making
    a successful Strength check.
Minor Leap
Type: Acrobat
Cost: 5 Stamina per 10 ft. / maximum 10
    ft. per level
Range: Special
Duration: Instant
Description: Using this ability, the
```

*acrobat is able to perform great
leaps horizontally or vertically. The
cost of the ability scales with the
distance leaped.*

Almost immediately Nia leaped straight up 20 feet and then came falling back down, only to land deftly in what Ethan could only describe as a superhero pose: One knee under her, the other one bent and her fist on the ground. She looked up at the group and grinned. "This is good!"

Ainslee huffed. "I don't even get to jump."

"Just watch your stamina," he told them. "Like my magic, all of those abilities use stamina. You don't want to run out, especially during a fight."

Nia then asked about his own ability and he read the description to them.

Summon Minor Elemental.
Type: Wizard
Cost: 5 Mana / 5 Stamina
Range: Special
Duration: 60 minutes
*Description: Caster can summon a
    creature of pure elemental energy. At
    the time of the summoning, the caster
    must choose the element that will
    shape the creature. The elemental
    will follow the caster's mental
    directions for the duration of the
    summoning.*

Ethan wanted to try out the ability, but wanted to wait until he had more time, and more *Stamina.* He doubted Cuthbert would give them any problems, but he preferred to be ready if the man did. After all, for all he knew, Cuthbert could be some sort of boss fight.

The group continued on but after only a few steps, Ainslee let out a loud breath. "Why is it Yuliana can make plants do things, you get to summon element things and Nia can jump really far but all I can do is yell and make us a little better in combat?"

Ethan shrugged and tried to think of the best way to phrase his answer. "You're a knight. Knights are more selfless than regular warriors. If you were a warrior, you'd have a more self or combat-centered ability, as it is, your ability reflects a knight's desire to help others."

"Selfless, huh?" the dwarf muttered. She cocked her head and then nodded. "Yeah, that's me."

Suppressing a grin, Ethan continued trekking up the increasingly steep path. Soon after they had passed the brigand's headquarters, the path had become steeper and he was already getting winded just keeping pace with the rest of the group. He glanced at the women. Yuliana was also breathing hard, so he didn't feel quite as bad.

After all, until a couple of days ago, he'd been a computer tech. The most strenuous thing he'd done is carry a computer and a printer at the same time. Now, he was hiking up mountains and fighting bad guys.

After two stops to rest and another hour, they reached about midway up the mountain. The road ended at the entrance to the mine. He was surprised how much it looked like the mine entrances he'd seen in old westerns. A square entrance braced by large timbers.

"Here's the mine," Ainslee said, looking around. "Where's this human we're supposed to get?"

"Cuthbert," Yuliana supplied.

The dwarf rolled her eyes. "Whatever."

They all glanced around the area, looking for any place

Cuthbert could be hiding but the road simply dead-ended at the mine shaft.

"He went inside," Nia said, sniffing the air.

"You're sure?" he asked. He didn't see any reason to doubt her scent ability but it seemed like an appropriate thing to ask before they delved into an abandoned mine.

"Of course," she said, folding her arms over her chest. "I caught his scent back in his shop. It was weak on the way up here but it is strong here at the entrance. He waited for some time and then went inside."

Ethan peered into the dark mineshaft and looked at the others. "I don't suppose any of you have torches?"

"Can you not summon the ball of flame like before?" Yuliana asked.

Ethan suddenly felt stupid. He was so tired from walking that he had forgotten that he'd summoned a ball of light before. Smiling, he brought up his HUD and checked his *Stamina* level.

Stamina: 10

It had been up to 20 when he was back in the village but now it was down to 10, probably from all the walking. Ethan sighed. He really just wanted to eat a good meal and then sleep in a nice soft bed. Or better yet, fall asleep and wake up back in his own bed and find this whole thing had only been a dream.

Dismissing his HUD, he focused on the ball of light like he had before and in a moment, it appeared hovering a foot away from him.

"Good, wizard-boy," Ainslee said. "Now go on and lead the way."

He frowned at the dwarf. The wizard never went first. The thief or the tank went first - everyone knew that. He smirked to himself. Everyone who had ever played any RPGs knew it. The thief would go first to look for traps or the tank would go first to soak up any damage from a surprise attack. Never the wizard.

He looked from woman to woman. Realizing it would take too long to explain the finer points of MMORPG and tabletop strategy and party order, Ethan cautiously started into the mine.

As stepped into the mine entrance, Nia moved up to walk next to him. She sniffed. "He definitely went inside. Stay right behind me so I can see."

"I thought you could see in the dark?" he asked.

"Outside, when there is moonlight or starlight, yes... in here, once we get away from the entrance, my vision will be limited," she replied, not bothering to look at him. "Now, come."

Ethan felt relieved that the foxgirl had taken the lead but at the same time felt a bit unmanly, like he should be leading the way as the man. Then he remembered that, despite her reluctance to kill enemies, Nia was probably the most highly trained warrior among them. Certainly far better than he was. Yeah. She could go first.

The shaft was wide enough that two of them could walk side by side, but the tunnel had a track laid in the middle of it. Ethan guessed it made it easier to get the ore to the surface. Unfortunately, it also forced them to walk single file inside the track or awkwardly hobble along with one foot on the track and one foot on the outside of the track.

"This track looks like dwarven construction," she said. "We have something similar in our world. If I had to guess, I'd say this rail system was made by dwarves."

"Shh," Nia hissed. "The prey may be near."

Ainslee seemed like she was about to retort but then nodded. When she spoke, her voice was a whisper. "Aye, sound carries in tunnels like this."

Following the track for several hundred yards, they came to a "Y" in the tunnel. Sniffing the air, Nia nodded to the left fork.

They walked down it only another fifty feet before they came to a four-way intersection. Sniffing, she started down the tunnel straight ahead but Ethan put a hand on her arm.

"Can you find your way back?" he whispered.

She chuckled quietly and then whispered back. "Yes, I will just follow your stink back to the surface."

The foxgirl moved forward and he followed her, unsure how to take her comment. As he walked, he bent his head down towards his armpit and sniffed. He frowned. She hadn't been kidding. He stank. Then again, he hadn't showered or taken a bath in days and the hike up here hadn't exactly been easy. He made a mental note to see if the inn offered a bath and a way to wash his clothes.

Then he stopped and felt Ainslee bump into him from behind. The dwarf cursed quietly. "What?!"

Ethan wasn't listening. He bent down and sniffed at his armpit again. He stank alright. But that wasn't the strange thing. The strange thing was, he smelled just like he did in real life. There were some other odors in there too - leather, blood and a few other things. But he smelled himself. Just like he had smelled on Earth.

Had the aliens really incorporated his own body smell into the game? He glanced back to Ainslee. "One second."

"Nia," he whispered. "Do you ... smell the same as you did on your planet?"

The foxgirl looked at him like he was a moron. "Of course. Why would I not?"

"You're sure?" he asked. "Exactly like you did on your world?"

"Yes," she growled. "I know my own scent!"

Ethan wasn't sure what to make of this. His simulation body felt just like his regular body. And it smelled like it too. He wasn't quite sure of the science of that, but there had to be thousands, perhaps even millions of factors that went into creating a person's unique smell. After all, that's why it was unique. Could alien technology really emulate all of that?

The alternative was that this was real. He was real. This was actually his body, on another world, with other aliens. And yet, magic worked here. And that was impossible. Wasn't it? And what about the HUD? That certainly wasn't possible. Unless. What if they implanted something in him. Some sort of tech that made the HUD appear to him. Maybe a bionic eye or a chip in his brain.

"What are you talking about, Ethan? Are you okay?" Nia asked, her face becoming concerned. "You are pale."

He didn't know how to answer that question. Was he okay? His mind was reeling from the sudden possibility. But that would explain why no one respawned. And why the other players, no not players, PEOPLE, had stayed dead. And why he was so sore all the time.

But the magic didn't make any sense. It defied the laws of physics. Then again, he remembered reading somewhere that technology was magic to those who didn't understand it. Was that what this was? Some sort of technology beyond his understanding? Or was this really just a super advanced simulation?

He looked around at the women. Now they were all looking at him with concern. Ethan wanted to explain to them his revelation but realized they had believed all of this was real from the start. He was the only one who had thought it was a game.

Flashing the women his best fake smile, he pushed the thoughts to the back of his mind. Ethan needed to think about this more. But now was not the time. There were better places to consider the possibilities than a mine shaft.

"Sorry," he lied. "I just need to check on my stamina and mana levels."

You have gained: Bluff.
Skill increase: Bluff +1%.

"Odin's Beard!" Ainslee swore quietly. "I thought something was wrong. Come on then! Let's move it!"

The group continued down the center tunnel but Ethan's mind was only partially paying attention. The other part was trying to come to grips with the fact that all of this might be real. And whatever happened to him in this world would have lasting consequences.

25

They followed the center tunnel through two more intersections before it came to another "Y" intersection. This time, Nia led them down the right passage. Ethan noticed that the tunnels had been getting narrower and now there was only enough room to comfortably walk in single file. If they had to fight, the passage size would severely limit them.

A hundred feet down the new tunnel, they came to a passage that looked recently excavated. Nia stopped. Sniffing, she turned to the group. "The brigands were here at this passage for some time."

"Wizard-boy," Ainslee called to him. She had moved a few steps into the new tunnel. "Bring your light here."

Rolling his eyes, Ethan did as asked. The dwarf was looking down at the scattered rocks the brigands had left to either side of the trail. As his light illuminated the area, she bent down and moved some rocks then stood back up shaking her head. "This isn't new construction. This is an old shaft that was sealed up."

"Sealed up?" Ethan asked, looking at the rocks. They looked just like rocks to him.

"Aye," she said. "Sometimes they seal up tunnels if there's something dangerous down them. Usually gas of some sort. You walk into a pocket of gas and you're out before you even know what hit you. Then you suffocate. Or if it's flammable and you bring a torch... boom!"

Involuntarily, Ethan took a step back from the tunnel entrance. Given his new revelation that the "game" might actually be real, he wasn't about to risk igniting gas with his little ball of light.

"We've passed quite a few sealed-up tunnels already," she said nonchalantly. "But I didn't think anything of it until I saw this one."

"We passed others?" Yuliana asked, glancing back into the darkness behind them.

"Oh, aye," the dwarf replied. "Maybe a dozen or so. You can tell by the extra boarding around them and the loose rock."

"Good to know," Ethan said.

"Our prey did not go down that tunnel," Nia hissed. "Come, this way."

Following Nia, they passed several more sealed passages, most of which had been reopened. Ethan guessed that the mining company had found the tomb and then sealed it up at some point. Cuthbert must have known about the existence of the tomb but not known which sealed-up passage it had been behind.

They followed the current tunnel another few hundred feet before they came to another four-way intersection. This time, it appeared that all of the intersecting tunnels had been sealed off at some point. The floor of the intersection was littered with the tell-tale signs of loose rock and broken boards.

The tunnel to the left looked as if it had been resealed by stacking rocks over the entrance. It was crude and amateurish work compared to what they'd seen elsewhere in the mine. Had the brigands opened it, only to seal it up again? Why would they do that?

"That's odd," Ainslee said, tilting her head.

"What's odd?" Ethan asked, stopping. Ahead of him, he heard Nia let out a frustrated breath before stopping and turning.

"It doesn't make sense that they would have something dangerous in three different directions. I've never seen a pocket of gas that would cover that large of an area."

"Please be quiet," Yuliana whispered, holding her hand up for silence. The elf had been quiet nearly the entire trip and it was uncharacteristic for her to speak up like that.

Ainslee turned towards the elf and seemed about to say something but Ethan held up a finger, signalling her to give Yuliana a moment.

Brushing the hair away from her ears, the elf tilted her head first one way, then another. Ethan remembered that she had excellent hearing and wondered what she might be hearing. Could she actually hear Cuthbert up ahead?

"There is movement," Yuliana said, her voice a low whisper. She looked at the re-sealed passage. "Behind those rocks."

"Movement?" Ainslee's eyes narrowed. "What kind of movement?"

"It is an odd sound," the elf said, her face screwing up in concentration. "If I was in my grove, I would say it was a large insect hive or a colony of spiders but this sounds too big to be either."

"Spiders?!" Ainslee's face went white. The dwarf turned and looked around the sealed passage. "Are they coming?"

"I do not think so," the elf said, tilting her ear towards the sealed passage. "It still sounds far away."

"I hate spiders," the dwarf muttered, eyes darting around the intersection.

"If there are spiders," Ethan said, "they're trapped on the other side of the passage. Let's just find Cuthbert and get out of here."

"Right," the dwarf nodded. Ethan saw her face was sweaty and wondered if it was more than just a dislike of spiders. Did she have a full-blown phobia of spiders? "Let's find Cuthbert."

Nia led them down the right passage for at least two hundred feet before it opened into a huge natural cavern. The space was at least fifty feet wide to his left and right. He could barely make out the edges of the cavern in the light. It stretched out in front of him only twenty feet, ending in a smooth, worked stone wall.

The wall of stone was smooth except for an archway that was carved out of the same stone. Thick and covered in some sort of writing or symbols, the archway framed two stone doors that were seven feet tall and four feet wide each. The right door had been pried open just barely enough to allow a human to squeeze through.

Nia pointed at the door. "Cuthbert went inside."

"That does not seem wise," Yuliana said softly. "The sounds come from inside."

Ethan barely heard them as he studied the writing. It was an odd style of writing that reminded him of a crude form of Arabic or maybe Sanskrit. "Do any of you understand this language?"

"I do not understand it," Nia replied.

"No idea." Ainslee shrugged.

Yuliana shook her head. "I have not seen writing like that before."

Ethan sighed. It was probably some dire warning to stay away, like the old inscriptions on the pyramids. Something along the lines of "Enter and die horribly."

"Come," Nia said, moving towards the open door. "Let us find this scoundrel."

Scenes from various movies started flashing through his mind. This would be the part where some mummy appeared or a giant swarm of flesh-eating beetles. Ethan pushed the scenes out of his mind and followed Nia.

His hands tightened on his staff. He had the brigand's crossbow slung over his back and briefly considered taking it down and readying it. But in this case, he could probably do more with his magic than with the crossbow. He knew the concepts of firing a crossbow. He'd even shot rifles with his dad when he was younger. But using an unfamiliar weapon in an unfamiliar environment seemed like a good way to end up shooting someone in his party.

Nia started to slip into the door but stopped and backed up. She turned to the group and stepped away from the door. "We have found Cuthbert."

Ethan gave her a confused look and she gestured to the door. He moved to the door and peeked in.

His ball of flame illuminated a ten-by-ten chamber. The chamber's walls, ceilings and floors were tiled. The tiles had intricate patterns on them but each of the tiles had a circle in the center. A man's body was on the floor, lying in a pool of drying blood. He appeared to have been punctured multiple times.

"Trap," he whispered. He looked at the holes in the floor and noticed how the blood seemed to drip into them but not fill them up. Holes for spikes. "That's some serious temple of doom stuff."

Ainslee pushed him to the side and stuck her head in. "He's dead. Some sort of traps."

Ethan looked down at the dwarf, who had basically just repeated what he'd said. Then a notification flashed on his HUD.

Quest Complete.

Stop the Graycloak Brigands III
You have learned that Cuthbert, the
    village general store owner, has
    found a tomb inside the abandoned
    silver mine. Confront him and bring
    him to justice.
Confront Cuthbert: (1/1)
You have found Cuthbert's body just
    inside the tomb. It appears justice
    has been served.
You gain 200 experience.
You gain +500 reputation with Residents
    of Hawkshead.
Congratulations!
You have reached level 3. Experience to
    next level: 255.
+1 Attribute Point.
New ability: Elemental Armor.

"Oh," Ainslee muttered. "Looks like I gained another level. Hmm... new ability. Charge. That sounds promising. Better than war cry."

"What about our other quest?" Yuliana asked. "Were we not supposed to bring him back to face justice?"

The dwarf groaned. "Please tell me we don't have to drag his miserable corpse all the way back to town."

"I think we might have to," Ethan said. "Otherwise, both quests would have updated."

"Well," Ainslee grumbled. "I'm not going to carry him the whole way by myself!"

"First," Nia said from behind them, "we should figure out how to get his body out without setting off the traps."

Ethan and Ainslee looked back at the foxgirl and then at the body. The dwarf shrugged. "That's a fair point."

In the end, they had used the two staffs to slowly pull the body back to the door. The weight of the body being dragged towards the door had caused six-foot-tall, sharpened metal rods to shoot from the floor, impaling the body. They quickly retracted but it took several minutes to pull the body back while it continued to be impaled.

Finally, they were able to drag it the rest of the way out of the chamber. By then, the body had been pin-cushioned so many times, it barely looked like Cuthbert.

"That's disgusting," Ainslee stated, looking at the body and making a face.

"I agree." Yuliana nodded. "Must we take this corpse back to the village?"

"We should," Ethan said. "We have a quest. And the villagers might want to actually give him a proper burial."

"Even a moron like this?" Ainslee made a face.

"We'll see," Ethan said. "Now the fun part. How do we carry the body?"

In the end, Ethan had come up with the idea. He had thought to make some sort of stretcher, but that lacked any sort of large cloth to put between the two quarterstaffs. Instead, he'd laid his and Nia's staffs down and then tied Cuthbert's arms and legs to the staffs using leather cording from his and Ainslee's bracers.

Ainslee grumbled but between the two of them, they were able to carry his body fairly easily, by resting the staves on their shoulders. They followed Nia and, true to her word, she was able to find her way back up to the mine entrance. Presumably, she did it by following Ethan's stink.

Once outside, they immediately started down the mountain to the village. The group reached Hawkshead just as it got dark. The entire trip, Ethan had been preoccupied with whether or not he was really on a different planet or whether he was in an alien simulation so detailed and so immersive that it rivaled reality itself.

As they stopped in front of the Crow and Pick inn, Ethan still had no clear answer.

26

Fearghas looked down at the body of Cuthbert and nodded. Several other of the residents looked down on the body with mixed emotions.

"I still can't believe he hired the graycloaks," said Froba, the miller. Her place was on the opposite side of the river, just down a trail he had seen before but hadn't had time to investigate. She was a stout, muscular dwarf with braided platinum-blond hair and pale blue eyes. If dwarves could be valkyries, Froba would have fit right in. Other than the ebony skin.

"And the kobolds," added Dudley the thatcher. He was a thin, balding man with gray eyes. The hair he did have was long and pulled back in a ponytail that fell between his shoulder blades. "I can't believe he paid off those dang kobolds!"

There was a murmur of agreement from the other members of the town who had come at Fearghas's insistence. There was Odelina, the butcher and tanner. She was a young woman, a few years younger than Ethan, with a head full of curly strawberry blonde hair and striking blue eyes.

Next to Odelina was her father, Ark, who might have once

been a strong, muscular man but whose muscle had gone to fat. Worse, his face was slack and he had a tendency to mutter to himself. Fearghas had said the man slipped on some blood in his shop, hit his head and had never been right since.

Hamish was there, next to Fearghas, and was muttering curses at the dead mayor under his breath.

Ethan had learned the only other residents were Fearghas' son Sawney and his wife, Elspeth. While many of the farmers came into town to have their animals butchered or to get their grain milled, the farmers didn't consider themselves residents of the village.

"Well," spat Hamish, "after all the trouble he caused us, I say he got what he deserved."

"And you say a trap did this?" Dudley asked. "So the tomb is inaccessible?"

"I don't know about that," Ethan said. "I never said it was inaccessible. I just said the first room was trapped."

"With six-foot-long steel spikes!" Froba huffed. "That sounds inaccessible to me."

Ethan already had an idea of how to bypass the spikes. He just needed the materials.

"We won't see a dime out of that tomb," Hamish grumbled. "Mark my words."

"You're assuming there was anything of value in there to begin with," Fearghas said. "All we know is that there was a tomb and the mining company walled it up."

There was more muttering from the villagers. After several minutes, Fearghas looked around. "So, I guess that means we need a mayor."

The villagers all looked around, their expressions clearly saying they didn't want the job. Fearghas looked from face to face and then he scratched his beard. He turned toward Ethan and his group.

"What about one of you?" Fearghas asked, his expression hopeful.

Ethan narrowed his eyes. "One of us what?"

"We need a new mayor," the innkeeper said. "How about one of you?"

Taken aback, he looked at the women, who seemed equally surprised.

"I'm not sure what a mayor is," Yuliana said, "but I do not think I want to be one."

"I cannot," was all Nia said and looked away.

Ainslee huffed. "Not my thing, lad. I can swing a hammer, an axe if I need to, but I leave the paperwork to those people who like it."

Ethan sighed. That left him. Was this like some type of town-building game? He hated those. But at the same time, if he were right about this being real, then having a village to use as a base of operations would be extremely helpful.

There were only a handful of people in the village. How much effort could it really take? He looked at the faces of the villagers, who were staring at him. Their expressions were mixed but most were hopeful. If these were real people, maybe he could do some good in this world.

"I will do it," he said and then immediately received a new prompt.

You have been offered the opportunity to take control of the town of Hawkshead.

Hawkshead
Current population: 9
Current buildings: 17
Do you accept? (yes or no)

He read the messages in his HUD and hesitated. Then he shrugged and clicked Yes.

```
You have seized control of Hawkshead.
Town Rank: 1
Town population: 10
Town morale: 18%
Town total buildings: 17
Town active buildings: 5
Town Output:
Food: 10
Metal: 0
Leather: 2
Wood: 0
Income from Taxes: 0
Income from Trade: 0
```

He wanted to read more but people were beginning to slap him on the back and wish him well as the new mayor. This took a few minutes before the residents backed off and all stared at him expectantly.

"So, mayor, when are you going to start clearing out the kobolds?" Hamish asked with a predatory grin. The residents looked at each other and nodded, murmuring in agreement and Ethan received a new quest.

```
The residents of Hawkshead has offered
    you the quest "Clear the Roads I"
The previous mayor paid off kobold
    tribes to prevent travel in or out of
    the village. The residents wish you
    to remove the kobold danger so
    travels and trade caravans can once
    again safely visit Hawkshead.
```

Eliminate Kobold Tribes (0 / 4)
Reward: 300 experience, +250 reputation
 with Residents of Hawkshead
Accept quest (yes or no)?

He nodded and accepted the quest, glancing back to see the women of his group were glassy eyed, reading the quest.

"We'll start looking into the kobolds tomorrow," he said.

The residents thanked him and patted each other on the back for about a minute before they turned and began bombarding him with things.

"Mayor, we need a blacksmith," said someone.

"Mayor, we need tools," cried someone else.

And then they were all talking over each other, each insisting their request was the most important.

Finally, he had to raise his voice to get their attention. "OKAY!"

The group quieted down and turned their attention back to Ethan. He waited for a moment and then spoke quietly and calmly. "Let's deal with the kobolds first..." A few of them started to speak but held up his hand and gave them a sharp look. "Let's deal with the kobolds first, and then we can prioritize the other things. In the meantime, if we are going to deal with the kobolds, we will need a good night's sleep. Is there a place where the ladies and I can get a good night's sleep? Possibly a bath?"

The residents nodded, muttering as they seemed to realize it was dark.

"Well, ah." Fearghas smiled uncomfortably. "Will you all be ... uh... sleeping together, or..."

"We will not be sleeping together," Yuliana said from behind him and he turned to see the women glaring at the dwarf with arms crossed over their chests. Nia was nodding vigorously too but Ainslee just smirked and eyed Ethan like a piece of meat. The dwarf's scrutiny caused him to blush.

"Begging your pardon, ladies," the innkeeper said sheepishly. "I was only inquiring so I knew what to offer for sleeping arrangements. Ahem... I have four rooms upstairs, but only three with beds."

Ethan looked at the women, who still glared at the innkeeper. They saw him looking and turned their glare on him. He raised his hands in a gesture of peace.

"What about Cuthbert's place?" Hamish asked. The dwarf looked down at the body. "It's not like he'll need it anymore. And, he is the new mayor."

There seemed to be a general consensus around the idea that Ethan should have the former mayor's house.

Tired and just wanting to get some sleep, Ethan nodded. "Fine. The ladies will stay at the inn for now and I will stay at Cuthbert's."

"Ethan's," Dudley said.

"What?" Ethan asked, not understanding.

"If it's your place now, we should call it Ethan's," he said.

"Fine," Ethan agreed. "Why don't we all get some sleep."

His stomach growled loudly and he looked between the residents. "Any chance I can buy some dinner first?"

"Oh yah," Fearghas said. "You and the ladies come on in and I'll have me wife warm up some leftover mutton."

The other residents smiled and said their good-nights before disappearing back to their own homes. Ethan and his companions followed the innkeeper inside and sat down at one of the tables while he went into the kitchen.

"So what's this about being the mayor?" Ainslee asked. "And why do we have to go out and risk our necks fighting more kobolds?"

All eyes turned to Ethan and he let out a breath. He was tired. His legs, shoulders and arms ached from carrying the former mayor's body back down the mountain and he was bone weary. He just wanted to eat and then sleep. Maybe sleep for a week.

Still, the women were expecting an answer so he took a deep breath and held up a finger. "First, no one else wanted the job so I took it because I thought we'd have a better chance of getting a decent meal and a good night's rest on a real bed.

"Second." He held up another finger. "We don't really have a plan and until we do, I figured this is as good a place as any."

He held up a third finger. "And third, even if we need to go elsewhere, it will be nice to have a base of operations we can return to."

The girls nodded, seeming to understand, or at least accept, his reasons. He continued. "As far as the kobolds. Assuming we want to stay here for a bit, we have no idea what Cuthbert's agreement with them was. The last thing we want is for a tribe of kobolds to come strolling into town and slit all of our throats while we sleep. Best to take the fight to them."

"We could just leave," Yuliana offered shyly, "without killing anything else."

Ethan nodded. "We could. But we have no idea how far we would need to go and whether or not the kobolds would try to stop us. Didn't they say there were kobolds to the south?"

The women looked at each other with blank expressions and shrugged.

"For now," Ethan continued, "let's get a hot meal and then get some sleep."

The foxgirl nodded. "That is acceptable."

Yuliana just bit her lip.

Ainslee let out a heavy sigh. "If only there was mead with the meal."

When it didn't appear that anyone else was going to ask him any questions, Ethan sat back in his chair and waited for the food to arrive. And after that, a real bed.

27

Ethan woke up the next morning to a pounding at the door. He blinked his eyes open and groaned. The light that came in through the windows told him it was daylight but he had no idea what time it was. He rolled over, wondering if he could ignore the knocking but it persisted.

Letting out an exasperated breath, he slowly sat up in bed. He paused. Ethan twisted left and then right. Then he moved his arms. When he had gone to bed, he'd felt sore all over. He had expected to feel sore today too but he felt only a mild aching in his muscles.

The pounding on the door continued and he threw his legs over the side of the bed. And it was a bed. A real bed. It wasn't nearly as comfortable as his own bed, but after sleeping on the ground and in a stall, it was like lying on a cloud.

He still wore the breeches and shirt he'd taken from the brigands. He'd simply been too exhausted last night to undress fully. He slowly walked out of the backroom and into the shop area, towards the door. He rubbed his eyes, trying to clear them before removing the chair he'd put in front of the front door to keep it closed.

A stocky shape burst in, followed by two more familiar figures. They were his companions, and they were dressed and ready to go.

Ainslee turned and faced him, her eyes evaluating him. She snorted and turned to the other women. "I told you he was still sleeping." She turned towards him. "You missed breakfast and Fearghas's wife just fed us an early lunch!"

"Are you well?" Yuliana asked. She was looking at him too, a bit less critically than the dwarf. She handed him a cloth-wrapped bundle.

"I'm fine," he said, covering a yawn. He unwrapped the bundle to reveal a large piece of cheese and some slice of hard bread. Was it breakfast or lunch? Or both? "Apparently, my body just needed a lot of sleep."

His stomach rumbled and he took a bite of the cheese. It was sharp but creamy and reminded him of cheddar. As soon as he had chewed enough to speak, he thanked them for bringing it.

"You have slept the entire morning away," Nia chided. "Did you not say we needed to hunt kobolds?"

Ethan let out a heavy breath. They were right, of course. He had slept way too late. The strange thing was, he never really slept late. Mostly because his cat got him up at 5am in the morning to get fed. But even when he was on vacation and sleeping in a hotel, he naturally seemed to get up before 8am.

Now they were saying it was almost lunch time. He started to wonder why he'd slept so long when he realized two things. First, he had done more physical activity in the last two days than he had in the last year. Second, he actually had no idea how many hours were in a day on this planet. For all he knew, their days were shorter.

"Give me a few minutes," he told them and lumbered back to the backroom. He ate as he got dressed, slipping on his boots and armor, before grabbing his staff and two of the daggers.

Returning to the main room, he found the women looking it over.

"Are you planning to re-open the shop?" Ainslee asked.

"What?" Ethan blinked, his head still fuzzy from sleep. Not for the first time, he wondered if they had coffee in this world.

"The shop, wizard-boy," the dwarf repeated. "Do ya plan to open it back up?"

Ethan looked around. "I hadn't really thought about it. I'm not sure how many supplies these people actually need."

"You might be surprised," Yuliana said. "There are many things these people lack that they might be willing to trade for."

"I'll think about it," he promised them and gestured to the door. "Shall we."

"About time," the dwarf huffed and stomped out.

"Are you okay with it?" he asked Yuliana.

The elf turned and shrugged. "For now. The dwarf and his wife told us stories of the hardships the kobolds had caused. They have caused many deaths. Perhaps they are like weeds, choking a plant. They need to be... pulled."

"Perhaps," he said. "As long as you are okay with it."

"For now," she said noncommittally. "For now."

The two of them followed Nia and Ainslee out into the street and Ethan closed the door behind him, only to see it swing open. He frowned. He'd need to get that fixed. Maybe Hamish would have some ideas. He was a cooper after all. Coopers made barrels and wooden things, right?

"Let's get going and find these kobolds," Ainslee said. "I want to get back here so I can take a look at the forge over there and see if it's worth salvaging."

"You're going to do some blacksmithing?" Ethan asked. He glanced over to the abandoned blacksmith's forge near the river.

"Wizard-boy," she huffed and turned to face him. She planted both feet on the ground and put her hands on her hips.

"I AM a blacksmith. Sure, this HUD thing may say I'm a knight. But I'm a blacksmith. Have been for fifty years." Her face softened and she looked wistfully at the blacksmith's forge. "Truth be told. I miss it."

"I suspect you'd have a lot of business if you did," he said, then he remembered how many people were actually in the village. "Well, comparatively speaking."

"Aye." The dwarf nodded. "I was talking to Fearghas this morning - while you were sleeping your pretty head off. The surrounding farms have been without any way to repair their tools or get new ones made, so there's a decent amount of work."

"We are letting the light go to waste," Nia said impatiently. "We should get moving."

"Do we know where we're going?" Yuliana asked.

"If we return to the place where the kobolds attacked, can you track them?" Ethan asked the foxgirl.

She frowned and shook her head. "I could have at the time, but the rain would have washed any scent away."

"I'm guessing that if the villagers knew where the kobolds' base was, they would have pointed it out," he said. He scratched his chin and realized he needed a shave. Yet another little thing that made him think this could be real. If only it weren't for the magic. He simply couldn't explain magic with any known laws of physics he'd ever heard of or read about.

He thought about the kobolds. Both times, kobolds had found and attacked them. It seemed logical to assume that if they went back up the road, at some point the kobolds would attack them.

The problem was, it was a day's journey to the last place they'd seen kobolds. He dreaded sleeping on the ground again, though at least this time they had cloaks. Ethan cast a glance back into the store. Was there some gear stashed away in there that could help them? Some bedrolls? Backpacks?

"This will take more than one day just to get there and back, let alone actually finding the kobolds and dealing with them," he said. "We should check the store to see if there's any gear we might need."

The women looked around at each other, none of them seeming thrilled at the idea of another overnight trip into the great outdoors.

"That seems like a prudent decision," Yuliana said and started towards the store.

"Let us be quick about this," Nia said and followed her.

Ethan was about to follow them when he felt a hand on his arm. He looked down to see Ainslee staring at the forge again.

"You're the mayor," she said questioningly. "If I get the forge working again, can I have it? I mean, until we find a way for me to get home?"

He glanced at the blacksmith's shop. Like the other abandoned buildings, it was in a state of disrepair but looked serviceable. Though she might need the thatcher to fix up her roof before she started sleeping there. He shrugged. "I don't see why not. I'd have to check with the rest of the villagers but as quickly as they gave me the store, I don't see why they wouldn't give you the smith. Especially if you're the one fixing their tools."

"Good." She grinned. She let her hand drop and then clapped him hard on his butt. "Thanks, wizard-boy."

Leaving the stunned Ethan behind, Ainslee hurried after the other women into the shop. He rubbed his stinging butt for a moment before following her. It had been a long time since a woman had slapped his butt. He kind of liked it.

He hadn't really thought about it up to this point, but each of the women were quite attractive in their own way. Much more attractive than the typical Earth woman who had actually said yes to go out on a date with him. And yet, they were all aliens. Like real aliens! He felt weird about even thinking about them in a sexual way.

Had the aliens who had abducted them put him with these three women for a reason? No. He remembered they'd found other men, other alien men. It was just sheer luck that he'd appeared further away from where the kobolds began killing them. The fact that there had been other alien males probably meant this wasn't some sort of alien attempt to witness some cross-species breeding rituals.

Then why were they here? Whether this was some insanely detailed simulation or they were all really on an alien world, why were they brought here? What was the aliens' purpose? He couldn't believe that aliens capable of traveling faster than light - which was the only way they could have reached Earth - would do so without a purpose. But what purpose?

And the aliens hadn't just travelled to his world, but obviously several worlds. He wondered if there had been others that arrived before or after they had or perhaps even in a different area. If so, how many worlds had they abducted people from? And again, he asked the question why? Why go through so much effort?

"Hey, wizard-boy!" came the dwarf's voice, breaking him out of his thoughts.

Going inside, he saw the three women looking through shelves and cabinets, looking for items they could use. He saw two dusty leather backpacks on one of the shelves that they must have scavenged from somewhere. At least that was something. Yuliana also found an old hatchet in the back of one of the cabinets and they laid that out too.

The four of them searched the main store area and then Ethan led them into the back, to a small store room he'd found last night before going to bed. He had been hoping it was a bathroom, but it hadn't been. Instead he'd found what appeared to be a chamberpot and had used that instead.

The crates in the store room held some mining gear, such as pick heads and leather bands with a candle holder attached to them. There was also a crate of candles. It was open and over half of the candles were gone - probably given to the bandits by Cuthbert. There was also an unopened crate of pewter mugs. Not much for them to use at the moment, but he did grab four of the mugs. They stuffed the mugs in one of the backpacks.

He then searched the bedroom and found four blankets, including the one from his bed, and rolled them up and stuffed them into the backpacks as well.

"Anything else here we should take?" he asked as he shouldered one of the backpacks.

Ainslee put the other backpack on and took a last look around. "No, nothing else worth bringing along."

"Great," he said, walking towards the door. "Let's get going."

28

The group assembled outside his new house. The sky was dark with clouds and Ethan prayed the rain would hold off. The memory of their previous trek through the rain was still fresh in his mind. The cloaks they wore appeared to have been treated with wax or some other material, to ward off the rain, but he doubted it would protect them from a serious storm.

Just before leaving Hawkshead, Ethan pulled up his HUD to check his stats. He was curious to see what getting a good night's sleep would do for his *Stamina*.

```
Strength: 10
Agility: 13
Hardiness: 13
Intellect: 19
Intuition: 14
Charisma: 10


You have 2 unallocated attribute points.
```

Health: 26
Stamina: 52
Mana: 41
Karma: 28

He whistled, causing the women to look at him questioningly. He smiled. "It looks like sleeping in a real bed restored my stamina back to full. Everything's full, for the first time since I got here."

"Yes." Yuliana nodded. "I noticed that everything in the HUD is at its utmost. But I do not understand what unallocated attribute points are. They appeared recently."

All three of the women turned from Yuliana to Ethan, obviously expecting an answer. He gave them a sheepish grin. "One second."

He quickly brought up his HUD again and looked at his stats. They seemed fairly obvious and his prime attribute was obviously Intellect since that seemed to affect his *Mana*. Of course, he'd gotten more use from *Stamina*, so maybe he needed to raise the score.

The stat that seemed most closely tied to *Stamina* was *Hardiness*. He couldn't think of another stat that made sense, except perhaps *Strength*. Tentatively he focused on *Hardiness* and a new prompt appeared.

Allocate 1 unused attribute point to
*   Hardiness? (yes or no)*

He furrowed his brows. There was no indication what the extra point would do. He guessed the aliens hadn't heard of tooltips. If he chose poorly, at least he'd only be wasting a single point. He chose yes.

+1 Hardiness.

He looked at his new stats.

Strength: 10
Agility: 13
Hardiness: 14
Intellect: 19
Intuition: 14
Charisma: 10

You have 1 unallocated attribute point.

Health: 28
Stamina: 56
Mana: 41
Karma: 28

The extra point in *Hardiness* had increased both his *Health* and his *Stamina!* Happy, he quickly put the remaining point in *Hardiness* as well. More *Health* and more *Stamina* seemed to be a good choice at this point - especially if this world was real. Even if it wasn't real, it seemed to have some sort of permadeath feature. Anything that helped him stay alive was a good thing.

Health: 30
Stamina: 60

The logical, computer tech part of his mind noticed the *Health* value seemed to be double his *Hardiness*, while his *Stamina* was exactly four times his *Hardiness*. Unlike the MMOs and RPGs he'd played, there didn't seem to be any extra *Health* for his level gains. If that were true, then his stats were even more important. He'd need to really think about where to place his future points.

"Ethan?" Yuliana said, snapping him out of his HUD.

"Sorry, things are different enough here that I wanted to check it out first," he apologized. "It looks like your Karma, Mana, Health and Stamina are directly related to your stats. Health and stamina are tied to hardiness, mana to intellect and karma to intuition. At least, I assume it is intuition since I don't use karma for anything."

The women nodded and he continued. "I got an extra point of mana both times I leveled up in wizard, so you probably get extra points based on your class. But it looks like our stats are very important for our overall power level and survivability."

"What do you mean, survivability?" Nia asked.

"When your Health reaches zero," he said. "You die. So the more health you have, the more damage you can take before you die."

Nia frowned. "That makes no sense. Enemies die when you stab them through the heart or cause them to bleed out. It does not depend on numbers."

Ethan shrugged. "While what you say is true, it appears that in this world things are a bit more granular. If you stab an enemy through the heart, I suspect that would be a critical hit and do more damage. I'm not sure how the extra health actually works but it seems like it should help us live longer."

The foxgirl screwed up her face. "Then what? We put all of our points into hardiness?"

"That's one way," he replied. "I'm guessing agility probably helps you avoid getting hit. It might make you react faster too. Strength probably increases the amount of damage you do and possibly how much you can carry. The other stats have uses too. It just depends on what you want your focus to be."

"Then what should we do?" the foxgirl demanded, in a tone which clearly spoke of annoyance.

Ethan took a calming breath. "For the first few levels, I think we can't go wrong with hardiness. The extra health and stamina could really come in handy at lower levels."

"How many levels are there?" Yuliana asked.

"I don't know." He shrugged. "Nothing in the HUD indicates the maximum level."

"Okay, fine," grumbled Ainslee, starting to walk south. "I put my points into hardiness. Let's go already?"

The others exchanged looks and followed after the dwarf, heading down the south road out of Hawkshead.

SIX HOURS LATER, they found an abandoned structure that might have been a farmhouse at one time but now was little more than a shell. The rain held out for what seemed like an hour before the temperature dropped and the sky opened up. The rain had come almost without warning and it had come down hard. Their cloaks helped keep the rain off them for a few minutes but they quickly became soaked.

They'd spent the next five hours trudging through the muddy road, passing farmhouse after farmhouse. On their original trek into Hawkshead, it had been dark and they'd missed all of the farmhouses. Now, even with the rain, the fields and herds were proof of over a dozen farms.

Yuliana's sharp eyes had caught the overgrown farmhouse and although most of the thatched roof was missing, at least part of it was intact and would protect them from the rain. They'd even found some remains of old furniture and some sticks that were dry, allowing them to start a fire.

The four of them huddled around the fire in silence. They were each too wet and miserable to talk and just stared into the fire. It was too stormy for Nia to hunt for game, but they'd found and collected some nuts and berries in the pewter mugs he'd packed.

They'd found several berry bushes earlier, as well as a nut tree. They'd eaten some of the berries and nuts where they'd found them and then collected the rest in the mugs for later. The berries were blackberries and raspberries from Earth.

His *Herbalism* skill identified the strange green nuts they found as concoria nuts. Concoria nuts were native to Nia's world and although she wouldn't eat them, the foxgirl confirmed the *Herbalism*'s skill description that they were safe. They tasted like something between a pistachio and a walnut. Bitter, yet with an odd sweetness at the end.

Eating until he was almost full, he handed the rest of his dinner to Ainslee. Yuliana had done the same when she had eaten her fill. In both instances, the dwarf was surprised, but gratefully accepted them.

"We should set watch again," he told them, as Ainslee handed the empty mugs back.

The group agreed and Ethan once again agreed to take first watch. He grabbed a mostly dried log from near the fire pit and put it into the flames. Then he watched as the women lay back on their blankets and turned away from the fire. It wasn't long before Ainslee's snoring began and drowned out the sound of the rainfall.

As he sat inside the shell of the farmhouse with the fire light obscuring anything beyond ten or fifteen feet and the dwarf's snoring obscuring any sounds, Ethan realized that something could sneak right up to them and he'd never know it. Keeping the crossbow cocked and ready, he leaned back against the wall and thought of home.

Once he started to feel himself get sleepy, he woke up Nia, who took the next shift and then retreated to his own blankets. Unlike the previous night, he was plagued by bad dreams. Things chased him in the darkness. Hungry things. Large things. Things that made chittering sounds and wanted to kill him.

He woke with a start as someone shook him and it took him a moment to recognize it as Yuliana. The elf backed away quickly, eyes wide and afraid. He looked down to see his hand covered in blue-white flame. Cursing, he dismissed the fire with a thought.

"Sorry," he apologized. "I didn't do it on purpose."

Yuliana nodded but still looked afraid. He silently berated himself but knew why he'd done it. In his dream, the dark things had found him. They surrounded him and wanted to kill him. But not just kill him, they wanted to devour him. Ethan shivered.

"Next time," Ainslee scoffed, "we'll just throw rocks at you until you wake up."

He looked down at his hand, which had just a moment ago been wreathed in blue-white fire. He hadn't consciously done that and wasn't even sure what it was or how much damage it might have done to anyone he touched.

"I was having a nightmare," he explained. "There was something in my dreams and it was trying to get me."

"Was it a snoring dwarf?" Nia said dryly, purposefully not looking at Ainslee.

"What did you say?" the dwarf demanded.

"I said I will look for some game for breakfast." The foxgirl grinned, careful to angle her face away from Ainslee. Nia slipped out of their shelter and disappeared around the corner.

"I don't snore!" Ainslee insisted.

Yuliana and Ethan exchanged looks, both of them suppressing a laugh. It worked for about thirty seconds before they both burst out laughing.

"I don't!" the dwarf said loudly, which only made them laugh harder.

29

Nia brought back two ducks, which she promptly defeathered and they cooked over the fire. The ducks had been wild and the meat was both gamey and greasy, but after nothing but berries and nuts for dinner, he enjoyed it.

While the meal was cooking, Ethan checked his HUD and wasn't surprised to see that his *Stamina* was down.

Stamina: 50

If he was right, he needed a good night's sleep in a comfortable bed to return to maximum. If his previous experience were any indicator, he wouldn't regenerate any *Stamina* until it was below half and then he'd only regenerate it to half his maximum. It was annoying, but those were the rules of this world.

"Thanks, Nia," Ethan said as he finished up his duck. He realized he hadn't really thanked her for all the hunting she'd done and without it, they would have been starving or eating nothing but berries.

Nia looked surprised but nodded. "I am Cha'to'mir'ta. It is my place to hunt."

"What does that mean?" Yuliana asked. The elf had saved some berries and nuts and had eaten those for breakfast, along with some wild carrots she'd found not far from the ruined farmhouse.

The foxgirl scratched her head, seemingly trying to think of how to translate that word. Ethan thought it was interesting that there were words that didn't seem to translate.

It was particularly interesting since he'd pointed out before that they all understood each other. That meant either they were all speaking English, or something was translating their individual languages. And yet, he'd watched and their mouths actually appeared to be speaking with the words they said, unlike the dubbed anime and foreign films he'd watched. So how was the translation being done?

"It means, seventeenth wife servant," Nia said finally.

"You're a servant?" Ainslee asked before taking the last bite of her duck.

"All of the alpha's wives are servants," she said. "We serve him, he protects us. That is the way."

"It looks to me like you do just fine protecting yourself," the dwarf retorted, licking her fingers clean.

"No," the foxgirl replied harshly. "It is forbidden."

"Then why do you know how to fight so well?" the dwarf snickered.

The foxgirl opened her mouth, closed it, opened it again and finally closed it. "I will check the perimeter."

Nia stood up abruptly, spun and stalked outside. The three of them watched her go. Yuliana turned to Ainslee. "You should not antagonize her like that."

The dwarf scoffed. "I didn't antagonize no one. I asked questions that needed askin'. I'm the strongest one here, sure, but

I've seen her handle her weapons. She's better than all of us put together. She just won't fight."

"We should get ready to go," Ethan said, forestalling another argument. "If we can find their village early, we might be able to get back to Hawkshead by evening."

The three of them gathered up their meager items. Before they had finished, Nia came back and quickly packed up her own items. They finished up in silence before setting out back down the trail.

Nia took the lead as they travelled, sniffing and searching the road for footprints. They travelled for two hours before the foxgirl called them to a halt suddenly. She ducked down and signalled them to do the same.

They had stopped in an area of tall grass to each side of the road and Ethan realized the smaller kobolds could be hiding all around them and they'd never know it. He pulled the crossbow off his back slowly, cursing himself for not cocking it earlier. Nia sniffed at the air, looking from side to side. She glanced back and appeared about to say something when three large forms burst from the bushes.

The creatures looked like wolves from Earth, except that they had two heads. They were each the size of a large dog and their fur was a mixture of colors, including green, that had allowed them to blend in with the grass so perfectly.

Two of the wolves were on the right, while the third was on the left. The furthest on the right went straight for Nia, while the other one on the right went for Yuliana. The one on the left came directly at him.

Ethan acted more out of some new instinct than actual thought. As the creature leaped at him, he felt the energy drain out of him but blue-white fire engulfed his entire body. And then the wolf-thing was on him, knocking him over and sinking its teeth into his right shoulder and left arm.

```
Forest orthrus bites you for 6 damage.
Elemental armor (fire) burns forest
   orthrus for 6 fire damage.
Forest orthrus bites you for 5 damage.
Elemental armor (fire) burns forest
   orthrus for 5 fire damage.
```

The forest orthrus quickly released Ethan and leaped back. The thing shook its head back and forth, both muzzles burning from where it had come in contact with flames.

Ethan was bleeding from the orthrus bites, but grimaced and pushed himself to his feet. The message in his HUD showed that the fire was elemental armor. He remembered that he'd received that ability but hadn't gotten to play around with it yet.

The forest orthrus who had attacked him was shaking its heads back and forth so he took a moment to scan the situation.

```
Forest orthrus
Level 3
Forest orthrus
Level 3
Forest orthrus
Level 3
```

Surprisingly, he saw Nia with two daggers in her hands, dodging deftly out of reach of the two heads and then darting in to slice at the creature. It was the first time he'd seen her using something other than the staff when they were fighting.

Ainslee had managed to put herself in front of the elf. She had the wolf-thing by the throat in a two-handed grip, keeping it from biting her, but wincing as the forepaws raked across her leather armor, tearing gashes in it. With an effort, the dwarf pushed the creature back and pulled out her short swords.

Turning back to the forest orthrus that now faced him, the creature was snapping at the air and shaking its head back and forth, probably trying to stop the burning. Still covered in the flames, he took a step towards the creature and it leaped back.

Ethan charged the creature. His thought was to tackle it and let the flames burn it. He had thought about going for his staff but wasn't sure what would happen if he held it in his hand. Would it burn it? His clothes and armor didn't seem to be burning, but he couldn't risk losing the weapon.

The forest orthrus deftly dodged to the side and made to snap at him before pulling up short. Instead, it leaped away from him, glaring at him. It circled around him, both heads snarling.

Sighing, he realized he wasn't quick enough to tackle the creature. Ethan was going to have to use up more *Stamina* if he wanted to kill it. He immediately thought of a fireball, but realized the orthrus were too scattered to get more than one at a time. He'd end up using a lot of Stamina and that would leave him weak.

Remembering the other ability he had earned, he tried to summon an elemental. He wasn't sure what to expect. In the roleplaying games he'd played, elementals were creatures or constructs composed of a specific element. They were usually somewhat formless and did their summoner's bidding - as long as they maintained control.

He willed a fire elemental to appear, focusing on the *Summon Minor Elemental* ability. Almost immediately, he felt the familiar weakness that came with his *Stamina* being used.

Skill increase: Fire magic +2%.

In front of him, a tongue of flame appeared. It grew to the

size of his forearm before dropping to the ground. It twisted and distorted until it morphed into the shape of what he could only guess was a large weasel, or maybe a mongoose.

The fire weasel hopped around like a real weasel, darting left and right and looking up at him. It wasn't exactly what he'd been expecting, but then again, he wasn't really sure what he'd been expecting.

"Attack the wolf," he told it and pointed to the orthrus, which now had its heads lowered, growling at the fire weasel.

The weasel spun and immediately darted at the two-headed wolf. The orthrus growled and snapped at the fire weasel but quickly retracted its head. Like real-life weasels, the elemental was both fast and dextrous. The fire weasel darted to the left and then leaped on the neck of the two-headed wolf.

Minor elemental (fire) burns forest orthrus for 5 fire damage.
Skill increase: Fire magic +1%.

The orthrus yelped and began trying to shake the elemental loose, whipping its heads from side to side. It yelped again, louder this time, as the fire weasel appeared to bite down on its neck.

Minor elemental (fire) critically burns forest orthrus for 18 fire damage.
Skill increase: Fire magic +1%.

The forest orthrus began to panic, throwing itself onto the ground and rolling back and forth. Despite the creature's desperate movements, the weasel stayed attached to the creature's neck.

*Minor elemental (fire) critically burns
    forest orthrus for 17 fire damage.
Skill increase: Fire magic +1%.*

The two-headed wolf's movements slowed, the thing's yelps turning into whines, then the creature stopped moving and lay still.

*Minor elemental (fire) critically burns
    forest orthrus for 19 fire damage.
Forest orthrus dies.
You gain 30 experience. Experience to
    next level 225.
Skill increase: Fire magic +1%.*

Bouncing up off the orthrus, the fire weasel hopped over Ethan and stared up at him. He saw that both of the other creatures were still up and that the slower dwarf seemed to have more injuries than the faster, more agile foxgirl.

"Get that one," he said and pointed at the wolf attacking Ainslee. The fire weasel's head looked over at the orthrus and it bounded over to the creature. It leaped up at the thing's neck but one of the canine heads caught the elemental in its mouth - and then immediately yelped and flung it away.

The distraction was enough that Ainslee was able to spring forward and drive one of her short swords into the creature's neck. The blade punctured the creature just between the two heads and the orthrus shuddered and then dropped to the ground.

*Forest orthrus dies.
You gain 15 experience. Experience to
    next level 210.*

The weasel looked at the body of the two-headed wolf and quickly scampered in front of Ethan, looking up at him.

He smiled down at the energetic little creature and then looked at Nia's fight. The foxgirl stood over the body of the forest orthrus with blood-stained daggers in each hand. She breathed hard as she looked down at the creature at her feet.

"See, you did fight," the dwarf bellowed, wiping her short-swords on the dead wolf's body.

Nia's head whipped around at the dwarf. "I killed prey. Prey is not an enemy. It is prey. Food. Furs. This is permitted."

"Right," Ainslee replied. "It's prey. Not an enemy. Sure."

"What is that?" Yuliana asked, pointing at the fire elemental. "Is it a demon?"

Ethan glanced down at the fire weasel, who continued to look up at him expectantly. "It's a minor fire elemental."

"It looks like a weasel," Ainslee said, squinting at the elemental.

He shrugged. "That was the way it appeared."

"Come," Nia interrupted. "We must skin these creatures and take what meat we can."

"You seriously want to eat wolf?" Ainslee asked, her nose drawn up and wrinkled.

Nia shrugged, bent down and began skinning the wolf. Ethan sighed. He knew what they'd be eating for lunch.

30

Only two of the orthrus pelts were salvageable but they got more meat than they could eat from them. The meat was smelly, to the point where both Ethan and Ainslee were hesitant to try it. Even after it was roasted over their makeshift spit, it didn't smell appealing. Nia didn't hesitate. The foxgirl ate her portion enthusiastically.

In the end, with both their stomachs growling, both he and the dwarf did eat it. Surprisingly, it wasn't nearly as bad as it smelled. It was almost like venison, but a bit more gamey. They each ate their fill, except for Yuliana, who hadn't been able to find any berries or nuts yet today.

The elemental weasel followed Ethan around the entire time Nia was skinning the orthrus and then as she was preparing their meals. It didn't do anything other than follow him around, much to the curiosity of the women. Eventually, its duration ended and the little creature winked out of existence.

"An elemental, huh?" Ainslee said, staring at where the fiery weasel had been. "It came in handy, I'll give it that much."

"How did you call it to you?" Yuliana asked.

"I got an ability called summon minor elemental," he

replied. "I used it during the fight and the weasel showed up. It was much more vicious than I expected."

"I too have an ability that says I may summon a creature," Yuliana said, and then read the description of the ability. "I received this when I earned level 3."

Summon Animal Companion
   Type: Druid
   Cost: 15 Karma
   Range: N/A
   Duration: Special
   Description: Druid summons a level-appropriate animal from the nearby area to serve as a companion. The animal companion can understand basic commands. The companion gains strength as the druid's level increases. If the animal companion dies, a new one can be summoned. A druid may only have one animal companion at a time.

"It sounds like you can summon some sort of animal with that ability." Ethan nodded. "But a regular animal, not one made of fire."

"I think I would prefer a normal animal," the elf said. "How do I summon it?"

"I just focused on the ability and making the elemental appear," he replied. "That should work for you as well."

She closed her eyes and her forehead wrinkled in concentration, then she opened her eyes and looked around. A pout formed on her lips. "It did not work."

"Maybe try it again, but think of a specific animal," he said.

She smiled and nodded. She closed her eyes and then

opened them, frowning. "The HUD says I have already summoned one."

They all looked around, but none of them saw any animals. Ainslee snorted, scratching her shoulder. "Is it a flea or something?"

Just then the brush to their side rustled and a large creature padded out. The creature resembled a cougar or mountain lion, except this mountain lion was a dark, forest green, with fiery orange stripes.

The big cat padded closer and stopped. It sat back on its haunches and looked at the party before settling on Yuliana.

Yuliana stared at the big cat with wide eyes. "Is that my animal companion?"

Ethan caught Nia moving her hands to the daggers on her hips but he shook his head. He turned to Yuliana. "Try asking it to do something."

"Like what?" Yuliana squealed. The elf was practically vibrating with excitement.

Ethan thought for a moment. "Tell it to lie down."

Nodding enthusiastically, Yuliana took a step towards the large cat. The mountain lion continued to watch her, unconcerned. "Can you lie down?"

The big cat regarded the elf for a long moment and then went down on all fours. It continued to look at the elf, who clapped her hands together excitedly. "It did it!"

"Now see if it will sit back up," he told her.

"What?" She turned towards him.

"See if the cat will sit back up," he told the elf.

"Why?" She wrinkled her forehead.

"To make sure that the cat lying down wasn't just a coincidence," he said.

She nodded and turned back to the mountain lion. "Sit up, please."

Giving them all a bored look, the cat deftly sat back up, still looking at Yuliana.

"It looks like it's your companion," he told her.

The elf slowly walked over to the big cat, who continued to sit there and look at her. She reached out a hand and the cat sniffed at it. Walking closer, she dropped to her knees and threw her arms around it.

The mountain lion seemed to sigh, but made no threatening move. Backing out of the hug, she began to scratch the mountain lion's chin and head. The big cat actually seemed to enjoy that and was soon purring.

"I've never seen a cat that big," Ainslee whispered. "It sure ain't from my world."

"We have big cats on my world but none that large," Ethan agreed.

"We have much larger cats," Nia snorted. "The males ride them into battle."

"Wait, what?" The dwarf's head snapped around to look Nia up and down. "Your people are fox people and you ride cats into battle?"

"Of course," Nia said in a matter-of-fact tone. "They are bred for riding."

"I wonder if they have riding cats on this world," Ainslee muttered.

"Speaking of creatures from other worlds. Have any of you ever seen a wolf like the ones we fought?" Ethan asked, finishing up his lunch.

"I have never even heard of such creatures," Yuliana replied.

"Me either," the dwarf, who had also resumed eating, mumbled with a full mouth.

Nia shook her head. "We have similar creatures, but they only have one head."

Ethan nodded. "Same here. We have many different species on my world, but none with two heads. There is a three-headed dog in mythology, but I'm pretty sure no one ever found any proof that it existed."

"What does that mean?" Nia asked. "Is it native to this world?"

"I'm not sure," he replied. "But just like they brought us here from different worlds, I wonder if they brought animals and plants from our worlds too. For all we know, nothing is native to this world."

"But none of us have seen that before, so maybe it is native to this world," Yuliana said. She was still scratching the big cat, who had rolled over to allow her to scratch its belly. The mountain lion was producing a deep, loud purring sound.

"Right. But we weren't the only ones brought here. Remember the other..." He almost said players, but caught himself just in time. He still thought of this in game terms but the others would not understand the references. "Remember the other people that the kobolds had killed. They came from different worlds too. And that was just one spot. For all we know, groups of people arrived in different spots. There could be hundreds of people stolen from their worlds here."

"What gives them the right to take us from our homes?!" Nia demanded, her tail suddenly puffy.

"And why would they do that?" Ainslee asked as she licked her fingers. The dwarf seemed surprisingly unfazed about the whole thing.

"I do have a theory," he said, taking a deep breath. He'd been trying to figure things out since he arrived. Most of his early theories hadn't really panned out. But he still had a few. "Do you know what a zoo is? Or a game preserve?"

The women gave him blank looks and he sighed. "It's a place where they put animals in cages or in certain areas so that people can view them."

Yuliana and Nia both looked outraged while Ainslee just shrugged. "Can't say I've really heard of people doing that."

"My people do," he said apologetically. He didn't actually have an issue with zoos, as long as they treated the animals humanely. In his eyes, the animals were treated better and lived longer than those in the wild. But he admitted, especially in his present circumstances, there was something to be said for freedom. And being left in your own habitat - or planet.

"Anyway." He cleared his throat. "People take animals, sometimes wounded or abandoned animals, and put them into pens or cages where people can observe them."

The girls all looked at him like he had three heads. None of them spoke, so he went on. "My theory is: We've been taken from our worlds and put in a type of preserve. Some sort of planet that they've designed for our species. If I'm right, they've also modified us to better survive on this world."

"Modified?" Ainslee scowled. "I don't like the sound of that. Like what sort of modifications?"

"Speaking the same language, for one. Obviously, we can't all possibly speak the same language normally. Somehow the aliens have done something to us or implanted something into us that allows us to communicate as if we were speaking our native language."

"Magic," Nia hissed. "They have bewitched us."

Ethan sighed, knowing he couldn't possibly describe the technology that his planet had, let alone some technologies that only existed, or that he thought had only existed, in science fiction. "You could think of it that way. But whatever they've done, I think it's so that we can better survive on this world."

Nia stood up. "This talk gets us nowhere. Let us go and find the kobolds and drive them from your land."

"I agree." Ainslee nodded, tossing away a bone. "This talk is making my head hurt."

Getting to his feet, Ethan slipped his backpack on and

grabbed his staff. He knew further talking at this point wouldn't serve any purpose.

It reminded him of the glassy-eyed stares and protests he received when he tried to explain internet security to computer-illiterate people. They didn't understand it and they didn't want to hear about it. He hoped it wasn't like computer security where the person ignored your advice until their computer was compromised and had to be wiped.

He would need to figure out a better way to explain things to them. Ethan had always been able to break down computer issues into things most people could understand. In fact, he prided himself on his ability to do so. The problem he faced here was the lack of any sort of shared culture that he could draw on to create analogies.

The group resumed their marching formation with Nia slipping into the lead. Ainslee moved in behind her. A smiling Yuliana came bounding up behind the dwarf, the cougar padding alongside of her. That left Ethan in the rear.

Ethan looked down at the mountain lion next to the elf. "What are you going to name him?"

"Her," Yuliana corrected as the big cat turned her head and glared back at him. "It's a she."

"Sorry," he told them both.

Yuliana looked up at the two moons that were always in the sky during the day. She turned around and smiled, pointing up at the largest moon. "I will name her Luna, after the moon."

"Luna." Ethan smiled. "That's a good name for a cat."

31

The five of them traveled south down the road, Ethan, the three girls and the mountain lion. The big cat padded along next to Yuliana like a dog. She didn't once growl or show any hostility towards any of the group and occasionally rubbed up against the elf like she was her mother. Ethan had to admit he was a little jealous. He liked cats and would have absolutely loved a mountain lion as a pet.

Sometime in the afternoon, Nia stopped suddenly, forcing them to a halt. She sniffed the air for a full minute, her feline head moving from side to side. Finally, she motioned them up to her and pointed to the ground.

"Kobold tracks," she told them. "Eight of them."

Ainslee squinted down at the tracks and scratched her head. "Eight? Are you sure?"

"I am sure," she hissed at the dwarf, eyes narrowed. "The mud has obscured the tracks but there are eight different scents."

"If you say so." Ainslee rolled her eyes.

"Why are there so many in a group?" Yuliana asked. The elf had bent down and was scratching Luna behind the ears.

Nia shook her head. "I do not know. But it is most likely a war party."

"A war party?" Yuliana repeated with alarm.

"The missing kobolds?" Ethan asked. In most of the games he played, there were never consequences for killing random bands of monsters. Since this was either real, or an extremely sophisticated simulation/game, it looked like there were consequences.

"If a hunting party or raiding party did not return," she nodded, "a good leader would send out more to find them or what had happened to them."

"How many of those little creatures do you think there are?" Ainslee asked.

"Enough that they've cut off the merchants that used to come to town," Ethan replied, remembering Fearghas mentioning it while they had eaten at the inn.

"I cannot say," Nia shrugged. "I do not know these creatures or how big their tribes are."

Luna let out a low growl, the mountain lion's ears flattening against her head. Nia moved her head suddenly, sniffing the air. She looked about to say something when kobolds exploded from the grass all around them.

These kobolds looked identical to the ones they'd fought earlier. Each had tribal patterns painted on their scales and each carried a spear. The creatures barked and snarled in their guttural language and Ethan was surprised that he actually understood the words. "Kill them! Kill them!"

Nia reacted instantly, dropping into a crouch and bringing her quarterstaff up defensively. Ainslee yelped and scrambled for her shortswords while Yuliana scrambled to pull the crossbow off her back. The mountain lion growled while putting herself protectively between the elf and the kobolds.

Ethan cursed. They'd walked right into an ambush. Or the kobolds had snuck up on them as they talked. Either way, he had reflexes honed by thousands of hours of video games. He let loose a fireball without even really thinking about it. The drain on his *Stamina* was palpable and he felt his legs go weak.

A group of three were coming at him, along with some sort of small hopping, horned creatures, and he aimed the fireball at them. The fireball flew into a group of three kobolds and exploded before they even knew what was happening.

```
You burn River Burrow Raider for 31 fire
    damage.
River Burrow Raider dies.
You burn River Burrow Raider for 33 fire
    damage.
River Burrow Raider dies.
You burn River Burrow Raider for 29 fire
    damage.
River Burrow Raider dies.
Skill increase: Fire Magic +3%.
You gain 30 experience. Experience to
    next level 180.
```

The fireball and screams of their companions caused the kobolds to hesitate and that was all the opening his group needed. Nia leaped at the two creatures closest to her on the right, landing in front of them and knocking them both down with a double hit of her staff.

Ainslee let out a yell and charged two more on the right. Brandishing her two short swords, she was forced to stop short as the creatures jabbed their spears forward. She slashed at them but the dextrous kobolds hopped back out of range.

"Use your plant magic to entangle them with the grass," he told the elf, who was still struggling with her crossbow.

"My what?" She looked over her shoulder at him.

One of the kobolds saw the distracted elf and charged her.

It only got two steps before Luna leaped on the little kobold and knocked it to the ground. The big cat locked her jaws about the thing's neck and ripped out its throat.

In the meantime, the remaining kobold on the left appeared to have realized that Ethan was the wizard and charged at him. He felt too weak to do another fireball without passing out so instead, he conjured a thin line of air right in front of the kobold at neck level.

The fast-moving kobold never saw the slight distortion that line of air gave off and ran straight into it, clothes-lining itself. The little creature went down in a heap, coughing and clutching at its damaged throat.

> *You critically pummel River Burrow*
>   *Raider for 19 damage.*
> *River Burrow Raider is choking.*
> *Skill increase: Air Magic +1%.*

Ainslee and Nia switched foes. The two Nia had knocked down with her staff were groaning on the ground, clutching at their groin or stomachs. Ainslee walked over and ran them through, ending their suffering.

Nia went to work on the other two, fending off spear strikes and retaliating with hard strikes to knees and elbows. The two kobolds began to fall back but one went down as Luna pounced on it, once again going for the throat.

The last one saw the rest of its war party dead or dying and turned to run. Nia used her Leap ability and jumped over it to cut off its escape. Panicked, the creature spun, only to find Ainslee's shortswords waiting for it.

Ethan looked down at the one on the ground clutching its throat. He pulled out his dagger and took a step towards the thing. The kobold's eyes went wide and it held up one hand, waving it back and forth. "No... kill... I..."

He stopped in his tracks. Ethan looked down at the kobold, who was staring up at him pleadingly.

"No... kill... I..." it repeated pitifully.

Ainslee stomped over, bloody shortswords in her hands. "Need help with this one?"

The kobold tried to crawl away but was still gasping and its attempts were weak.

"What are you waiting for?" hissed Nia from behind him. "Kill it!"

"Wait," he barked and held out an arm to stop Ainslee from moving forward. The dwarf glared at him.

The kobold looked at him hopefully. "Spare... I... serve... you..."

"Oh great," Ainslee said, throwing up her hands. "They talk now?"

"They talked before," Nia growled. "But they speak in low tones."

"You are not killing this one?" Yuliana asked with a raised eyebrow. Luna was next to her and looked down at the kobold hungrily.

Ethan gave the kobold a hard look. "How can I trust you?"

The dwarf spun and gave him an incredulous look. "You're not seriously considering sparing that thing are you? It'll kill us in our sleep!"

"I agree," Nia spat. "These are cowardly creatures. They are not worthy of our trust."

Sighing, he bent down and looked at the little creature. It was thin and pitiful-looking. Its only clothing was a leather loincloth. He frowned. Were his companions right? Would he be an idiot to trust this creature?

"How can I trust you?" he repeated to the small creature.

"I... swears," it pleaded. "I... serve."

He stood up and turned to the women, who were giving him hard looks. Except for Yuliana. The elf seemed more curious than anything else and her face softened. "Let's give it a chance."

Nia and Ainslee both started to speak at the same time but he held up a hand and lowered his voice to a whisper. "It may have useful information about the kobold village."

The foxgirl and dwarf seemed to consider that and then Nia nodded, followed by Ainslee. "It's your throat."

He turned back around and held out a hand. The kobold flinched away but when it saw he didn't intend to hurt it, just lay there and stared at his hand. Ethan sighed. "Take my hand."

Hesitantly, the kobold did so and Ethan pulled the little thing to its feet. It looked from person to person, and at the big cat who still had a bloody muzzle. It turned back to him. "I serve! You not sorry, magic-man."

"We'll see about that," Ethan said. He hadn't felt right about killing the thing but he wasn't convinced he could trust it either. He motioned from Nia to Ainslee and finally to Luna. "If you do betray us, any of them will be happy to kill you. And that's IF I don't burn you to a crisp. You saw what I did to the others?"

The kobold swallowed and glanced over his shoulder at the three charred bodies near the grass. "Yes. You great magic-man. I serve!"

The kobold bent down to retrieve its spear but Ethan cut him off. "No. No weapons for now. Not until we know we can trust you."

"No spear?" the kobold asked, the scaled ridges that served as reptilian brows furrowed.

"Not for now," he replied and reached down and picked up its spear. "I'll hold on to this until you earn our trust."

"I earn trust." It bobbed its head up and down. "I serve."

"Right," he said, still unsure how he felt about the little creature. "Do you have a name?"

The kobold stood up and puffed its chest out. "I is Par'karr."

"Parker?" Ethan tried to repeat the name.

"Par'karr," it repeated.

"Par - karr" he said slowly, trying to get the pronunciation correct.

Par'karr nodded his head, Ethan assumed it was a he, up and down. "Yes! Yes! I Par'karr!"

The women glanced at each other and then looked at him. Nia shrugged but gave him a look that told him she would be watching the kobold.

Ainslee let out an exasperated breath and turned away. "Fine. Fine. It's your funeral."

He looked at Yuliana, who smiled. "You are kind to spare the Par'karr. But be careful."

Nodding, he turned to look down at the kobold. He would be careful. "Okay, Par'karr. It's time to start earning your keep. We need you to show us where the kobold village is."

The kobold swallowed and looked around like a deer in the headlights. The kobold seemed torn for a long moment but then Par'karr let out a breath and nodded. "I tell you. But you not like answer."

32

A inslee threw her hands up in the air. "There's more than one kobold village?!"

Upon questioning Par'karr, they had learned that there had been multiple villages for years. According to the little kobold, recently one clan had gotten stronger and had been systematically wiping out the others. Par'karr's village was the last to fall.

Par'karr cowered away from the irate dwarf and shook his head. "No. Now just one. My village gone. We were last."

The kobold looked around the bodies of the other kobolds and his shoulders slumped. "Me am last."

"So these other kobolds wiped out your village?" Ethan asked.

Par'karr nodded sadly.

"Do you know where the other village is?" he asked.

The little creature looked around and shrugged. "Par'karr not warrior. Me not leave village. Me is herder."

"Herder?" Ainslee snorted. "What do you herd?"

"Me herd rabbits!" Par'karr replied indignantly, his little head raised proudly. "Me summon rabbits too!"

Ainslee burst out laughing and even Nia snickered. The kobold deflated, head sinking once more. "But Par'karr's rabbits gone now."

Ethan had been squatting to be on eye level with Par'karr, but now he stood up and heard his joints pop. He looked down at his knees. If this was a simulation, that was an insanely small detail to add. Yet one more reason why this all might be real.

"What do you want to bet the tribe that's been wiping out all of the others is the one that Cuthbert hired," Ethan said, turning to face the women.

"You think Cuthbert did something to upset the balance?" Yuliana asked as she stroked Luna's fur. The mountain lion stood by her side, relishing in the attention.

"Like what?" Nia asked.

"Better weapons maybe," he replied. "The bandits all had matching armor and weapons. I don't think that was a coincidence. I think those items came from Cuthbert. I'll bet you he made a deal with the kobolds: I'll give you weapons to defeat the other tribes, if you make sure no one comes down the road."

As the women digested his words, he turned back to the kobold. "Par'karr, did the other tribe have special weapons? Something that they hadn't had before?"

Par'karr bobbed his head up and down. "They have swords when they attack village. Some. Not have before."

He nodded and turned back to his companions. They all had grim expressions.

"This will make them harder to fight," Nia said. "How many are there?"

They all looked at Par'karr. The kobold grew nervous under their collective gazes and kicked a stone with his clawed toe. "Me not really know. Many attack our village. Too many to count."

"It's not really much help," Ainslee said. "We should just kill it."

"No!" Ethan and Yuliana said at the same time and Par'karr ducked behind Ethan.

The dwarf rolled her eyes. "Fine. Keep it. Just don't expect me to trust it!"

Ethan looked at Yuliana and flashed her a smile, which she returned. At least there was one other person who didn't want to immediately kill the little kobold.

"We need to find the remaining village," Nia said. She stared down at the kobold. "Do you know which direction it was from your village?"

The kobold nodded and pointed west. "Yes, Cave Clan that way."

"Cave clan?" he asked.

"Yes." Par'karr nodded. "They not live in huts. They live in caves."

"That will make sneaking up on them more difficult," Nia said. "Like going into a org-to's lair."

"One way in, one way out." Ainslee nodded. "And it could be a maze of tunnels inside."

"And we have no idea how many of them there actually are," Ethan added. "There could be ten or there could be a hundred."

They all grew quiet and thoughtful for several minutes. Finally, Nia broke the silence. "We need to scout out their cave and see if there are any hidden entrances. Perhaps a way in that is not guarded."

Ethan nodded and looked at the sky. If he was right, it would be dark soon. Better to wait until morning. "Let's find a place to camp and then we can track down the kobold cave in the morning."

～

THE NEXT MORNING, Ethan was a little surprised that Par'karr was still there. They'd let him stay in the camp with Luna keeping a watchful eye on him. He had thought the little kobold might flee but instead, had been up bright and early.

The morning brought more dark clouds but it didn't feel as humid as it did the other days and he hoped any rain would pass them by.

The group had found a campsite surrounded by several wild Kortha berry bushes, an edible berry from Yuliana's homeworld. The elf had been ecstatic when she'd seen the plant and had quickly gathered many handfuls. Ethan had tried them and they tasted tart, like cranberries but with a strangle-sweet aftertaste.

The rest of them had eaten fish from the river that Nia had speared, both for dinner and breakfast. The fare was satisfying, if a bit light and most of them supplemented their dinner with a few handfuls of berries.

After breakfast, they set out towards the west to try and find the Cave Clan's lair. Ethan was reminded of his roleplaying days and adventuring into dungeons and caves full of creatures and treasure. Only, in this world, there seemed to be many enemies but very little treasure.

After a couple of hours, Nia found kobold footprints leading west. They followed them west into a hilly region. Once in the hilly region, the tracks had criss-crossed with many other sets of tracks. Nia let out a low growl and turned to the group. "I can no longer follow the tracks, there are too many of them. I must go by scent from here on."

Ethan nodded. "Lead the way."

They followed Nia for another half an hour before she signalled them to stop. She motioned them closer and then pointed over the hill in front of them.

"They are close," she said. "Very close. Maybe just over this hill. Stay here while I scout them out."

They all nodded and the foxgirl dropped to all fours and began crawling up the hill. They watched her reach the top and then crawl to different spots, obviously seeing something that interested her. Nia continued to creep around the top of the hill for several minutes before returning to them. She didn't look happy.

"There is a cave entrance in the hill beyond this one," she whispered. "It is guarded by four kobolds that I could see, but I heard more further in the cave. If we kill the guards, the rest will surely be alerted."

"So what's the plan?" Ethan asked her. She was more experienced at real fighting and stealthy tactics and he was ready to trust her judgement.

"I was hoping you would have a plan." Nia frowned. "You are the wizard."

Par'karr and the women all turned to stare at him, waiting for a plan. He sighed and tried to think of what he might be able to do.

What they really needed was reconnaissance. They needed intelligence on enemy forces. But how to get it without letting the entire Cave Clan know they were here. He had no spells that seemed to fit the bill. All he had was elemental magic and fireball didn't really seem to be able to help out much.

Luckily, an idea came to him. He wasn't sure if it would work, but it was worth a try. He summoned an elemental, but this time instead of a fire elemental, he summoned an air elemental.

Air shimmered and solidified in front of him into the shape of a large bird. It could have been a hawk or a raven, but its semi-transparent form made it hard to get a good look at its actual shape. Summoning the air elemental was the easy part. Now came the hard part.

In some of his role-playing games, magic-users had been able to see through the eyes of familiars or other summoned creatures. If he could do the same, he would have a way to reconnoiter the cave with minimal risk. If it could be done.

"I'm going to try something," he told the others as he sat down on the ground. "If this works, I may run out of stamina and you might have to carry me out of here."

"You mean I'll have to carry you," Ainslee groaned. "Fine, wizard-boy. Do your magic stuff."

Ethan nodded and closed his eyes. He thought of the air elemental bird and focused his mind on it. He could sense it. Whether he was sensing magic or somehow knew because it was his spell, he wasn't sure. But he could definitely feel the air bird.

Skill increase: Air Magic +1%.

He focused on the elemental and imagined he could see through its eyes. He concentrated as hard as he could and then opened his eyes. Only, it wasn't his eyes that opened. It was the air bird's. And he was seeing through them. It worked!

You have gained: Clairvoyance
Skill increase: Clairvoyance +1%.

Ignoring the HUD messages, he mentally commanded the elemental to fly up. Obediently, the air bird did so. It flew straight up. He commanded it to fly straight, then left, then right. Each time, the elemental followed his exact command. He smiled. At least, he thought he smiled. He wasn't sure if it were his real body or the elemental.

He directed the bird to fly over the hill, reveling in the sensation of flight. It was like being in a really high-resolution flight simulator, only he was controlling it with his mind.

Ethan/bird elemental flew up and over the hill and he saw the cave entrance Nia had mentioned and flew straight towards it. The kobolds didn't notice the semi-translucent elemental until it flew between them and into the cave. Behind him, he could hear them crying out.

"Bat!" "Hawk!" "Pigeon!"

Luckily, the cave was lit by torches that were placed regularly along the tunnel. He flew, or rather the elemental flew, down the tunnel, staying close to the roof and flying over the heads of several more kobolds.

He flew through several tunnel branches before the one he was following opened into a huge cavern. He flew to the top and surveyed the large cave that currently held a large number of kobolds. If he had to guess, he'd say there were at least eighty of them. And they were all facing a large kobold who was yelling.

"The hill clan, the river clan, the meadow clan," he yelled. "They no more!"

The crowd of kobolds cheered.

"Now," bellowed the large kobold, which Ethan bet was the chieftain. "Now, we take valley back! Tomorrow, we prepare and the next day...we march on humans! We burn farms! Then we burn village! Then kobolds rule valley!"

Once again the kobolds cheered.

Letting go of his hold on the air elemental, Ethan felt the magic of it dissipate. He snapped his own eyes open and gasped. He looked around, disoriented and weak. Blinking against the bright sunlight, he struggled to get to his feet.

Your minor elemental (air) has been dismissed.

"They're coming," he breathed, trying to catch his breath. "They're coming for the village!"

33

D espite his shaky legs and overall feeling of weakness, Ethan forced himself to walk along with the women. They had immediately left the hills of the Cave Clan and headed back to the road. Once they hit the road a few hours later, they started back to Hawkshead.

"Are you sure there were a hundred?" Nia called back to him. "Sometimes the herd may look larger than it actually is."

Ethan had told them what he'd seen and heard. He wasn't sure of the exact number but he'd counted 8-9 per row and there had been 12 rows. Some of them might not have been warriors, but they had to assume all of them were. Plus, there were probably guards, scouts and hunting parties that might not have been with the main group.

He looked at the foxgirl. "It's got to be at least 100, possibly more."

"Those are not good odds," Nia replied, turning back to the road.

"More like impossible odds," Ainslee chuckled mirthlessly. "This might be a good time to go check out that city they told us about."

"And leave Hawkshead to the kobolds?" Yuliana asked.

"They're going to die either way," Ainslee replied. "I don't feel like I need to die for them. I mean, I barely know them."

"We have to at least warn them," Ethan said.

"Yes, we must," Yuliana agreed.

"Warn village, then go hide?" Par'karr asked hopefully.

"The pass just south of the village is narrow," Nia said. "If we did not leave in time, we would be trapped in the village."

"We have two days," Ethan argued. "Maybe we can help them get ready."

"And risk getting caught with no way out?" Ainslee snorted. "I don't think so."

They lapsed into silence again as Ethan wracked his brain for a plan or something the villagers could do to prepare. He wasn't a tactician, except maybe in boss fights. And this was no boss fight. It was more like a large-scale battle in one of those wargames. Wargames he didn't really play.

He had magic, but no time to sleep and restore his *Stamina*. Or maybe he could sleep, once they got to the village. Maybe a few hours would work. If not, he was next to useless. He had no real skill with weapons. The only thing he had to offer was his magic.

They continued walking, not stopping for lunch or dinner. Instead, they grabbed berries and occasionally took long drinks from the river. The river did actually restore his *Stamina*, but like before, it never went above half.

As they marched into the night, he summoned orbs of light to illuminate their path. Ethan thought about what Nia had said about the pass being narrow. Hadn't the Spartans held a narrow pass with only 300 men in that movie? Of course, those had been 300 warriors who had trained since birth and, in the movie, had abs of steel.

But maybe he could use a little ingenuity to turn the tables. After all, he came from the most advanced civilization of anyone he'd met. He needed to put that knowledge to use. Ethan needed to come up with a plan.

The night wore on and they stopped at every farmhouse and warned them. They told the people what was coming and to come to the village. He wasn't sure that would make a difference, but if the farmers stayed in their homes, the kobolds would surely get them.

Most of the people thanked them, but his group was threatened multiple times. Only their armor and the weapons they carried kept some of the farmers from trying to run them through with wood pitchforks or rakes. But at least they listened.

The suns were just rising when the exhausted group finally made it into Hawkshead. No one appeared to be awake yet. They trudged to the inn and began banging on the door until they heard cursing on the other side and the door was yanked open.

Fearghas stood there in a sleeping robe and a long hat on his head that reminded Ethan of something Scrooge wore in several of the movie versions. His eyes were red with sleep and in his hand he held his table leg cudgel.

The innkeeper opened his mouth, probably to curse them, but saw their somber expressions. "What is it? Something is wrong?"

"The kobolds are coming to wipe out the village," Ethan told the dwarven innkeeper.

"What? Don't be daft! They've never so much as set foot in the village. Why would they wipe it out?" the dwarf said with a yawn. Then his eyes grew wide. "And why do you have a kobold with you? And a mountain lion!"

"He's the last survivor of his tribe," Ethan replied. "The tribe that Cuthbert armed wiped out the other tribes, which I'm guessing were holding each other in check. Now that the Cave Clan has wiped out the other clans and are coming for the farms and villages. Oh, and the cat is Yuliana's companion."

The dwarf shook his fist angrily. "If Cuthbert wasn't already dead, I'd kill him myself. That scoundrel. Bringing this down on the village."

Moving back from the door, the innkeeper held it open and motioned them inside. "You might as well come in. Me and the Mrs. are already up. I'll see if she can whip you up some breakfast since it looks like you walked all night."

Fearghas watched Par'karr and Luna with narrowed eyes but allowed them to enter. He shut the door and turned the back. Dragging the cudgel on the floor, the innkeeper disappeared into the backroom and they heard him stomping up stairs.

They all sat down at the only cleared table and Ethan pulled up a chair for Par'karr to sit on. The little kobold seemed extremely curious about the entire place, his head darting around and taking in the room. "This is... house?"

"It's an inn," Ethan explained. "It has rooms where many people stay."

"Like communal huts!" The kobold nodded.

"Not quite like that," Ethan replied. "But close enough."

The kobold continued to take in the room and a few minutes later, they heard Fearghas and his wife stomping down the stairs. The innkeeper came into the room and Ethan saw Elspeth walk past the doorway and into the kitchen.

"I'm going to get the others up," the dwarf said, heading for the door. He stopped and chuckled. "No reason they should sleep late if I can't."

Thirty minutes later, they were finishing up some scrambled eggs and bread as the common room began to fill with people. Ethan immediately recognized some of the people as farmers. The farmers had listened to them after all.

Fearghas had returned and was arguing with several of the

other townspeople. Voices grew loud and finally the innkeeper bellowed out loud enough for everyone to hear. "Ask the mayor. He brought the news."

Farmers quieted down and looked around while the town people all looked at Ethan. Soon, everyone was looking at him, waiting for him to speak.

Swallowing, Ethan stood up and pushed in the chair. The sound it made seemed especially loud in the sudden quiet of the common room.

"The...uh..." He cleared his throat. "The kobolds are coming. They plan to burn down all of the farms and then burn down the village."

Pandemonium erupted as people began cursing, asking questions and talking to each other. One angry voice, he recognized it as Hamish's, called out. "You went and done stirred them up!"

More noise erupted and this time it sounded angrier and more than one person pointed at Ethan. He needed to get this mob under control before something bad happened. "Listen! Listen!"

He waited for the talking to settle down before continuing. "We didn't stir them up. That was Cuthbert, the former mayor. He gave them weapons in exchange for keeping travelers and caravans from reaching the village. They did that but they also used those weapons on the other kobold clans and wiped them out. Now they want to reclaim what they believe is their valley - and that includes the farms and the village."

The people began talking again, but at least there wasn't any finger pointing this time. Ethan let it go on for several minutes before calling for silence again. "You really only have two choices. You can leave." He paused for dramatic effect. "Or you can stay and fight."

The farmers and townspeople all began talking. Through it he heard several repeating themes.

"Can't leave. Got no place to go."

"We ain't no militia. How are we supposed to fight?"

"This mayor's out of his mind!"

Hamish's voice called out over the others, causing a momentary lull in the yelling. "What about you, mayor? What are you doing?"

Everyone went silent and turned to Ethan, even his own companions. He looked to his group and then looked out at the mob of people in front of him. There were men, women and children among the group and he realized he couldn't just abandon them to be slaughtered.

He took a deep breath. "Whatever you all decide, I am with you. If you want to leave, I'll go with you. If you want to fight..." Ethan paused, knowing he may be signing his own death warrant. "If you want to fight, then I'll fight with you."

That elicited some more somber talk between the people. Several of them glanced his way several times. Finally, Fearghas stepped forward. "This is my inn. It's all I got. I will stay and fight."

"Aye," Hamish said as he stepped next to Fearghas. He clapped a hand on the innkeeper's shoulder. "Me too. I got no other place to go and no money to start over. I will fight."

"I will stay too," said one of the farmers, who stepped forward with his two children and his wife.

One by one, the people stepped forward to say they would fight. Ethan saw the desperate and haunted looks in the farmers' faces. None of them had any place to go and if they tried the journey to the city, which Fearghas had told him was a two-week journey, most of them wouldn't make it. And that was if they could make it past the kobolds.

Staying and fighting was the only chance these people had. They all realized it. They just didn't like it. And they didn't expect to win.

*You have received a new quest "Defend
    Hawkshead I"*
*The kobold Cave Clan is coming to
    destroy the village of Hawkshead. The
    villagers and farmers are looking to
    you to save the village.*
*Prevent the village from being destroyed
    (0/1).*
*Reward: 500 experience, +500 reputation
    with Residents of Hawkshead, +500
    reputation with Farmers of Arrowpoint
    Valley*
Accept quest (yes or no)?

Looking at the mob of people and then at the quest, Ethan sighed. The people were looking to him to lead them. To come up with a plan that would allow them to live. And he was a normal average guy. Just a computer tech with no experience leading or fighting. A geek. A gamer.

He chuckled to himself and accepted the quest. Ethan saw the women's eyes had gone blank too as they must have also gotten the quests.

He chuckled at the absurdity of the situation and of him leading a town. They were all doomed.

34

Unable to come up with a plan on the spot, he had told the assembled crowd to search all of the buildings to see if they could find any weapons. He'd sent several of the young men to run up to the old mining company and fetch the remaining armor and weapons from the brigands. There wasn't much there, but it was something.

Next, Ethan made a quick tour of the village. Even to his untrained eyes, he knew it wasn't defensible. Whoever the original settlers of the village had been, they hadn't had defense in mind when putting up the buildings.

He did note that the river running through the village was too fast and too wide to easily ford. The only easy crossing was the stone bridge. He didn't know any easy way to destroy the bridge, but at least it was a choke point.

After looking at the village, his group went to the pass. The pass was a narrow passage between two sheer rock walls. The pass was about fifty feet long and the road that ran between them was only large enough for a single wagon. It was a good choke point with no way around it. If only they had some Spartans to defend it.

He yawned. Lack of sleep was catching up with him and it was getting harder to focus. Ethan would need to get some sleep soon, if for no other reason than to regenerate his *Stamina*.

Stretching his stiff neck, he glanced up at the top of the rock wall to his left. There were plants hanging over the edge of the wall. He looked to the right. There were plants there too. Did that mean there was room up there to stand? If so, that changed things dramatically.

Ethan started formulating a plan. It was a simple plan, but it just might work. But they would need to start making preparations now.

"You have a plan?" Yuliana asked, head tilted and eyebrow arched.

Ainslee snorted. "Either that, or he figured out a way for us to all get our arses out of here."

"I have a plan. " He smiled.

The dwarf put her hands on her hips. "Let's hear it, wizard-boy."

He pointed to the tops of the rock walls. "I want to place archers or even stone throwers up there, provided there's enough room.

"Is there even enough room up there?" the dwarf asked, looking between the walls.

"I was thinking I can get some of the men to build a ladder out of trees and we can check it out. It'll take some time, but if there is room up there, we might be able to surprise them with the high ground," he said.

Nia looked between the two walls and without a word, leaped halfway up the right wall. She hit the wall lightly and must have used her claws to grab the sides before jumping again and disappearing over the top edge.

The other three stood at the bottom with their mouths open for a long moment. Then Nia poked her head over the edge. "There is enough room up here for maybe four or five men."

Nia disappeared for a long moment and then jumped across the space separating the two walls and landed on the other side. They heard a thud and then some hissing.

"Nia!" Ethan shouted. "Are you okay?"

The foxgirl's angry face popped over the side. Even from where he was, he could see that her face was covered in burrs. Nia angrily pulled one from her fur and tossed it down. "There are thorny bushes that attach to you up here. They will need to be cleared but then four or five men could stand up here too."

Nia jumped down, landing in that familiar superhero style pose with one knee bent and fist on the ground. He winced. That had to be hard on the knees. The foxgirl grimaced as she stood up.

It was easy to see why. She had burrs stuck all over her body. Even the leather jerkin she wore over her chest and back was covered.

"Is this some sort of magic?!" Nia demanded as she began pulling the burrs from her.

Ethan shook his head. "No, just a type of sticker plant. We have all sorts of them on my world."

"We have none!" Nia snapped as she pulled several more off. "They are like living creatures!"

After a little hesitancy, Nia allowed them all to help pull the burrs from her. It took them almost ten minutes to pull the three-inch-wide burrs off the foxgirl but finally she was free of the little thorny spheres.

"Okay," he said. "We don't need a ladder built. But I will need you to jump back up there with some rope so that we can get people up there."

Nia frowned but nodded.

"If you put rope at top," Par'karr said, looking up at the

walls. "Me climb up and clear stickers. They not stick to kobolds."

Ethan looked the little kobold up and down and realized the creature's scaled skin probably gave the burrs nothing to latch onto. "That would be great, Par'karr."

The kobold grinned broadly. "Par'karr help!"

"That's not going to stop them all, wizard-boy," Ainslee pointed out. "And some of those kobolds had bows."

"True." He nodded. "But that's only part of my plan. Come on."

Ethan began walking back to the village. He needed to check with the villagers on whether or not they actually had the items he needed for the next part of his plan.

"What is the rest of your plan?" Yuliana asked. As usual, the mountain lion padded along next to her and the elf had her hand rested on Luna's neck.

"I'm going to burn them." He grinned.

"Burn them?" The elf looked at him quizzically. "With your fireballs?"

"No. I have no idea how many fireballs I can create before I run out of stamina," he started to reply.

"And then you're a tired lump," Ainslee cut in.

"Yes." He smirked. "Then I'm a tired lump. I'm actually thinking of a more mundane way."

"Mundane way?" Yuliana asked.

"I'm thinking Molotov cocktails." He grinned. The women stopped and exchanged confused looks but then hurried after him.

The group went back to the inn and Ethan asked Ainslee and some of the farmers who had axes to start chopping down small trees, saplings and large branches. He wanted them stripped and the ends sharpened.

Both Odelina and Hamish had ropes, so Ethan instructed Nia and Par'karr to knot the rope so it would be easy to climb and then go back to the walls and start clearing the tops of the rock walls.

He asked Yuliana to tally up the weapons and especially the bows and arrows, since those would primarily be their ranged weapons.

Then he talked to Fearghas and Elspeth about oil and hay. His idea was simple. Scatter hay all around the ground of the pass. Then, when all of the kobolds were in the pass, they would drop Molotov cocktails on the ground and set as many kobolds on fire as they could, while also lighting the hay to cause even more chaos.

Once the kobolds were in disarray, the men could rain arrows down on them until they retreated. With the fire and arrows raining down from above, it might be enough to repel them. If not, they'd set up abatis, a row of sharpened spikes, at the end of the pass. Combine that with some long sharp sticks that the men could stab the kobolds with through the abatis, and they might just have a chance.

But he wasn't deluding himself. If the kobolds broke through the abatis, the villagers would be hard-pressed to fight them off. Ethan was hoping that if enough of the little creatures died in the fire and then at the abatis, they would leave.

"Oil doesn't light like that," Fearghas said with a shake of his head. "Not sure what kind of oil you got at wherever you're from, but our oil is mostly animal fat. You really got to work to light it up. Once it's lit, it stays lit, but it's the devil to light."

Ethan frowned and slumped back in his chair. He'd been counting on being able to make Molotov cocktails that the men could hurl down. Now, it seemed like that wouldn't work. So much for his shock and awe plan.

"Sorry, lad," the dwarf said. The dwarf suddenly looked thoughtful and eyed Ethan up and down before speaking again. "Now, there is something that might do what you have in mind." The dwarf paused. "Dwarven spirits."

"Dwarven spirits." He grinned.

Ethan looked the dwarf in the eyes. "Do you have some dwarven spirits?"

"You don't think I'd give the good stuff to those graycloak brigands, do ya?" He grinned. "I make it down in the basement with me still."

"And it's more flammable?" Ethan asked.

"You could say that," the dwarf chuckled and then looked around the room before lowering his voice. "Almost burned down the whole place a few times. But it burns fast."

Sitting back in his chair, Ethan considered the dwarf's words. He thought he remembered reading somewhere that Molotov cocktails were made from motor oil and gasoline. He couldn't remember why, but maybe if he added some oil to the dwarven spirits, that would help it burn long and possibly stick to their enemies.

"How much do you have?" Ethan asked.

"Two hand kegs." The dwarf smiled.

"How much is in a hand keg?"

Fearghas got up from his chair. "Let's go down to the basement and I can show you."

Ethan followed the dwarf down into the basement. It was dank and smelled of ale, mead and something Ethan couldn't quite place. The closest thing he could associate with the smell was bourbon.

The dwarf showed him over to a large wooden table near what could only be some sort of still. Sitting on the table were small wooden casks that appeared to hold about two gallons. "One's full. The other..." Fearghas gave him a sheepish look. "... about half full."

"How strong is it?" Ethan asked. He remembered that the proof had to be fairly high for alcohol to burn easily.

Fearghas grinned but didn't answer. Instead, he walked over to the table, grabbed two mugs and poured some of the brown-gold liquid into them. He handed one to Ethan and then clanked their mugs together. "Cheers, lad."

The dwarf threw back his cup, drinking the contents down. He brought the cup down and smiled. "Good stuff."

Ethan smelled the liquid. It smelt smoky and strong, almost like straight grain alcohol. Trying to imitate the dwarf, he slammed the mug back and gulped down the dwarven spirits. At least, that was what he intended to do.

The harsh, smoky alcohol burned all the way down his throat and he couldn't help coughing as it scorched his throat. Fearghas erupted into laughter as Ethan struggled to cough and catch his breath.

"Good... stuff," he croaked, his throat still burning. "I think that will work. Just keep it away from Ainslee."

35

After an hour of testing, Fearghas and Ethan found that mixing 50% oil and 50% dwarven spirits was the right mixture to create a longer-lasting fire that ignited quickly. Unfortunately, that used up almost all of the half keg. Gauging by the amount they used, they could make two dozen of the improvised molotov cocktails. Ethan hoped it was enough for his plan.

By that time, the men had chopped down dozens of saplings and some thicker trees. Ethan showed them where and how to place them into the ground so they were pointed at waist level to the kobolds.

The ground was still slightly muddy from the recent rainfall, so they were able to push the sharpened sticks into the ground. This created a pointed barrier that he hoped would slow the kobolds down long enough for the men to get some stabs in.

Ethan had them stack bales of hay to make shields they could stand behind in case the kobolds threw spears or had bows. The bales were far enough away from the oil-soaked hay the children and women lying down in the pass would be hiding in, that it shouldn't affect them. Just in case, he told the men to make sure they had buckets of water from the river to drench their bales when they saw the fireworks go off.

Next, he checked on their collection of weapons. It wasn't much. They had several short swords and daggers, a few large knives they'd found in the abandoned houses, six bows, and two crossbows from the brigands. There were also a number of axes and hatchets, but most of those were in use by the men chopping trees. There weren't nearly as many weapons as he had been hoping for.

The people around the weapons looked at Ethan hopefully. He could see the fear on their faces. These were not fighters. These were common people in a life and death situation, and it showed. But for now, his plan - the only plan anyone had offered - gave them hope.

At the moment, Ethan was mustering all of the confidence he could. He'd been in situations with customers where he had no idea what was wrong with their computers, but he'd found that as long as he appeared confident, the customer didn't get upset. The moment he looked panicked, so did they.

This situation was a little more important than some accountant losing their records or some mom losing her children's baby pictures because their hard drives crashed. This was literal life or death. He still hadn't decided whether this was a simulation or real life, but in the end it didn't matter. Those others they'd found the first day were dead. Simulation or reality didn't seem to matter, death was permanent.

Yuliana and several of the farmers and most of the villagers were nearby, waiting for him to say something.

"This is all we could find," the elf told him, motioning to the collection of weapons.

Ethan looked down at the variety of weapons. With the exception of the few bows and crossbows, they were all close-range weapons. Close-range weapons that would be in the hands of inexperienced people.

Ethan wracked his brain, summoning up all of his role-playing games, dungeon mastering and MMO experience. Was there something that could help him? Some nugget of wisdom he had inadvertently learned?

Then it hit him! In medieval times and in many fantasy games, the local militia men and even foot soldiers all carried spears. There was a reason for that. Sure, one of the reasons was cost. A metal spear head was much cheaper and took much less skill to make than a sword. But the main reason was, it was easy to use and gave the person a much longer reach.

He surveyed the weapons again and called over Ainslee, who was helping to stack hay bales around the barricade. The dwarf looked relieved and hurried over.

"What do you want, wiz-" the dwarf started but Ethan and Yuliana both gave her a hard look. Ainslee had almost called him wizard-boy. Ethan being a wizard was supposed to be a secret. She made a face and then continued. "What do you want WITH me?"

He snorted at the lackluster save. "Did you ever work with weapons before?"

The dwarf surveyed the pile of weapons and shrugged. "A bit, but mostly axes and hammers."

"Think you can take these apart and mount the short swords and daggers on the end of some of those long thin saplings?" he asked.

The dwarf screwed up her face as she looked at the hodge-podge collection of weapons.

"They don't have to be pretty or last longer than the battle," he told her. "But a metal tip is going to puncture those kobolds much better than a sharpened stick."

"I guess I could pull apart the pommels and handles and try

to mount the blades in the poles," she mumbled. "But it won't be pretty."

"It doesn't have to be," he told her. "It just needs to hold together for the fight."

"I guess so. But I'm gonna need some tools," she said.

"We'll get you whatever we can," he told her.

"Aye," Fearghas said and elbowed Hamish. Both dwarves had come over to look at the weapons and to, presumably, hear what Ethan would say.

"Yah, the lass wants." Hamish grinned and tried to make eye contact with Ainslee. But Ainslee was looking down at the pile of weapons, moving things around and muttering to herself.

"Great," Ethan said. "Grab whoever you need to help you."

Ethan tried to stifle a yawn but failed. Yuliana looked at him with concern. "You should get some sleep while people work on things. You will need your stamina for the fight."

He started to object but another yawn interrupted him and he nodded. "Maybe you're right."

"Yah, mayor," Fearghas said. "Everyone's got their orders. You get some rest. You look dead on your feet."

Nodding, he started to turn and then spun back around. "Scouts! We need scouts!"

"Scouts?" Yuliana repeated.

"We need to know when to get people ready," he told her. "I'll check with Nia and Par'karr."

He walked past the barricade and back to the pass, where he found the kobold and the foxgirl still clearing away brush and trees.

"Par'karr! Nia!" he called up to them. "Let some of the farmers or villagers finish that up. I need you two for something else."

The foxgirl growled and threw down a large shrub before leaping down and doing her superhero landing. Par'karr stared open mouthed at what Nia had done, then looked at how far down it was.

Shrugging, the little kobold shook its head and ran over to the rope. The deft little creature scurried down until it was about ten feet from the bottom and then dropped and did a similar landing - though perhaps not quite as graceful. Standing up, the little kobold gave them a toothy grin and ran over.

"Par'karr helping!" he told Ethan and looked to Nia for confirmation.

Nia rolled her eyes but Ethan saw the corners of her mouth curling up. "Yes, Par'karr helped!" She looked to Ethan. "What do you need now?"

"We will need scouts," he told them. "Someone to warn us when the kobolds are approaching."

Ethan looked down the rocky road that led down the slope. The good thing about the position of the town was, there was no other way to get in, so the kobolds would be forced to use the road. The bad thing was that the road wound around the mountain, obscuring a direct line of sight.

Nia seemed to understand. "You need someone to go out and watch for them, then run back as soon as they are spotted, yes?"

"Yes." He nodded. "You two are the logical choices."

Nia nodded.

"Shall we go now?" the foxgirl asked.

"Par'karr can go," he said. "I'm going back to get some sleep and you should come with me. It will be dark in a few hours and your night vision will be more useful at night."

He saw the corner of the foxgirl's mouth flinch and her eyebrows rose. "You want me to come to sleep with you?"

Ethan felt his face grow warm and knew he must be turning red. That wasn't what he had meant at all. Not that she wasn't attractive, in a primal way. He rubbed his forehead with his fingers. He was tired, so tired. And now he had embarrassed himself.

"No," he sputtered. "That's not what I meant. I mean... you should come back... to the village with me and... you know... sleep in your room... by yourself... not with me."

The foxgirl emitted what seemed like a cross between a laugh and a purr, but nodded. "Yes, I will come back to the village with you. You are right. I can see much better in the dark."

"I'm trusting you, Par'karr," he said. "To warn us. Can you handle that?"

The little kobold stood up straight. "Me can handle! Me run back! Warn you!"

"Good," he said. "Find a spot a mile or so away. If you see them, run back as fast as you can so we have time to get prepared."

"Me will!" said the kobold and turned and raced off. He got about a hundred yards before he stopped, turned around and ran back. He went over to the rock wall and grabbed his little spear before grinning at them and running back down the hill.

"You think we can trust the kobold?" Nia asked, her eyes following the retreating kobold.

"I think so," he said and watched the little kobold go around the bend in the road. There was something about the little kobold that he did trust. Ethan couldn't quite put his finger on it, but he did trust Par'karr. He really hoped he wasn't being foolish or naive. He lowered his voice to a whisper. "I hope so."

He and Nia turned to go back to the village. As they did, the foxgirl turned to him. "It happens sometimes that our alpha will give his wives to another alpha. But my alpha is not here to give me to you. So we cannot sleep together."

"Wha-?" he muttered, unsure if he had heard her correctly.

"You are the alpha of the village," she said. "I am the seventeenth wife. It is not uncommon for twelfth and lower to be traded as terms of an alliance. But my alpha is not here to trade me. So we cannot sleep together."

"I told you," he replied. "That's not what I meant."

The foxgirl waved away his objection. "You are a male. That is all you think about."

He opened his mouth and then closed it without saying anything. While that might be true in a normal situation, this was far from a normal situation. In fact, nothing about this was normal. He wasn't even normal any more. He could do magic and he fought kobolds and two-headed wolves. That was not normal!

Of course, with her having put the thought in his mind, he let his eyes rove up her body, noting the toned physique. But when his eyes reached her eyes, he realized she had caught him leering.

There was no judgement in her eyes, just a bit of mischief. When she spoke, her voice had a note of triumph. "See, I told you that's all males think of."

His face hot, he snapped his eyes forward. Staying silent, Ethan didn't trust himself to reply. He had embarrassed himself enough for one day.

36

Ethan woke up a few hours later with a start. He'd been having that dream about being chased again and he found he was sweating. Blinking and slightly disoriented, he looked around.

It was dark in the room, which meant the sun had gone down. He heard a light snoring near the foot of his bed. Was someone in here with him? Sleeping on the floor? He yawned and summoned a small ball of light.

Looking at the source of the snoring, he found a small form huddled in an old blanket on the floor, at the foot of the bed. It was Par'karr. The little kobold's eyes were closed and his chest rose and fell in a steady rhythm. Ethan frowned. If Par'karr was back, how long had he slept?

"Ethan!" came Yuliana's frantic voice from the front room. "Are you awake?"

"Yah. I'm awake," he called out. As he did, Par'karr stirred in his sleep.

"They are coming!" she said, her voice cracking with fear. "Nia said they will be here in half an hour."

"I'll be right out," he called, jumping out of bed. He nudged the kobold awake as he slipped into his leather breeches.

The little kobold scratched and yawned. It turned to him with slitted eyes. "It morning?"

"They're coming," Ethan said as he slipped his boots on.

Par'karr hopped up, turning around in a full circle until he spotted his spear in the corner. He hopped over to it and snatched it up. Holding it in a ready position, he turned to Ethan. "Me ready!"

"Almost ready," Ethan grunted and slid his jerkin over his head. Grabbing his knife belt and quarterstaff, Ethan stumbled towards the door. He let the ball of light fade as he walked through the front room so none of the villagers would see it.

Stopping in front of Yuliana, he quickly checked his HUD.

Stamina: 56

He knew the ball of light he created didn't use four *Stamina*, so he must not have gotten enough sleep. Ethan would have to make do.

Yuliana looked up at him and he could see she was terrified. Before coming to this world, she'd tended a grove. She'd never had to deal with this sort of large-scale violence. There wasn't even the simulated violence of video games. This was all new for her.

Ethan placed a hand on the elf's shoulder. Part of him was scared too, but he forced it down. He let his customer service skills take over and he forced a smile. "Everything will be alright. We'll get through this. You will be back here with the villagers, healing them."

The elf smiled up at him but it didn't reach her eyes. She turned and took a step back so she was next to him, revealing a sea of faces looking at him. Many of them were carrying torches, which illuminated the area in a flickering orange-yellow light. Some looked haggard, like they hadn't slept. Others looked like they had just been woken up.

He saw Nia, learning against Ainslee. The foxgirl was breathing hard and it was the first time he'd seen her out of breath. She must have run the entire way. He gave her a nod and she returned it.

He looked out at the villagers. They were all staring at him. Waiting for him to speak. To tell them what to do. To save them. He suppressed a smirk. No pressure.

Struggling to keep a calm and brave face, Ethan took a deep breath. He hated speaking in front of people and he hated being responsible for so many people. But now wasn't the time to second guess himself. Now it was time to put the group leader face on and pretend this was a dungeon raid and he was talking to his buddies.

"The kobolds are on their way," he said. The crowd must have already known this but still there was muttering, moaning and even some crying from the assembled crowd. He waited for a moment and then continued. "I want the women and men who won't be fighting to take the children over the bridge. The entire thing is covered in the oiled hay. If the kobolds break through, then light it up and go to the mines. Find someplace and hide out as long as you can."

More crying, though this time it sounded like children instead of villagers. "Men and women who will be fighting, you've been broken up into squads?"

He'd given instructions to Hamish and Fearghas before he'd lain down. They were to pick out the men and women who would use bows or throw stones really good. Those people would be on the ridge. The others - those who could fight - would be behind the barrier with spears. Ethan was hoping they had done as he asked.

There were half-hearted nods and mutters but then a

familiar voice called out. It was Hamish. "Yah. We're ready to do our part, mayor."

"Yeah," came another voice. This time he recognized it as Odelina. He spotted the butcher to his left. The woman was armed with her bow. He knew from Fearghas that Odelina was a good hunter and always had venison, rabbits or even an occasional elk to share with the villagers. She was one of the ones who would be joining him on the ridge.

"We're ready," came Fearghas' voice as he muscled his way to the front. He had his cudgel in his right hand and was slapping it into his left. "Ready to teach those kobolds a lesson."

Ethan smiled and nodded. "We're fighting for the village but we're also fighting for our lives. Show them no mercy because they will show none to you."

He waited for some sort of reaction or cheer or some acknowledgment that they'd even heard him. When nothing was forthcoming he sighed. That's what happened when you had an average *Charisma* score. "Alright. You know where you need to go. Everyone get to their stations and get ready."

The people began to move in different directions and Ethan watched them go. All except for Fearghas, Hamish and Odelina. The three villagers came over and stopped in front of him.

"We did what we could while you slept," the innkeeper said. "The mackerel cocktails are up on the ridge, we broke two getting them up there but there's still plenty."

"Molotov cocktails." Ethan smiled.

Fearghas waved away his correction. "Whatever they are. They're up on the ridge. I have a hooded lantern up there on each side. We can open them when the kobolds are in position and light the mack...molly love cocktails."

"Good job," he told the innkeeper, not bothering to correct him this time.

"I'll be up there too," Odelina said, giving him a wink. "I'm pretty handy with a bow."

He flashed her a smile. "So I hear."

"And I'll be down here with this rabble, skewering kobold devils," Hamish muttered. The dwarf's eyes went to Par'karr, who was on the other side of Ethan. He coughed. "Uh, no offense."

"Me not offended," his kobold companion said. Par'karr stabbed his spear in the air several times. "Me skewer kobold devils too!"

Hamish grunted. "Ah, yah. Just be careful you don't get mixed up with the other kobolds."

"Thanks for all your help," he told the villagers. "If you want to get your posts, I have a few last-minute things to talk over with the ladies."

Fearghas gave him a sly wink. "Of course, we'll get going."

As the villagers moved off towards the barrier, Nia and Ainslee walked over. The foxgirl was still breathing a little heavy but looked mostly recovered.

"Good job with the warning," he told her.

Nia gave him a weak smile and nodded. "They were easy to spot in the dark with their torches. You were right. There must be a hundred of them."

He nodded grimly. "And there's no way I can convince you to go full lethal on them?"

"They are not prey," she retorted sharply, but then her face softened. "I will do what I can. But I cannot kill them unless they are prey. I will be behind the barrier, if any kobolds get through."

"Well," huffed Ainslee. "I have no compunction about it. I'm going to grab me one of those spears and run me through some kobolds."

He smiled at the dwarf. "Skewer all you want."

They all turned and looked at Yuliana, who blushed under

the attention. "I will heal all I can."

As she said it, Luna came from around the corner and leisurely walked over to rub up against the elf. "Luna will protect me if any kobolds get through."

"We must go," Nia interrupted. "They will be here soon."

"Good luck, you three," he told them.

"You know," Yuliana called after him, "you may need to use your..." The elf lowered her voice. "...wizardry."

"Yeah." Ethan nodded. "I guess I'll cross that bridge when I get to it."

"Bridge?" the women asked and looked to the north.

He sighed. "Not that bridge. It's a figure of speech in my world. It means, I'll deal with it when I have to."

The women shrugged and they set off for the barrier. When they reached it, he left them and continued on to the pass. Par'karr came with him.

"You coming to the ridge?" he asked the little kobold.

"Yes," he bobbed his head. "Me good thrower. Use rocks to chase away bashna!"

"Bashna?" he asked.

Par'karr furrowed his brow, or what would have been his brow if he had hair. "Hmm... like.. Small wolf. Purple and red fur, with long tail that has stinger. They like rabbits. They not get Par'karr's rabbits! Me chase them away!"

"Good to know," he chuckled as they reached the rope. He gestured up. "You first...." His words trailed off as he saw a mass of torches round the bend in the road. They were here and only a few hundred yards away.

"Go, Park'arr," he hissed. "Go fast!"

The two of them scrambled up the rope as quickly as they could and then Ethan turned and pulled the rope up. Without it, the rope wouldn't be able to scale the walls. He and the villagers would be safe until they revealed themselves.

He hoped.

37

"**D**o you have any sort of special night vision?" Ethan whispered to Par'karr as the army of kobolds approached.

"Night vision?" Par'karr repeated, his tone confused.

"Can kobolds see well in the dark?" Ethan rephrased his question.

"Yes," the little kobold whispered back. "Kobold see better than humans. Still need light. Not see if no light. Unless moon bright."

Nodding, he turned back to the oncoming mass of torch-bearing kobolds. Ethan remembered that when he had sent the air elemental to scout the kobold cave, they'd had the passages and caverns illuminated with torchlight. There would be no point if they could see in absolute darkness.

Par'karr's admission confirmed his earlier suspicions. The kobolds needed some light to see. Their eyes just processed it better. Like a cat's eyes. Or, in game terms, that meant they had low-light vision, not some ability to see in total darkness like darkvision or infravision. Ethan wasn't sure how that helped him at the moment, but he filed away the information.

Carefully setting his Molotov cocktail down, Ethan wiped his sweaty palms on his jerkin. He had been too busy or too tired to feel nervous before but now, with the conflict only minutes away, he found that he was nervous. Maybe more than nervous. Maybe there was a little fear there too.

This would be an all-out conflict, not some simple skirmish with a few kobolds or wolves. And if his plan failed, if the kobolds got into the town, then they'd eventually find their way to the mine. If they did that, they'd find the women and children. And their deaths would be on his head.

No! Ethan had to remind himself that Cuthbert, not him or his group, had put this into motion when he'd given weapons to the kobolds. If they hadn't gone after the kobolds and learned of their plans, all of these people would probably have died in their sleep.

But still. It was Ethan giving them hope. It was his plan. Maybe one of the others could have come up with a better plan. After all, Nia was more of a warrior than he'd ever be. Maybe she could have come up with a better one. Maybe.

The kobolds were closer now. Only 50 yards away from the pass. Ethan forced himself to focus. He would need to give the signal for the attack. Taking slow deep breaths, he watched the kobolds continue into the pass.

The creatures moved in a staggered, chaotic formation. They seemed to be clustered up in small groups, rather than in any real skirmish line. The kobolds were just in range of his *Analyze* skill and the gamer in him couldn't waste the opportunity to analyze them and get some skill ups.

Cave Clan Raider
Kobold
Warrior
Level 2
Skill increase: Analyze +1%.

He got dozens of skill ups as the kobolds went past him. As more and more of them entered the pass, the vanguard started to reach the far end. Depending on how good their eyesight was, they would see the barricade. It was time to spring the trap.

"Light!" he yelled and the hooded lanterns were thrown open. The mass of kobolds halted the moment they saw the light from the ridges, turning and peering up at the top of the ridges. Even from where he was, he could hear the muttered voices of the kobolds far below.

"Keep moving!" boomed a voice from the back. Squinting, Ethan could see a larger kobold towards the back. He recognized it as the same one who had been giving the speech in the cavern, the chieftain.

The oil-soaked cloth for his Molotov cocktail lit and Ethan held it away from his body. He waited until all six of the others had their cocktails lit as well before waving his in the air to signal the other side.

Someone on the other side waved theirs, signalling that they were ready too. Ethan looked over the edge and saw that the kobolds were moving towards the village again, but slower this time. Most of them continued to cast glances up at the stone walls. They were worried. And with good reason.

"Throw!" Ethan shouted and tossed his Molotov cocktail. He had aimed at the chieftain and, despite his normal lack of physical prowess, his aim was true. The clay jar filled with dwarven spirits and oil soared through the air directly at the big kobold. Then, at the last second, it shot to the left.

His Molotov cocktail hit some random kobold near the leader. It bounced to the ground and shattered, igniting that kobold and several around it. At the same time, the other villagers' jars hit all around the pass, exploding into flame and igniting the oil-soaked hay.

The villagers quickly grabbed another round of Molotov

cocktails and began lighting them. Ethan didn't move. He was staring at the kobold just to the right of the leader. The one who had made a gesture, just as his cocktail had gone off course.

But the gesture wasn't what had gotten Ethan's attention. It was the glowing blue tip of the stick in the creature's hand. Could that be some sort of wand? And if so, did that make the creature a magic user like him? Maybe even a wizard?

"Par'karr!" he hissed, gesturing at the little kobold who was grinning and lighting his second cocktail.

Par'karr glanced between his Molotov cocktail and Ethan, obviously torn. He frowned and handed his jar to one of the other men before hurrying over to the edge with Ethan. "Me help?"

"Maybe," Ethan replied and pointed out the glowing tip of the wand as the kobold wielding it flicked and swished the wand, causing some of the jars to slam into the stone wall. The Molotov cocktails that did broke open and spilt their contents on the rock instead of the kobolds. "Who or what is that?"

The kobold glanced down and then ducked back, eyes wide. "That medicine man. Make big magic like you."

Ethan grimaced when the kobold mentioned him doing magic but none of the men seemed to notice. They were all too busy raining down fiery death on the screaming kobolds below. "So it's a wizard?"

Par'karr shrugged. "Medicine man. Make magic. Fire magic. Water magic. Sometimes make things move."

Fire. Water. Air. Those were the elements. The same elements his own magic allowed him to manipulate. It had to be a wizard. But what was it doing with the wand? How was it using it? And why wasn't it looking fatigued? It was using a lot of magic. More than Ethan could have used without tiring. Did the wand have anything to do with that?

Before he could think of it any longer, one of the farmers

who was about to throw his Molotov cocktail was suddenly yanked from the edge by invisible hands. The man screamed as he fell, but that ended abruptly when he hit the ground. His Molotov cocktail hit a second later and burst into flame but the man was already dead and didn't flinch.

The medicine man was yanking people off with air. He turned the other men. "Stay away from the edge. Throw your jars from... Ahh!"

His words cut off as he felt invisible hands yank him from the ledge. He would have gone flying if it weren't for Par'karr's quick reflexes. The little kobold grabbed his hand, nearly being pulled over himself. The kobold used one hand to grab onto the stump of a sapling they'd cut down but in doing so, his grip on Ethan's hand slipped.

Ethan began to fall down, but the kobold's quick action had swung him against the wall. The wall was sheer, but still had small outcroppings that Ethan desperately tried to grab onto. Doing so scraped his fingers raw and he thought he might have lost a fingernail.

You are scraped for 1 damage.
You are scraped for 1 damage.
You are scraped for 1 damage.

The action caused him both pain and physical damage, but it slowed him down enough that when he hit the ground, he didn't break anything. Despite not breaking anything, he still felt the jarring pain lance up his legs.

You take 5 falling damage.

Unfortunately, he landed on some of the flaming hay. Fortunately, it was a small patch and he was able to jump to a bare spot to his right.

Fire burns you for 2 fire damage.

His *Health* was now down 10 points, and he hadn't even started fighting yet. Spinning, he saw that the medicine man was continuing to try to pull men from the ledges using air magic. But the shaman wasn't the only one with air magic.

"Two can play at that game," Ethan grumbled. "You want to go all dark side force, so be it!"

He wasn't sure if there was magic in the wand itself or the kobold was using it as some sort of focus. But given the wand's glowing blue tip, it was probably doing something to aid the shaman. The first step was to rid him of it.

Remember his favorite wizarding series and lightning-scarred boy's favorite spell, he grinned. He held out his finger like it was a wand and flourished it a bit. Swish and flick was a completely different spell, but he did it nonetheless. At the same time, Ethan reached out his own magic. He grabbed the wand in a grip of air and yanked it out of the medicine man's grip. "How's that for a disarming charm!"

Skill increase: Air magic +1%.

The medicine man's eyes went wide and he yelped as he watched his wand go sailing away. Ethan didn't hesitate but focused on grabbing the creature's throat with air, holding his arm out and squeezing his thumb and index finger together. He made his voice sound deep. Just call him Darth Ethan! "I find your lack of faith very disturbing!"

You crush Cave Clan Medicine Man for 7
    air damage.
Skill increase: Air magic +1%.
Cave Clan Medicine Man is choking.

The medicine man's eyes bulged as he felt the effects of Ethan's air choke and looked around wildly. Ethan, for his part, was focusing on the medicine man but also keeping a wary eye out for any kobolds who might attack him. At the moment, they were doing exactly what he had expected, they were running out of the pass.

You crush Cave Clan Medicine Man for 8 air damage.
Skill increase: Air magic +1%.
Cave Clan Medicine Man is choking.

The medicine man squirmed in his grasp of air, eyes wide and clutching at his throat. He was really channeling his inner dark side but this was an enemy. An enemy who had personally killed one of the farmers he was protecting. And tried to kill Ethan too. So he didn't feel too bad about it.

You crush Cave Clan Medicine Man for 8 air damage.
Skill increase: Air magic +1%.
Cave Clan Medicine Man is choking.

As Ethan continued to squeeze, the medicine man's movements became more sluggish and his eyes became unfocused. He continued to struggle weakly until his eyes closed and his body sagged.

You crush Cave Clan Medicine Man for 9 air damage.
Skill increase: Air magic +1%.
Cave Clan Medicine Man is choking.

He looked at his HUD. No experience yet. It was still alive, just unconscious. A little longer and it would be dead.

"Look out!" came Par'karr's voice from above.

Ethan looked just in time to see the chieftain barreling towards him, sword raised. He barely had time to get an air shield up to prevent being beheaded by the large kobold. But even with the air shield, he was thrown back against the wall hard.

"You magic man too," the chieftain hissed. The large kobold looked him up and down, forked tongue flicking in and out of its mouth. It gave him a toothy grin. "If I drink your blood, maybe I get magic."

Ethan swallowed hard. He was face to face with a kobold chieftain and he had nothing but a knife and whatever remained of his magic. This was going to hurt.

38

The chieftain was a head taller than the other kobolds and proportionately larger as well. Around its neck, the big kobold head wore a necklace of large claws or teeth, possibly from a bear or other large animal. Like the other kobolds, it wore no armor, probably depending on its scales to protect it.

It was armed with a steel short sword, almost identical to the ones the bandits had carried. No doubt a weapon that the treacherous Cuthbert had supplied them. Ethan cursed the man. His greed had gotten the former mayor killed and could very well be responsible for the destruction of the entire village.

Ethan brought up his HUD and examined the chieftain.

Tigna'Rorn, Cave Clan Chieftain
Kobold
Warrior
Level 5

Skill increase: Analyze +1%.

You have reached Rank 2 in Analyze.
+1 Intuition.

You have received a new quest "Defend
  Hawkshead II"
You have found Tigna'Rorn, the chieftain
  of the kobold Cave Clan, who led his
  tribe against Hawkshead. Killing him
  would scatter and dishearten the
  kobolds, preventing the kobolds from
  regrouping.

Kill Tigna'Rorn (0/1).

Reward: 375 experience, +300 reputation
  with Residents of Hawkshead, +300
  reputation with Farmers of Arrowpoint
  Valley

Accept quest (yes or no)?

He barely had time to accept the quest before Tigna'Rorn, the kobold chieftain, lunged forward. He aimed a strike at Ethan's head, but then changed the sword's trajectory to instead try to slice the blade across Ethan's thigh.

Only game-honed reflexes, and magic that acted on his thoughts, saved him from a deep gash in his leg. He deflected the strike, but had wasted some of his *Stamina* trying to parry the feint. Counting, Ethan threw a punch of *Air* to the kobold's throat.

You pummel Tigna'Rorn for 11 air damage.
Skill increase: Air Magic +1%.

Through either instinct or luck, the kobold chieftain lowered his muzzle just as Ethan threw the *Air*. Instead of the throat, the ball of air caught him in the mouth. He watched in satisfaction as one of the creature's front teeth went flying and blood ran down his muzzle.

Shaking its head, Tigna'Rorn leapt back. The big kobold slashed reflexively to keep Ethan from following but Ethan had no intention to follow him. He was feeling weak and drained and brought up his HUD to check his *Stamina*.

Stamina: 23

Ethan grimaced. Less than half of his *Stamina* remained and he hadn't made a dent in the chieftain's health. He eyed the big kobold but also kept an eye on the other kobolds running back and forth in a panic. Arrows were being rained down on them from above, though none came near the chieftain. Probably because the big kobold was too close to Ethan.

Tigna'Rorn was flicking his forked tongue in the place where his tooth used to be. He grinned at Ethan. "First blood yours, human. But last blood count more."

"Sure," Ethan muttered. He called on his *Summon Minor Elemental* and summoned the fire weasel again. The elemental formed between him and Tigna'Rorn. As it did, he felt the strength go out of him. He checked his *Stamina*.

The weasel looked to Ethan for directions. He pointed at the big kobold. "Get him!"

Stamina: 18

Now, Ethan had less than a third of his *Stamina*. He needed to be careful with the rest of it. Conserve it if he could. Around the two combatants, kobolds continued to run all around as they were cut down by arrows and rocks.

The fiery weasel bounded toward the chieftain, leaping at the kobold's throat. Unfortunately, the kobold was fast and side-stepped the elemental and sliced his sword across its torso.

> ***Tigna'Rorn slashes minor elemental***
> ***(fire) for 5 slashing damage.***

The elemental made no sound and didn't seem to be affected by the blow, but when it landed, the weasel looked smaller somehow.

Ethan tried summoning another elemental so they could flank the chieftain. When he tried, he felt a weird jarring sensation and instantly received a message on his HUD.

> ***You already have a minor elemental***
> ***(fire) summoned. Do you wish to***
> ***dismiss it and summon another***
> ***elemental? (yes or no)***

He cursed. It appeared he could only have one at a time. So much for creating an army of elementals. He would need to think of something else.

The elemental weasel leaped at the chieftain again, but once again Tigna'Rorn dodged nimbly out of the way and managed another slash on the weasel.

> ***Tigna'Rorn slashes minor elemental***
> ***(fire) for 5 slashing damage.***

This time the elemental hit the ground and lunged at the kobold's nearby leg. It seemed to bite into the chieftain's leg before Tigna'Rorn kicked it off.

> *Minor elemental (fire) burns Tigna'Rorn*
> *for 7 fire damage.*
> *Skill increase: Fire magic +1%.*

Twisting in the air, the weasel landed on its feet and squared off against the large kobold. The two circled each other for a moment before the weasel once again darted in. Tigna'Rorn leaped to the side, scoring a long slash across the side of the weasel.

> *Tigna'Rorn slashes minor elemental*
> *(fire) for 9 slashing damage.*

The fire elemental was almost half the size as it had originally been now but it didn't seem to be affected otherwise by the blows. Ethan guessed the creature's size was an indicator of its health. The smaller it got, the less health it had left. He needed to do something.

Ethan pulled his long knife free of its sheath. He would have preferred his quarterstaff, with its longer reach, or even the crossbow. Unfortunately, both were at the top of the ridge. The knife would have to do.

Watching, Ethan waited until the chieftain's back was to him and then lunged forward and attacked. Somehow, the large kobold sensed him coming and side-stepped, slashing Ethan across the ribs.

> *Tigna'Rorn slashes you 6 slashing*
> *damage.*
> *Leather armor absorbs 3 points of*
> *slashing damage.*

Left hand clutching the slash across his ribs, he slashed in the air as he backed away. He could feel the warm blood flowing through the fingers of his left hand. The wound didn't seem that bad, but he checked his *Health*.

Health: 14

He swore and the chieftain gave him a wicked grin. Tigna'Rorn brought up his sword close to his muzzle and his forked tongue darted across the blood, licking it from the blade. "First taste is sweetest. But me enjoy all your blood!"

The chieftain was obviously trying to intimidate him, but it cost him. The fiery weasel leaped onto the kobold's shoulder and bit Tigna'Rorn's neck.

Minor elemental (fire) critically burns Tigna'Rorn for 13 fire damage. Skill increase: Fire magic +1%.

The kobold yelped and brushed the elemental off his shoulder with his sword, knocking the weasel to the ground. Now the elemental was a third its original size.

Tigna'Rorn slashes minor elemental (fire) for 5 slashing damage.

Ethan realized that after another blow or two, the weasel would disappear. Should he summon another one? Would that be enough to finish off the kobold chieftain? He knew he couldn't muster a fireball. That would probably leave him unconscious. But what else did he have?

He remembered his elemental armor ability but fire wouldn't really help him against the kobold's sword. The fire wasn't hot enough to damage the metal nor was it intense enough to heat the metal to a point where the kobold would drop it. And even if he did drop it, the chieftain could probably kill him with his claws and teeth.

He slipped on the oiled hay beneath him and fell back against the wall. He caught himself with his hands and didn't go down, but the knife slid from his grasp to clatter on the stony ground.

Standing upright, Ethan looked up in time to see the weasel take another slash from Tigna'Rorn and fall back. The kobold chieftain was moving confidently. He knew the weasel wouldn't last long.

> **Tigna'Rorn slashes minor elemental**
> **(fire) for 6 slashing damage.**

The fire elemental was now a quarter the size it had been. One more blow, two at most, and it would be gone. He turned and looked for his knife and stopped when he caught sight of his hands. They were the same gray color as the wall. He looked to the wall and then his hands.

Was that elemental armor? He'd been thinking of elemental armor when he touched the rock. Could it be earth elemental armor? He tapped his hands together and didn't feel a thing. They were hard and solid like rock and yet he could move them like normal.

Movement from the corner of his eye caught his attention and he turned just in time to see the weasel cut down in the middle of a leap.

> **Tigna'Rorn slashes minor elemental**
> **(fire) for 7 slashing damage.**
> **Your minor elemental (fire) has been**
> **dismissed.**

Tigna'Rorn whirled and gave him a grin. "Your magic weak. Now you die."

Willing the elemental armor to cover him, he felt and saw his skin turning gray and craggy. It didn't hurt. In fact, like with his hands, he felt nothing. Not the clothes on his body. Nothing. Well, nothing except for more of his *Stamina* draining away.

Stamina: 13

The kobold stopped advancing and tilted his head, looking at him. "What magic is this?"

He wasn't sure how much protection the elemental armor would offer so Ethan dived for his knife. As he did the chieftain stepped forward and slashed at him. The blade slid across his armor, tearing a gash in it and then across his side.

Tigna'Rorn slashes you for 0 damage.
Leather armor absorbs 3 points of
*   slashing damage.*
Elemental armor (earth) absorbs 5 points
*   of slashing damage.*
Skill increase: Earth magic +1%.

Ethan didn't feel a thing and, according to his HUD, he hadn't taken any damage. That was good. Very good.

Grabbing the dagger, he stood up and took another slash across his chest. Once again, he took no damage and he saw the confident expression disappear from the chieftain's face.

Tigna'Rorn slashes you for 0 damage.
Leather armor absorbs 3 points of
*   slashing damage.*

> *Elemental armor (earth) absorbs 5 points*
> *of slashing damage.*
> *Skill increase: Earth magic +1%.*

He lunged out with his dagger several times, but the kobold sidestepped each time, countering with slashes to his arms and chest.

None of the blows did any damage but Ethan could sense the magic of the armor weakening. Was there a limit to how much it could absorb? He swore. How close was he to the limit? He needed to get the upper hand. But how?

He tried some feints, but they must have been obvious to the trained kobold and he ignored them, slashing at Ethan to force him back. It would be a stalemate until his earth armor disappeared. Then the chieftain would kill him.

An idea occurred to him then. He flipped the knife around in his fingers and tossed it straight at the kobold's face. His aim wasn't perfect - he'd never thrown a knife before - but it was enough to do its job. The kobold ducked his head to avoid the flying knife. And that's when Ethan tackled him.

Ethan had used the knife as the distraction and so the kobold was surprised when the earth-skinned human slammed into him. They both tumbled to the ground but he landed on top of the creature and began to pummel his head with his stony fists.

> *You crush Tigna'Rorn for 11 earth*
> *damage.*
> *Skill increase: Earth magic +1%.*

The kobold's head snapped back and his eyes went out of focus for a moment, then he began to claw at Ethan's face.

> *Tigna'Rorn slashes you with claws for 0*
>   *damage.*
> *Elemental armor (earth) absorbs 5 points*
>   *of slashing damage.*
> *Skill increase: Earth magic +1%.*
>
> *Tigna'Rorn slashes you with claws for 0*
>   *damage.*
> *Elemental armor (earth) absorbs 5 points*
>   *of slashing damage.*
> *Skill increase: Earth magic +1%.*

"It's clobberin' time!" Ethan yelled out. He was still unsure how long the elemental armor might last, and began raining punches down on the kobold chieftain.

> *You crush Tigna'Rorn for 13 earth*
>   *damage.*
> *Skill increase: Earth magic +1%.*
>
> *You crush Tigna'Rorn for 10 earth*
>   *damage.*
> *Skill increase: Earth magic +1%.*
>
> *You crush Tigna'Rorn for 12 earth damage.*
> *Tigna'Rorn dies.*
> *Skill increase: Earth magic +1%.*
> *You gain 50 experience. Experience to*
>   *next level 130.*

Ethan hit the kobold a few extra times, not realizing the thing had died. He realized he was screaming and clamped his mouth shut. He looked up to see other kobolds looking at him, fear in their eyes. As their eyes met, the kobolds turned and ran back out of the pass.

"Tigna'Rorn dead! Magic man kill him! Run! Run!" they screamed and disappeared into the night.

Climbing off the chieftain's body, he backed away until he was against the stone wall. He looked down at his hands, covered in blood, and then back at what remained of Tigna'Rorn's body.

He had killed the kobold chieftain with his bare hands. He felt revulsion, but also relief. The enemy was dead. He was alive. He should feel good but instead he felt like he was about to be sick. Somehow, beating the kobold to death with his fists just made it all too real.

Swallowing down the bile, he looked up to see villagers looking down at him from the ridge. They weren't firing arrows or throwing rocks, just staring down at him. Ethan remembered he was covered in rock and swore quietly. So much for hiding the fact that he was a wizard. The truth was out.

39

E than climbed slowly to his feet. Despite his rocky exterior, he was sore and tired. The fight had taken a physical and emotional toll on him. Glancing around, he saw that most of the fires in the pass were starting to go out or only burning in small pockets.

It looked like most of the kobolds either fled or had been killed by the fire. Those which hadn't died in the fires had been killed by arrows or rocks launched from the ridge. His plan had worked. So why didn't he feel better about it?

Sounds of battle from the direction of the barricade snapped him back into the moment. Letting out a heavy breath, he reached down and picked up his knife. He looked up on the ridge. "There's still fighting at the barricade! Come on!"

There was a moment's hesitation and then the ropes were thrown down and the archers began descending. While they did, Ethan looked around for the medicine man. He needed to finish that spellcaster off before the kobold caused any more trouble.

Walking over to where the medicine man's body should

have been, he found the spot empty. He looked around but there was no sign of the magic user. Ethan swore. Of all the kobolds he hadn't wanted to get away, the chief and the medicine man were the only two he really didn't want escaping.

What about the wand? Had the medicine man taken the wand with him? Ethan scrambled over to where he remembered it landing and looked around. There were charred kobold corpses but no sign of the wand. Swearing again, he kicked one of the kobold corpses and caught a flash of something beneath it.

Squatting down, he rolled the kobold's body to the side. There on the scorched hay was the wand. Gingerly, he reached down and picked it up.

After a moment, Ethan frowned. He wasn't sure if he'd expected something special to happen, but nothing did. On this world, apparently the wand didn't choose the wizard. Or maybe he needed a lightning bolt scar on his forehead first.

He held up the item and examined it with his *Appraise* skill.

```
Crude Wizard's Wand
Type: Wand
Range: Special
Damage: Special
Durability: 6 of 10
Special: A wizard's wand allows the
    wizard to focus his Mana through the
    Chymera crystal at the tip to cast
    spells.
Skill increase: Appraise +1%.
```

Ethan read and then re-read the description several times. If he understood it correctly, the crystal would allow him to use *Mana* instead of *Stamina* to cast spells. That would come in handy.

"Here your staff!" came a high-pitched voice from behind him and Ethan turned to see Par'karr grinning and holding Ethan's staff.

Standing, he took the staff from the little kobold. "Thanks."

"You not need it." The kobold made a fist and punched out several times. "You kill chieftain with bare hands."

"And magic," Ethan replied, looking down at his stone-covered hands. He could still see the blood on his hands.

"Yay! Big magic! Make you stone!" Par'karr nodded cheerfully.

The other villagers were down from the ridge now and looking at Ethan. He let out a frustrated breath and pointed at the barricade. "Go help them!"

Scrambling, the villagers rushed to do what he instructed and Ethan wasn't happy to see that many of the villagers' eyes now had fear when they looked at him. It was exactly the reaction he had been hoping to avoid since learning about the wizard-killing brain-suckers.

He glanced around one last time, hoping to see the medicine man's body before turning back to face Par'karr. "Let's go help them."

"Right!" The kobold nodded, brandishing his little spear.

The two of them followed the archers through the pass to the barricade where a small force of kobolds were still fighting. With the arrival of the archers, the kobolds were being cut down from behind, but there were at least two dozen left, sparring with his companions and some of the villagers.

Ethan checked his stats in the HUD to see what type of condition he was in.

Health: 14
Stamina: 13

He was at less than 50% of his *Health* and under 25% of his

Stamina. Glancing at his skin, his skin was still covered in rock but he had no idea how long it would last. Where was a Player's Handbook when he needed it?

"Come on, you apes, you wanna live forever?!" he yelled and charged at the kobolds.

Ethan, Par'karr and a few of the villagers from the ridge charged the kobolds, with Ethan's longer strides putting him in the front. He reached the first kobold and slammed his staff down on the back of the kobold's head.

> **You critically crush Cave Clan Raider for 14 damage + 11 damage flanking bonus.**
> **Cave Clan Raider dies.**
> **You gain 10 experience. Experience to next level 120.**

The kobold dropped like a sack and Ethan saw from the message on his HUD that he'd killed it. Par'karr stabbed the one next to him through the small of the back with his spear. The creature spasmed and tried to spin around but Par'karr's grip on the spear prevented it from turning.

Ethan swung his staff like a baseball bat, catching the skewered kobold raider in the throat. The creature's eyes went wide and it dropped its own spear, clutching at its ruined throat as it emitted strangled gurgling sounds.

> **You critically crush Cave Clan Raider for 11 damage.**
> **Cave Clan Raider is choking.**

Par'karr pulled out his spear and stabbed the raider through its chest. The enemy kobold shuddered and then dropped lifelessly to the ground.

Cave Clan Raider dies.
You gain 10 experience. Experience to
next level 25.

Ethan felt something poke gently against his hip and looked over to see a wide-eyed kobold staring at him, its spear poking at his side. Thankfully, the elemental stone armor was still active and the blow did no damage.

Cave Clan Raider pierces you with spear
for 0 damage.
Elemental armor (earth) absorbs 5 points
of piercing damage.
Skill increase: Earth magic +1%.

Twisting his body, Ethan brought his staff back around like a baseball, hitting the kobold across the side of the face, snapping its head back. Ethan grinned and yelled, "Swing, batter, batter! Swing, batter!"

You crush Cave Clan Raider for 5 damage.

Par'karr leaped forward while the raider was stunned and stabbed the other kobold in the abdomen. The cave clan raider squealed and tried to leap back but was skewered through the back by a long spear from one of the villagers.

Cave Clan Raider dies.
You gain 10 experience. Experience to
next level 100.

Another kobold raider charged at Ethan from his right but stumbled and went down to the ground as an arrow from one of the archers pierced it through the leg. The creature started to push itself off the ground so Ethan slammed his staff into the kobold raider's head.

```
You critically crush Cave Clan Raider
    for 9 damage.
Cave Clan Raider dies.
You gain 15 experience. Experience to
    next level 85.
```

Ethan felt a thrust against his back but there was no pain. But this time, he saw the stone that covered his exposed flesh seemed to evaporate. The message in his HUD confirmed his fear.

```
Cave Clan Raider pierces you with spear
    for 0 damage.
Leather armor absorbs 3 points of
    slashing damage.
Elemental armor (earth) absorbs 5 points
    of piercing damage.
Skill increase: Earth magic +1%.
Elemental armor (earth) is dispelled.
```

Cursing, he stepped back and swung his staff at the kobold, catching a glancing blow as it hopped to the side to avoid his clumsy swing.

```
You crush Cave Clan Raider for 1 damage.
```

Unfortunately for the cave clan raider, it hopped right into Par'karr's spear. Then, immediately afterward, was struck in the back by an arrow. Par'karr pushed and the raider slid off his spear to lie unmoving on the ground.

Cave Clan Raider dies.
You gain 15 experience. Experience to
next level 70.

He barely had time to acknowledge the new messages. Another kobold charged Ethan and he brought his staff back, ready to strike it. Instead, a thick arm lashed out with a short sword and sliced the creature across the abdomen as it ran. The thing stumbled, hands going to its sliced midsection before stumbling down face-first into the ground. A blood-spattered Ainslee stepped out from around a bale of hay.

"There you are, wiz..." She stopped and looked around. The bloody dwarf shrugged. "Well, it's not like people don't know now, right, wizard-boy?"

He gave her a weak smile. Unfortunately, she was right. The proverbial cat was out of the bag. "I guess so."

"I am glad to see you are well." Yuliana stepped out too and smiled at him. She saw his side and her face grew pained. "You are hurt but I'm sorry, I have no more healing."

The rest of the kobolds had tried to flee and had been cut down by the archers. As he looked around, the villagers were glancing around, trying to find more enemies. He nodded to the elf. "It's okay, pretty tapped out myself."

Yuliana came to him then and looked over his side. "Take off your armor."

Obediently, he took it off, wincing as the rough leather scraped against his wound. He looked at it and made a face. It looked worse than it felt and his shirt underneath was soaked in blood.

"Shirt too!" the elf demanded. She pulled out a long strip of cloth that had probably been a bed sheet from one of the abandoned buildings.

Ethan silently prayed that they'd listened to him and boiled the sheets before turning them into bandages. He pulled off his shirt and flinched as the blood-soaked fabric was removed from his skin.

Yuliana carefully dabbed some sort of yellow-gray paste on the wound and then took the long bandage and wrapped it several times around his injury before tying it off.

He looked down and smiled at her. "Thanks."

"You're welcome," she replied and returned his smile. "I understand you slew the chieftain and turned the tide of the battle."

Shrugging, he looked around. "I killed him. But how are the casualties over here?"

The elf's face fell. "We lost three of the men and a woman. All farmers."

He nodded soberly. "I think we lost a few others from the ridge who were pulled off by a magic-using kobold medicine man."

"And yet we are victorious," came Nia's voice from behind him.

Turning, he saw the foxgirl coming towards them. She was significantly less bloody than the dwarf though there were splatters of blood. Next to her was Luna. The mountain lion's muzzle was stained red. The big cat had obviously seen some action as well.

"You okay?" he asked.

"I am fine," she said and flashed him an evil grin. "But many kobolds are not."

A few farmers with spears came to stand next to her. "You should have seen her! She was amazing! Knocking them down, tripping them. All we had to do was stab them!"

Nia looked like she was about to retort when a voice boomed out from behind, causing him to turn yet again.

"Ha!" Fearghas bellowed. "We did it! Who knew dwarven spirits could come in so handy!"

Ainslee's eyes went wide and she spun towards the innkeeper, hands on hips. "YOU HAVE DWARVEN SPIRITS?!"

40

Fearghas grinned at Ethan and his group as he surveyed the carnage. "I'll be honest, I gave your plan a 50/50 chance. Glad to see I was wrong. The village is safe."

Quest Complete.
Defend Hawkshead I
The kobold Cave Clan is coming to
   destroy the village of Hawkshead. The
   villagers and farmers are looking at
   you to save the village.

Prevent the village from being destroyed
   (1/1).

You gain 500 experience.
You gain +500 reputation with Residents
   of Hawkshead.
You gain +500 reputation with Farmers of
   Arrowpoint Valley.

Congratulations!
You have reached level 4. Experience to
next level: 370.
+1 Attribute Point.
New ability: Enchanting.

The innkeeper looked around as the other villagers hauled away the corpses of the kobolds. Leaving them out would most likely attract predators and the last thing they wanted right now were wolves, bears or whatever else in this land ate carrion, to be running through the village streets. "Do you think the kobolds will be back?"

Ethan shook his head. "No, I killed their leader and we decimated their tribe. I doubt they'll be a threat any longer."

"You killed the chieftain?!" Fearghas smiled. "Well, that'll put a damper in their style."

Quest Complete.
Defend Hawkshead II
You defeated the Cave Clan chieftain,
Tigna'Rorn, which will prevent them
from regrouping under a strong leader
and continuing to harass Hawkshead.

Kill Tigna'Rorn (1/1).

Reward: 375 experience, +300 reputation
with Residents of Hawkshead, +300
reputation with Farmers of Arrowpoint
Valley

You gain 375 experience.
You gain +300 reputation with Residents
of Hawkshead.

You gain +300 reputation with Farmers of
Arrowpoint Valley.

Congratulations!
You have reached level 5. Experience to
next level: 1595.
+1 Attribute Point.
New ability: Mana Affinity II.

He saw the messages and smiled. The gamer in him relished the idea of gaining levels and he was interested to check out his new abilities. He'd gained two levels and had gained two new abilities. The *Enchanting* ability especially intrigued him. Would that allow him to craft magic items? If so, that would be awesome!

There was also the wand that he'd taken from the medicine man, who had turned out to be a wizard. The description had mentioned channeling *Mana*. Considering the side effect of running out of *Stamina* was incapacitation, being able to harness his *Mana* stat would be a huge boon.

But both things would have to wait until later. At the moment, there was work to be done around the village.

"What about the other kobold tribes?" Fearghas asked. "Do you think our show of force will scare them off?"

Out of the corner of his eye, he saw Par'karr deflate. No doubt the little kobold was thinking of his own village, which the Cave Clan had destroyed. He reached down and squeezed the kobold's shoulder. Par'karr looked up and he nodded at the little kobold, who nodded back.

"The Cave Clan took the weapons that Cuthbert gave them to block the roads and turned them against the other tribes in the area," Ethan told him. He gestured to Par'karr. "That includes Par'karr's tribe."

Fearghas looked between Ethan and the little kobold and

then hung his head. He looked at Par'karr. "I'm sorry about your village. Your folk and mine gave each other a wide berth. I can't say we were friends, but we weren't enemies until one of ours betrayed both of us."

Ethan was touched that the innkeeper was so understanding and it appeared that Par'karr was too. The kobold gestured to Ethan and the women. "Me have new tribe now."

Ainslee rolled her eyes but Yuliana reached out and patted the little kobold on the head. Ethan smiled down at the little kobold.

The innkeeper nodded and turned back to Ethan. "So then we're safe from other kobold attacks and the roads are open?"

"I think so," he replied. "At least, I doubt there will be any coordinated attack as before."

> *Quest Complete.*
> *Clear the Roads I*
> *The previous mayor paid off kobold*
>   *tribes to prevent travel in or out*
>   *of the village. The Cave Clan*
>   *eliminated the other three tribes and*
>   *you have scattered the Cave Clan*
>   *tribes. Travelers and trade caravans*
>   *can once again safely visit*
>   *Hawkshead.*
>
> *Eliminate Kobold Tribes (4 / 4).*
>
> *You gain 300 experience.*
> *You gain +300 reputation with Residents*
>   *of Hawkshead.*
> *You gain +300 reputation with Farmers of*
>   *Arrowpoint Valley.*

"So we aren't cut off from the rest of the world?" the innkeeper asked hopefully.

"You shouldn't be," Ethan replied, seeing the completed quest.

This was another one of those things that tipped the scale in favor of this being some sort of alien simulation. How would quests work in the real world? It didn't make any sense. But neither did magic or black holes and multiple suns.

"You fools gonna sit around gabbing all night or you gonna help?" Hamish growled as he went by carrying a kobold body.

"We can talk more tomorrow. We'd better help or we'll never hear the end of it," the innkeeper said as he looked after the surly cooper. Fearghas hurried away, leaving the group alone.

"Do we have to help them?" Ainslee whined. "We just defended their village."

He was tired but he was also the mayor and needed to be seen helping. But the rest of his group didn't. While Ethan had felt obligated to help, the women hadn't been and had helped anyway. They deserved a little rest. "I need to stay up and help but why don't the rest of you get some rest. You've earned it." He looked at the blood-smeared dwarf. "Though you might want to wash up a bit first."

Ainslee looked at her blood and gore-stained torso and chuckled. "You aren't wrong about that. I'll see you all for breakfast."

Without any further ado, the dwarf spun and walked off towards the river. When the others didn't move he turned to them. "You three can get some rest too."

"I will help," Nia said simply. She looked tired, but the foxgirl looked adamant.

Yuliana smiled. "I will help as well."

"Me help!" Par'karr chirped. "Par'karr good helper!"

"Yes, you are," Ethan agreed. He looked at the elf. "Yuliana, the best help you can give right now is healing. Can you drink water and restore some stamina and then heal whoever needs it."

The elf shook her head and her lovely face screwed into a frown that was almost a pout. "I was drinking water during the battle. It did restore stamina but then stopped working."

Ethan frowned. There was probably some limit to how much *Stamina* a person could restore before needing to rest. "Do you remember how much stamina you restored before it stopped working?"

The elf screwed up her face for a moment, obviously trying to remember, but then shook her head. "I'm sorry, everything was happening so fast, I don't remember."

"It's okay." He smiled. "Once we have some time, we should test that out to see what the limit is. That's information we should know." He gestured to the inn. "Why don't you go get some sleep then. Come back when you have some more stamina and heal anyone who still needs it."

"Does that include you?" she asked with a raised eyebrow. Nia and Yuliana both gave him hard looks, daring him to object.

"You chief." Par'karr nodded, pointing at Ethan. "You get healing first!"

"No," he replied but held up his hands to placate any objection from the women. "Heal whoever needs it most first. I don't want to lose anyone else." Remembering the herbs he'd found before, he unbuckled the small pouch from his belt. "Maybe take these herbs around before you go to bed and see if anyone needs them to stabilize until you can heal them properly."

The elf took the pouch and nodded. That actually gave Ethan an idea. "Nia, if you're going to help, do me a favor and tell the people to strip off any gear or equipment the kobolds have and put it in front of the inn. We can go through it and raise our appraise skill and look for any other herbs or other items that might be useful."

"I will do that now." Nia nodded. "Some of the people are already taking the equipment with the kobolds."

The foxgirl ran off without another word. Yuliana watched her go and then walked off too. She began going over to the wounded, examining them and dispensing the herbs.

"What we do?" Par'karr asked.

"We help move bodies," he replied and started towards the barricade. At least, that's what he intended to do.

"You didn't tell us you were a wizard," Odelina said as the butcher stepped out between two buildings. Her tone was accusatory but not hostile.

Suppressing a sigh, he turned to face the butcher. Once he'd revealed himself as a wizard, Ethan had known there would be questions and possibly even accusations, or even a call for his resignation as mayor. For all he knew, they might even run him out of the town or try to kill him.

The tall woman stopped a few feet from him. Odelina had been one of the archers on the ridge; now her bow was nowhere to be seen. Hopefully that meant she wasn't going to try to kill him. "Is that a problem?"

The woman shrugged. "Not now. But bad things happen to wizards. And the people around them."

"So I heard." Ethan nodded. "I learned about that a few days ago."

"My mum was a wizard," Odelina said, her eyes far away. "One night a couple of years ago - this was when we lived in Helmsford..."

"Helmsford?" he asked.

The butcher looked annoyed but explained. "It's a town just north of Castlehaven, between there and Moonpoint. Anyway, something woke me up in the middle of the night. I went into my parents' room to find my mom dead on the floor, a hole in her where her eye had been and her brain missing. My da quivering in the corner. He was never quite right afterwards. I took him and whatever we could bring with us and moved out here. I came here to be away from that stuff."

"I'm sorry," Ethan said and meant it. No child - no matter how old - should have to lose a parent, especially not in a gruesome fashion. Then something she had said set off warning bells in his head. She'd said this happened a couple of years ago but the farmers mentioned it only going on for about a year. "Wait, you said this happened two years ago. I was told this just started a year ago."

Odelina scoffed. "No, it was going on before. But it was rare and scattered. My mom just thought it was a rumor...."

The butcher trailed off, a faraway expression on her face for several seconds before she shook her head and snapped out of whatever memory she'd been locked into. "I wanted to warn you to watch your back. No one knows what happened to my mum, or what it did to my da, but it's not just you that you need to worry about."

"I..." Ethan started but the butcher waved off his words.

"I said my piece," she told him. "That's all I got to say about that."

Turning, Odelina disappeared back between the buildings. Ethan watched her go and wondered, not for the first time, what in the world could be killing wizards in such a gruesome way. Were mindflayers a thing in this world?

Mindflayers were a tentacled race in Dungeons and Dragons. They had psychic powers and an appetite for the brains of sentient creatures. If elves, dwarves and kobolds were real in this world, could mindflayers be real too? And if so, why only the brains of wizards?

"Come on," he told Par'karr. "Let's help them carry bodies and round up the belongings."

The kobold nodded and followed after him. They began helping the villagers clear away the corpses but Ethan's mind was on whatever was eating the brains of wizards.

41

The next morning, Ethan had wanted to sleep in, but a pounding on his door disturbed him from his sleep. In this case, it was a good thing because he'd been having that dream where he was running from something that wanted to eat his brain. Rubbing the sleep from his eyes, he had the sinking feeling that sleeping in might be a thing of the past.

Sitting up in bed, he saw that Par'karr was curled up at the foot of his bed. Ethan shook his head. He needed to make a bed for the little kobold, especially if he was going to be staying with him in the long term.

"Mayor!" bellowed Hamish's voice.

Sighing, he wiped the sleep out of his eyes and hopped out of bed. His body was sore, but not as sore as it had been. He padded across the floor of the front room in his bare feet and opened the door.

Fearghas, Hamish, Froba and Dudley stood there. Hamish's mouth was open as if he were about to yell again and he snapped it shut. Ethan looked up and saw that it was barely daylight. Why was everyone up so freaking early?! "Yes? Why are the innkeeper, the cooper, the miller, the thatcher at my door at the crack of dawn?"

Hamish opened his mouth to speak, but Froba slapped him across the chest. "Shut your trap, Hamish. Let Fearghas ask him."

The cooper looked indignant but shut his mouth and crossed his arms over his chest.

Fearghas cleared his throat. "Pardon the intrusion, mayor..."

"Ethan," Ethan corrected.

"... Mayor Ethan..." Fearghas continued.

"Just Ethan, please Fearghas," he sighed. "It's early. Please get to the point."

"Ahem, right, may... er... Ethan," the innkeeper continued. "There were a couple of things we needed answering."

"Get on with it," Hamish said tersely.

"Right," the innkeeper said, obviously trying to choose his words carefully. "We were, uh, wondering what you planned to do with the people whose farms were burned down?"

"What do you mean?" Ethan yawned. He shook his head. "Sorry."

"I mean." Fearghas wrung his hands nervously.

"Odin's beard, man," Hamish broke in, his face red. "Are you going to be imposing any taxes on us to rebuild the farms?! Because we haven't paid..."

Froba smacked him in the back of the head with her palm. "Hamish!"

"Wha?!" He glared at the miller indignantly.

"Let Fearghas speak." She returned his glare. Hamish kept up his glare for almost a minute before finally withering under Froba's stare. He lowered his head and Froba gestured to the innkeeper.

"What Hamish was trying to get to, was that we haven't really paid any taxes since the silver mining dried up," Fearghas told him. "Mostly cuz none of are making any money."

"And you'd like to keep it that way," Ethan said tiredly. It didn't take much of his customer service experience to tell that the group wanted to keep the status quo.

They all nodded their heads vigorously. He hadn't even thought about taxes or checked his town control menu. There just hadn't been time.

"Truth be told," Dudley said, his eyes downcast. "We haven't had much use for money since then. We're pretty self sufficient here."

"The only time we really need money," agreed Fearghas. "Is when the traders would come. And then, we usually got more coin than we dished out."

Ethan nodded, starting to get an idea of how things had worked. This was like an old west pioneer town. The people here were self sufficient and worked mainly off the barter system. To them, money was something they needed when dealing with people from the outside.

But he didn't understand the relationship of the farms to the town. Were they part of the town? Did they owe it any allegiance? Did they give nothing to the town but expect help in return? "Are the farms part of the town?"

The assembled villagers all looked at each other. They began exchanging shrugs and Ethan held up his hands. "Did they pay taxes back during the silver mining?"

"Yah," Hamish said, scratching his head. "I think so. Right? I mean, back when we had a constable."

"You had a constable?" Ethan asked.

"Aye," Froba answered. "Had to. Miners get rowdy when they're drunk."

"Ha!" Hamish snorted. "And they're always drunk!"

The villagers had a chuckle but stopped when they saw Ethan wasn't laughing. They all looked at him, waiting for him to say something.

"If they paid taxes," he said. "They must technically be considered part of the town. If that's the case, then..."

"But..." Hamish started but stopped when Ethan glared at him.

"... then..." Ethan continued. "We should help them. BUT, I don't see how taxes or money will really help - especially if there are no caravans right now."

Once again, the villagers bobbed their heads up and down.

"However," he said. "It seems like we're all in this together. So I don't think it's unreasonable for us to help them out any way we can - short of taxes and coin."

Dudley sighed. As the thatcher, Ethan guessed he'd be in great demand but if the farmers' houses were destroyed - and possibly fields and livestock gone too - they would have nothing to pay him with.

"I'm not sure how yet," Ethan said. He'd gotten some coin from the bandits but he had no idea of the worth yet. He could have a small fortune or enough for a coffee and a bagel. "But I'll reimburse anyone who helps out the farmers to rebuild their farms."

Ethan looked out at the town. There were many buildings that were completely deserted. Most of them were already in use by displaced farmers. If any of them wanted to make that permanent, he wouldn't complain. "And we should offer houses to anyone who needs shelter for now."

The group nodded, though less enthusiastically than for his previous ideas. He wondered what they might have against people moving into the village.

None of them made a move to leave and he sensed they needed more from him. He sighed. "What else?"

"Well." Fearghas smiled. "It wasn't much, but the traders did bring in some goods that we can't get elsewhere. Plus, they did bring in the little bit of coin that we did make here."

"But two trade caravans were ambushed by the kobolds,"

Hamish growled. "They won't send more until someone goes to Castlehaven to tell the trade guild that things are back to normal."

"That's fine, who..." Ethan started. He had been about to ask who they could send to tell the trade guild but judging by the sickly-sweet smiles they directed at him, he realized they already had an idea of who they wanted to send. "I see. You want me to go to this Castlehaven and tell the trade guild that it's all clear."

"Well... we... uh... I mean... you're the mayor..." They all muttered and looked away or down but the message was clear enough. That was exactly what they wanted.

"How far is Castlehaven?" he asked.

"Two weeks."

"Yeah, about two weeks."

"Yes, two weeks, give or take a day."

"Two weeks!" Ethan replied, maybe a little harsher than he intended since they all took a step backwards. Two weeks to a town meant he would be on the road for over a month - at a minimum!

Ethan took a deep breath and calmed himself. He remembered that there were no planes, trains or automobiles on this world. At least, he doubted it based on the level of technology he'd seen so far. Was a two-week journey really unreasonable given the lack of modern conveniences? He wasn't even sure how to translate that into miles.

"I'll talk it over with my companions," he told them and they returned what he thought were forced smiles.

"Something else?" he asked, letting some annoyance slip into his tone.

"May... er... Ethan," Fearghas said. "We all saw what you are. And don't get me wrong, we appreciate what you did and all. I mean, we don't have nothing personal against wizards. But, we wanted to make sure... I mean... that is... you will be going with your companions to the city, won't you?"

And there it was. They were like the farmers. They were afraid that whatever was hunting wizards would come to the village and start sucking brains. He remembered what Odelina had told him last night. It's not just you that you need to worry about, she had said.

Ethan looked at the villagers. They looked apologetic and yet scared, much like the farmers. These were good people, but the idea of some brain-eating, wizard-killing assassin coming to their village had them spooked.

"Of course," he sighed. "As mayor, it is my responsibility to re-open trade with the outside, so obviously I will go myself."

> **You have received a new quest "Re-open Trade with Helmsford"**
> **Your town needs trade to survive. You have told your villagers that you intend to go to Castlehaven personally and re-open the trade route.**
> **Re-establish Trade with Helmsford (0/1).**
> **Reward: 500 experience, +250 reputation with Residents of Hawkshead, +250 reputation with Farmers of Arrowpoint Valley**
> **Failure: -150 reputation with Residents of Hawkshead, -150 reputation with Farmers of Arrowpoint Valley**
> **Accept quest (yes or no)?**

That was interesting. Had he just given himself a quest? And this new quest had a consequence for failure. Great! Yet another thing he had to worry about.

"Was there anything else?" he asked.

The group shook their head, their smiles genuine now. They'd gotten what they wanted. He hadn't imposed any taxes and he'd agreed to leave the village and open up trade with the outside world.

Ethan hoped the women would agree to come with him. Should he have asked them before he agreed? Maybe. But in the end, he'd only obligated himself. They would stay if they wanted to. But he did hope they came.

He went back inside his house and smiled as he saw the kobold, still sleeping. He thought Par'karr would come with him, if no one else did.

Walking gingerly, so as not to wake the little kobold, he got back into bed and tried to fall back asleep. At least, that was the plan. But after tossing and turning for what seemed like an hour, he finally got up, got dressed and went outside.

It was time to do some town and character sheet management.

42

Ethan walked north to the river and sat down on the bridge with his legs dangling over the side. There were more people up now. They gave him nervous smiles as he passed and some muttered a "Hullo" or "Morning".

They were afraid of him, or rather, they were afraid of whatever was after him. He cursed silently. Ethan needed more information on whatever it was that was killing wizards. He wasn't about to sit quietly while something stabbed him through the eye and sucked out his brain.

The farmers and villagers here had no idea what was going on. Even Odelina, who had been in the same house when her mother was killed, had no idea what had done it. He needed to find someone who had. Someone who was investigating these killings.

Luckily, he was going to what he guessed might be a place to get some answers. Castlehaven. The place was an actual city, according to Fearghas. If he was lucky, they'd have answers there. He'd have to ask around once he got there, discreetly, of course.

Now, it was time to check out his new abilities and levels. He brought up his HUD and examined his character sheet.

```
Strength: 10
Agility: 13
Hardiness: 15
Intellect: 19
Intuition: 15
Charisma: 10

You have 2 unallocated attribute points.

Health: 30
Stamina: 60
Mana: 48
Karma: 30
```

Not much had changed since the last time he'd looked at it. His *Mana* had gone up without his *Intellect* going up. How had that happened? He switched to his ability tab.

```
Mana Affinity I
Summon Minor Elemental
Elemental Armor
Enchantment
Mana Affinity II
```

He had gained the *Enchantment* ability and the *Mana Affinity II* abilities with his last two levels and brought up their information.

```
Mana Affinity II
Type: Wizard
Cost: N/A
```

```
Range: N/A
Duration: N/A
Description: Provides 2 points of Mana
   per character level.
Special: This does not stack with other
   Mana Affinity abilities. Only the
   highest-level ability is active.
```

The increase in *Mana* made sense. Looking at *Mana Affinity I*, it only gave him 1 point of *Mana* per level. At his current level, that would have been 5 points of *Mana*. Now, with Mana *Affinity II*, he received 10 points of *Mana*.

Next he checked out his *Enchantment* ability. Extra *Mana* would be nice, once he figured out how to use it instead of *Stamina*. But the idea of being able to enchant things gave him all sorts of ideas! He began imagining all sorts of magical items!

```
Enchantment
Type: Wizard
Cost: Special
Range: Special
Duration: Special
Description: Allows the enchantment of
   mana into items through the use of
   Chymera crystals bound to the item.
```

He frowned. The description was short and extremely lackluster. It told him absolutely nothing about how to actually do it! He let out a growl of frustration and silently cursed the aliens. Yet another thing he needed to research when he got to the city.

Swapping back to his stats, Ethan considered where to place his two attribute points. He considered *Stamina* again but hesitated. He had just gained the ability to use *Mana*. Maybe he should invest in *Intellect* to get more *Mana*.

He looked at the other stats. Other than *Hardiness*, he hadn't really had a need for the other physical stats. Nor had he found a use for *Intuition*. That really just left *Intellect* or *Charisma*. He smiled. The smart move would be to put the points in *Intellect* for more *Mana* or *Hardiness* for more *Health* and *Stamina*.

He shrugged and placed both points in *Charisma*. It may not be the smart thing to do, but it seemed to him that if he was going to be the mayor of a town, he should have some *Charisma*. Plus, he was going to the city to negotiate new trade caravans - provided it worked the same way as it did in the MMORPGs and Tabletop roleplaying games he'd played. He confirmed and then waited.

Nothing happened. He didn't feel any more attractive, nor did he feel any more charismatic. It was like when he gained *Intellect*. Did he really get smarter? He didn't feel any smarter from the *Intellect* boosts and he didn't feel any more stately, attractive or eloquent from the *Charisma* boost.

Disappointed, he closed down his character sheet and opened up the town menu.

```
Hawkshead

Town Rank: 1 (13%)

Town population: 27
Town morale: 41%

Town total buildings: 17
Town active buildings: 13

Town Output:
Food: 10
```

```
Metal: 0
Leather: 0
Wood: 0

Income from Taxes: 0
Income from Trade: 0
```

Not much had changed, except for the number of town population, the town morale and the active buildings. All of those had gone up. Also, there was a percentage next to the town rank. What did that mean?

Food hadn't changed but was now red. Did that mean they produced enough food for 10 people but now they had 27, so they were 17 short? That wasn't good. Maybe he could ask some of the farmers to hunt.

He looked at the menu for the town section.

```
People
Buildings
Resources
Financial
Alliances
```

He checked out People first. That option brought up a list of jobs and whether they were filled or vacant.

```
Jobs - Town Level 1
Baker - vacant
Blacksmith - vacant
Butcher - filled (Odelina)
Carpenter - vacant
Constable - vacant
Cooper - filled (Hamish)
Groom - vacant
```

Innkeeper - filled (Fearghas)
Miller - filled (Froba)
Storekeep - filled (Ethan)
Tailor - vacant
Thatcher - filled (Dudley)

Unassigned workers: 13

According to the menu, he had six vacant jobs. What would happen if he filled them all? Could he fill them all? He tried clicking on a vacant job but nothing happened. He tried clicking on unassigned workers but nothing happened. That figured. He'd have to fill it the old-fashioned way.

Next, he looked at the Buildings menu. It brought up a list of the buildings and their status. That was more depressing than the People menu.

Baker - 0%
Blacksmith - 0%
Butcher's Shop - 20%
Cooper - 15%
House - 100%
House - 180%
House - 120%
House - 100%
House - 100%
House - 0%
Inn - 100%
Miller - 15%
Stables - 0%
Temple - 0%
Thatcher - 5%

Ethan wasn't sure he understood the information. The

percentage for the houses might be capacity, which made sense given the sudden influx of people. Were percentages for the business the capacity of what they could operate at? If so, other than the Inn, none of the other businesses were near capacity.

As he thought about it, the Inn's capacity made sense. Currently, their rooms were filed with the women from his party. So in a way, it was at full capacity. Once again, he could not interact with the buildings, only view the statistics.

He moved on to Resources. Bringing it up, he could see that he'd been right earlier. He was short on food, and surprisingly wood.

Food: 10 of 27
Metal: 0 of 0
Leather: 0 of 0
Wood: 0 of 95

Surplus: -17

Was the wood what he would need to repair the farms? If so, that was a lot of wood. And did it mean logs? Or planks? There was no sawmill around, so hopefully logs would do. He'd need to ask some of the villagers.

Next, he brought up the Financial menu. It was both straightforward and depressing.

Town Coffer: 0

Income from Taxes: 0
Income from Trade: 0

Trade agreements:
None

*You have no money in the town coffer. Do
you wish to change the tax rate? (yes
or no)*

He finally found something he could interact with, but of course all he could do was change the tax rate. Oh yeah, that would endear him with the villagers. It also looked like whatever trade agreement they'd had was now gone.

Finally, he brought up the Alliances menu. That was equally bare.

Allies:
None

Enemies:
None

Feeling depressed, he closed down the town menu. There didn't seem to be anything he could do from the town menu. Everything would have to be done the old-fashioned way. That meant, he'd have to physically tell people to do things. Ugh. Somehow, he had become management. He hated management!

Getting up, he walked back into the village. He had wanted to play around with the wand and see if he could figure it out but it seemed other things needed his attention.

He stopped in front of the inn. A pile of equipment, mostly weapons, from the kobolds lay just outside the door to the inn. He remembered asking them to stack up the loot. But now, looking at the pile, he suddenly dreaded going through it. But on the plus side, if he leveled up his *Appraise* skill, it meant another point of *Intellect*.

He sighed and sat down near the pile and began going through the items. The first thing he noticed was that he was not getting as many skill ups. Previously, it seemed every time he examined an item, he would gain a rank. Now, it averaged to about every other time.

Yet with so many items, mostly spears but also a few short swords and bows, Ethan eventually saw the message he had been waiting for.

You have reached Rank 3 in Appraisal.
+1 Intellect.

He continued going through the items, picking out the items that might be useful to the village while putting the others in a separate pile. He was almost through the entire pile when he heard a small voice.

"Mister mayor," said Sawney. Fearghas's son was peering at him through the open door. "Da would like to know if you want breakfast."

Before he could open his mouth to answer, the smell of cooking eggs reached his nose and his stomach growled loudly. Sawney giggled. "Your belly says yes!"

Ethan grinned at the little dwarf. "You're right. My belly is definitely saying yes."

Standing up from the pile of items, he followed the little dwarf into the inn to get some breakfast. The rest of the items could wait.

43

"Are you serious?!" Ainslee sputtered, flecks of eggs spraying from her mouth. "You want to go away for a month?!"

"We need to re-establish trade with Castlehaven," Ethan said. He lowered his voice and looked around to make sure Fearghas or his family weren't nearby. "And maybe get some answers on our situation."

That shut up the dwarf as she continued chewing her eggs. The women all looked thoughtful and Ethan used the pause to take another bite of the scrambled eggs Fearghas' wife, Elspeth, had cooked them.

"You really think we might find answers in this, haven of castles?" Yuliana asked.

"I don't know," he said. "But Castlehaven is a bigger town so they may have libraries or some other sort of records."

"Libraries?" Yuliana asked, raising her eyebrows. Nia looked up too.

"Buildings with books." Ainslee rolled her eyes. "Lots of books. Blueprints too, if they're like our libraries."

The dwarf suddenly narrowed her eyes and looked at

Ethan. "Oh wizard-boy, let's say we go to this town. I want a set of blacksmith's tools. And an anvil."

"You still want to open the smithy?" he asked. He remembered the town menu and how that building wasn't used and no one was assigned as a blacksmith. If the dwarf did open it, that would be one less job he had to worry about.

"I do." She nodded. "Unless we find a way home in Castlehaven."

"I'll do my best," he told her. "I have no idea how much money we have or its comparative value. But I think that should be one of our priorities."

"I'm in then." The dwarf grinned, a little bit of egg falling from her mouth.

"I will go with you as well. I do not know what I would do here without you," Yuliana said and then blushed. "I mean, without our group."

Elspeth had brought the elf some spinach and herbs from her garden, which the elf greatly appreciated and was slowly nibbling at.

"You are the alpha here," Nia said. "If you tell me to come with you, I will come."

Ethan frowned. "Do you want to stay here?"

The foxgirl considered the question for a minute before shaking her head. "No."

"Then come along." He grinned.

Nia nodded. "Very well. I will come."

"Good, then it's settled," he said. "We can leave tomorrow morning."

Ainslee groaned. "Couldn't we wait a few days?"

Lowering his voice, he leaned in. "I think they want me gone as soon as possible."

The dwarf made a face and then seemed to remember the reason. She made a slurping sound. "Oh, right. The brain sucking thing."

Ethan chuckled mirthlessly. "Yes, the brain sucking thing."

"Fine! Fine!" Ainslee said and shovelled the last bit of her eggs into her mouth. "We wan weave womorrow."

ETHAN ASKED the women to get things ready for their journey, while he talked with the villagers and played mayor.

After gathering up some of the farmers and older teens, he had them form up hunting parties using bows and spears. He wasn't sure how successful they'd be, but until they got the farms in working condition, it would have to do.

Par'karr, at his prompting, showed some of the non-hunters how to build rabbit pens and "herd" the rabbits. The little kobold was too happy to show off his skill. In the end, they used the discarded kobold spears to make pens and then filled them with rabbits that Par'karr spent the rest of the day catching.

He also told Fearghas and the other villagers to allow the farmers who wished to rebuild to cannibalize the old mining headquarters, as well as anything they could rip out of the mine. It wasn't much, but it might give them a headstart on some things.

By the time he went to bed, he had the villagers and farmers all working together and felt like a real mayor. He once again had dreams of something hunting him, but this time it was closer and it chased him for what seemed like the entire night.

When he finally awoke the next morning, he was covered in sweat. He didn't feel rested, nor particularly safe. He dressed and slipped on his armor before waking up the still-snoozing kobold.

"We go now?" Par'karr asked sleepily.

"Soon," he said. He picked up the haversack where he'd

stored the bedroll and what money they had. Then he started for the door. "Join me outside when you're ready."

The kobold hopped up, grabbed his spear from against the wall and ran over to him. "Me ready."

He chuckled, remembering how light the kobold travelled. "Yes, you are."

They ate breakfast at the inn, more eggs, before leaving. Feraghans and his family wished them a good journey but none of the other villagers came to see them off.

Each of the women had a backpack too, donated from the villagers, and presumably carrying their own bedrolls and supplies. Even Par'karr was given a small backpack that had belonged to Sawney.

"It fits you good." The little dwarf grinned.

"Me thanks you much," Par'karr thanked him and poked out his little kobold chest. "Me ready for adventure!"

They all chuckled at the kobold's enthusiasm and turned to the south. The journey to Helmsford was before them and who knew what dangers awaited them. With a last glance at the village,

Ethan signaled his group to move out. Another adventure awaited.

44

EPILOGUE

It skittered across the countryside with its insect legs. Though smaller than the warrior caste, it nevertheless had the same forelegs, triangular head and killing mandibles. But unlike the warrior caste, it had wings and could fly short distances. This helped it find its target. Or run it down if it tried to escape.

Pausing, it scanned the area with its two bulbous compound eyes while testing the air with its two large antennae. It didn't see its target, but it smelled it. Or rather, it smelled the magic. Wizard magic.

The Queen had directed it here, to this small mountain area, to find a wizard. It didn't know how the Queen knew. It wasn't its place to ask. Its only concern was following the Queen's orders to the best of its ability.

It moved west, following the scent of magic. Yes, it was getting closer and its mandibles snapped at the thought of reaching its target. Not that it would be using its mandibles. The Queen was very clear. This one's brain was to be brought back so that the Queen could digest and absorb its memories.

It had done this countless times before, though recently it

had been sent further and further away from the hive to collect the wizard brains. It didn't know why that was and it didn't care. It lived only to serve the Queen.

Movement caused it to freeze. Its large, faceted eyes had seen movement through the trees and they scanned them now, looking for its target. Its antennae moved back and forth, sampling the air. Yes, the target was close. Very close. But it was not alone. Other scents mingled with the smell of magic. The smell of a wizard.

It wouldn't matter. Although it was not of the warrior caste, it had ways to deal with obstacles. The Queen had seen to that. It had not run into anything yet that could stop it. It had sneaked through entire armies to reach targets before. The few beings with its target would pose no threat.

Hurrying from tree to tree, it closed in on its target. The figures were not moving quickly, not running as they some-times did if they caught sight of it. No. These figures were not aware of it. It would have the element of surprise.

It spent the next several minutes getting closer to the target, slipping through the shadows. The scent of magic was strong now. Almost maddening. And yet, it knew it could not kill and consume this target. It must bring back its brain and feed it to the Queen.

Closer and closer it crept until it was behind the lines of figures, hidden in the trees. It watched, its large eyes rotating as it took in their weapons and assessed the danger. It had its own magic, a gift from the Queen, that it could use to counter the wizard's magic. But if it struck fast enough, the target may not even have a chance to use its magic.

Sensing the time was right, it rushed forward with amazing speed. It reached the figure in the back, a slight figure and attacked. Opening its sharp mandibles, it snapped them closed around the figure's neck, severing its head from its body in a spray of blood.

The body and head dropped to the ground and the other figures began to spin but it was already moving. Darting forward, it slashed its sharp foreleg across the nearest figure, tearing a long, fatal gash down its front.

Moving on, its other foreleg slashed at the next figure's legs, slicing them in half and leaving the figure on the ground screaming. As it darted past, one of its rear legs jabbed through the figure's chest, ending its pitiful cries.

And then it was on the next creature, spraying a toxin from underneath its mandibles that caught the figure in the face. It dropped instantly, its body convulsing. The neurotoxin would cause permanent neural damage to the creature but it didn't care. Its only concern was the final figure. Its target.

The wizard was summoning magic and it released darts of ice that streaked towards it. Casually, almost without thought, it summoned fire to melt the ice darts, even as it closed in. The wizard tried to scramble away but it was quicker.

Before the wizard could summon any magic, it was upon it. Strong forelegs grabbed the wizard, careful not to use too much pressure and kill the target. With strength that defied its size, it lifted the struggling wizard until its head was even with the target's head.

It spread apart its mandibles and pushed a long, sharp appendage out from its jaws. In a motion almost too fast for the wizard to follow, it drove its head forward. The tube-like appendage penetrated the target's eye and lodged into its brain.

The target went still, other than the occasional twitch, as it sucked the contents of the wizard's brain. It felt indescribable ecstasy, not just from sucking the brain but also from knowing that it would greatly please the Queen when it presented her with her prize.

Minutes passed until it had emptied the target's skull of all brain matter. Slowly, it withdrew its appendage and retracted it back between its mandibles. As it did, it looked at the corpse of its target.

It was an odd creature. It had scaled skin, a short muzzle and a long tail. It remembered encountering these before. Kobolds. Yes, that was what it was called. A kobold.

It let the kobold wizard drop to the ground and started to turn away. But then its antennae caught the scent of other magic. Wizard magic but different. Another wizard?

It did not matter. It could only carry a single brain and its mission was over. It was compelled to return to the Queen. Return and feed her. It shuddered thinking about the pleasure it would get from feeding the brain to its Queen.

Turning south, it ran back towards the hive... and its Queen.

<<<<>>>>